Coming Around

Ginger Williams

PublishAmerica
Baltimore

First printing

ISBN: 1-60441-821-4
PUBLISHED BY PUBLISHAMERICA, LLLP
www.publishamerica.com
Baltimore

Printed in the United States of America

To Danny, my childhood sweetheart, best friend, lover, husband, father of my children, PawPaw to our grandchildren, enthusiastic travel companion, personal Mr. Fix-it, and, oh yea, my very own barbarian. (Read on. You'll understand).

Acknowledgement

To Terry and Barry Limarzi, who took my Pdf and converted it to a Rtf, and in doing so, saved my life. That was very cool.

Chapter 1

Iris Corrigan stood at the balcony of the cruise ship *Whimsical* awaiting departure from Miami. The whistle blew and an announcement was made that it was time for any visitors to say their goodbyes to departing passengers and walk down the ramp to the dock. Crew members were making final preparations to free the ship from land. Then she would be free to do as she was made to do, glide gracefully, majestically and yes whimsically, across the Caribbean, to exotic ports of call.

There was so much noise and laughter, voices raised in fond farewells and bon voyages, that Iris even began to respond a little to the thrill of it. Perhaps respond was overemphasizing her reaction, but at least she was awake, sober, and not crying at the moment. Maybe the cruise would turn out to be a good idea after all.

People began to pack in shoulder to shoulder all along the lengthy railing and everyone was holding a drink of some kind, it seemed. Iris finally, after the third server asked if she would care for a drink, ordered a margarita on the rocks, no salt. She had always been health conscious. Iris had spent so much time alone lately that she thought the drink might help her relax.

With so many strangers pressed against her like cattle being herded back to the barn, she was beginning to feel panicked. At last her drink arrived with big chunks of lime, lemon and even an orange-wedge hanging off the edge of the glass. She said "thank you, it's perfect," to the beautiful, young server.

Most of the time they brought her drink with thick salt all around the edge and she would have to send it back, but these people obviously paid attention and knew how to deserve a tip, which she happily forked over. The drink itself would be charged to her suite.

As she used the drink umbrella to spear the pieces of fruit, so she could suck the juice out of them, she noticed the powerful quivering of the *Whimsical* as she moved sideways away from the dock and out into the open water. If Iris had any second thoughts about whether or not she should have taken this trip, it was officially too late to back out now.

She watched with the other passengers as Miami became smaller and smaller and a lot of people began to move away from her to various parts of the ship, which was fine with her. She had kept her distance as much as possible, from everyone, being content to sip her margarita and take in the beauty of the bright blue sky, and shimmering water and feeling the warmth of the southern sun on her slender arms which she kept propped up on the ship's railing. Her elbows were slightly bent, as if trying to take up as much room as possible for herself. No one except the waiter had intruded upon her solitude, for which she was greatly relieved.

But, just because Iris hadn't looked at any of her fellow passengers, that didn't mean that she had gone unnoticed. William Pendleton, along with just about everybody else, had made his way to the main deck to witness the departure of the cruise ship from Miami, and soak up the gaiety that was as contagious as a baby's smile. He was like Iris herself, standing quietly and alone, sipping on a Jack Daniel's over ice and lost in the beauty of the day. He was enjoying the feel of the ship and trying not to let the memories of previous cruises he had taken with his beloved Rebecca, intrude upon his peace and tranquility. Not that they weren't good memories, it just made him feel too lonely to go down that road. After all, he had come on this trip not expecting to actually have a good time, but to perhaps at last, begin the healing process.

He never in his wildest imagination had ever thought he would outlive his wife of thirty years, especially considering he had been eight years older than her. Rebecca had only been fifty one when she was killed instantly in a car crash, bringing not only her life to an abrupt halt, but his as well. She had been gone almost a year and he would turn sixty on board the *Whimsical* in a few days.

William's glass was empty and as he turned to gain the attention of the nearest server, he saw her. The crowd had thinned out somewhat so that there were only about a dozen people between them. She was as still as a statue and he sensed almost as rigid. It was as if she was in a trance. He wondered if he had been wearing that same haunted look just a moment ago, as he had thought of Rebecca. Somehow he knew she was traveling alone as well, and that her heart was as heavy as his. He couldn't help but wonder who she grieved for.

Iris was lost in her own deepest, darkest thoughts and was not the least bit aware of her surroundings any longer. She had taken the plunge into the depths of the emotional hell she'd been revisiting every day for the past nine months, or so. She'd promised herself that she wouldn't waste her time on this trip with thoughts of her now ex-husband, David. Ex-husband...she had to let that sink in for just a moment. It was a word that had always applied to the men in her friends' lives, but not hers. No, never hers, not David.

Iris Kemp and David Corrigan had met in high school, fell in love, got married right after graduation, and had proceeded to have the perfect family, the perfect marriage, and the perfect life...end of story, or so she had always believed. But then what in the bloody hell did she know about anything? Obviously nothing. At least, not until Valentine's Day of this year. God, but she would always hate fucking Valentine's Day!

That was the day, after almost thirty three years of marriage, that David told her he was leaving her. They were both about to turn fifty, and had been married since they were seventeen. David assured her that he wasn't seeing anyone else. Although, he did seem to have trouble looking at her as he explained. "It's just that I've been married all of my life, and I feel I've missed out on so much," he had told her. He thought they both needed some time apart. He felt that they were at a crossroads in their lives, and before they just settled for another possible three decades of marriage, they should make absolutely certain that was what they both wanted.

"In other words," her best friend Peggy had told her, right after Iris had run next door, burst into Peggy's house without even knocking, and blurted out between bone racking, flood quality sobs, what David had said to her, "he's screwing a woman about half his age, has probably already bought her a new convertible, and while discussing the divorce with his lawyer, has mentioned in passing, that he'd also like for him to be drawing up the legal documents necessary for him to adopt her children." Iris unraveled herself from Peggy's comforting arms long enough to dart into her hall bathroom and throw up.

As it turned out, Peggy was right on the money. Iris thought that it was because Peggy herself had been married three times, twice taking someone else's husband and had also been the recipient of a couple of new cars as a show of good faith until her lovers had obtained their divorces. And let's just say her kids had gotten accustomed to a new last name more than once. But the real reason that Peggy had been so clairvoyant was that almost everyone in their little Tennessee town of Springhill had known, it seemed, except Iris.

As an additional slap in the face, her divorce became final in June, on what would have been their wedding anniversary. Iris slipped into a deep funk, shutting out not only her friends, but her family as well. Her grown children rallied around her in support, but she didn't think she was healthy company for her grandchildren in her present condition and proceeded to become almost a recluse.

She had never worked outside her home, as David and his best friend since he was twelve years old, had slowly but surely built up a nice construction business, and it had been profitable enough that Iris could be a stay at home mom for her children. She prided herself on how well they had turned out. David had attended their games of soccer, baseball and basketball, but had left the day to day raising of his family totally up to Iris. All three of them had grown into responsible, successful adults with happy, healthy, beautiful children of their own. Iris loved her six grandchildren so much, that she sometimes feared her heart would simply burst open, it swelled so when she looked at them.

If only she had possessed a crystal ball that would have told her David was going to fuck her over, but good, she might have had the foresight to establish a career for herself after her children grew up and left home. As it was, with her house paid for and a decent alimony check each month, she had been able to wallow for months in luxurious self pity.

She had always been well organized and soon developed a routine that worked well for her. She slept all day, in the guest room she had turned into her bedroom, since she could not bring herself to sleep alone in the bed she had so passionately and willingly shared with David, then get up about dark. She would go downstairs to the kitchen, in her pajamas (she had stopped sleeping in David's t-shirts finally) and make herself two pieces of buttery toast while mixing a pitcher of margaritas. No salt, of course, because salt's not good for you, and Iris had always been health conscious.

Then, she would go outside, barefoot and pajama clad, and curl up in the swing on the front porch, placing the pitcher of margaritas within easy reach, eat her toast, refill her glass at least three times and let the warm, humid Tennessee night, caress her wounded spirit while the tequila worked on the rest of her.

As hard as she tried to drown the memories of a lifetime with David, her mind just refused to be beaten down. Each night, for some reason, only the good memories rose up to torture her. It was almost like he had died and every bad moment between them had been forgotten and only the good ones remained. Sometimes she felt guilty because she wished he had died, instead of just walking out and leaving her. At least then she could have still respected him, and herself.

She had no idea where this self-loathing had come from. In trying to explain how she felt to Peggy, she said, "I understand fully why I hate David, he deserves it. But, I don't." Maybe, she thought, it was because his leaving her made her feel so stupid and ugly. She had always thought she was blessed with outstanding, natural intelligence, and while she didn't consider herself beautiful and had never been vain, she had always been pleased with her reflection in the mirror.

But now, she no longer cared about her appearance or the fact that she had always kept an immaculate house. It was as if everything she had done, and done well dammit, she had done for David. And now, without him in her life, if was as if she had suddenly ceased to exist. How could she matter to herself if she no longer mattered to him? God, how she hated him for making her feel this way, and despised herself for allowing him to.

About daylight, she would make her way into the house, before any of her neighbors would come out to pick up their newspapers from the driveway or sidewalk. She had long since stopped taking the paper or watching the news on television for that matter. It's not that she no longer cared what was happening in the world. Oh wait, yes, that's exactly what it was. That, and the fact that she had already been the recipient of too much useless and painful information lately.

Her friend and neighbor of twenty something years, Peggy, had been a fountain of unsolicited news. It seemed not only was Iris' husband someone else's husband now and the father of her children had become the father of someone else's children, but the house he had so skillfully built for her, while still very nice (but suddenly too large) paled in comparison to the small mansion he was building for his thirty two year old slut. God, she was the same age as their oldest daughter, Sarah.

But, Peggy's latest news flash had forced Iris to shut down the communication grapevine between her friend's house and her own. She no longer answered the phone when Peggy's number came up on the caller ID or went to the door for anyone except her children and grandchildren. The one exception besides family was the teenaged boy who delivered her small supply of groceries to her house each week. Thank God that she lived in a small town, where for a minor fee and of course a tip for the grocer's son who brought them all the way into the kitchen for her, this type of service was still fairly common.

Then there was the downside to small town life. She hadn't been able to stand the whispering, the pitiful looks and sympathetic comments of the other shoppers, most of whom she had known all her life. She hadn't done her own grocery shopping since February.

Yes, Peggy's last tidbit of news had come as quite a shock to Iris. It seems that David, who was turning fifty in August, just as she was, was going to become a father again. After they had produced three babies in three consecutive years, David had had a vasectomy. That was thirty years ago, when they had both been twenty. When David married his slut, (Iris refused to acknowledge her real name) he immediately had the vasectomy reversed, at his new wife's insistence. He obviously had stopped using his "big" head completely and was deferring to his "little" head for all his major decision making.

Iris knew that while David loved their three children, his life hadn't exactly revolved around them. He certainly hadn't won any father-of-the-year awards. She could only imagine that he had thought, after so many years and at his age, the reversal wouldn't work. Ah! The wonders of modern medicine! The slut had become pregnant in no time flat. In response, Iris said to Peggy, "I hope they have a house full of little ones. Couldn't happen to a nicer guy. Perhaps the slut can eventually negotiate a discount for buying in bulk. Pampers for the babies and Depends for David." Everything considered, she thought she was being generous.

When Iris turned fifty in August, her children insisted on giving her a special gift. They wanted to throw her a big party, but she had told them not only "no" but "hell no". But, they knew her well, and having grown more than a little concerned because all she seemed to do was sleep, drink and cry, they came up with the idea of sending her on a cruise.

Sarah called a family meeting and said, "If there's ever any hope of Mama returning to some sense of normalcy, then something had better be done fast." They had long since given up on their mother pulling herself out of the deep mire she had been bogged down in for the past six months. But then, she shouldn't have to do it alone. After all, Iris had been there for each of her children throughout not only their childhood years, but throughout their entire lives.

Their father may have supported them and paid for their educations, but it was Mama, as they called her, who was and had always been, their confidant, cheerleader, advisor, friend, and until they married and had families of their own, she had been the center of their world. She was the stable force, the very axis around which each of their worlds had turned. "It's our turn now to step up," Sarah added.

Their parents had started going to the Caribbean islands soon after the last one of them left home. In the beginning, they hadn't been able to afford vacations and then later on, the family vacations had been either to the Smokey Mountains in east Tennessee and North Carolina, or down to Siesta Key beach, near Sarasota, on the southwest coast of Florida. Their mother's mother had lived there for many years, but since their grandmother died, none of them had been back. It just wouldn't be the same with their Nanny gone.

They knew that Iris had more than a fondness for many of the islands she had visited in the past ten years or so. As a matter of fact, it seemed she was never as happy as when she was planning her next trip to Sint Maarten or Aruba, or one of the cruises that would take them to three or four islands in a single week. She would always return home bearing souvenirs for the grandchildren and love them up real good, declaring how much she had missed them. But, at the same time, she would seem wistful and a little melancholy for a few days as if she was surprised to find herself back home in the real world. Her children suspected that if it wasn't for the grandkids, their mother would want to live on one of the islands full time, and that Tennessee would become her occasional vacation destination. But Iris was a devoted mother and grandmother and the thought of ever being away from them for long, would never cross her mind.

Sarah's brother Jake, the youngest, pointed out, "She won't go on a cruise alone if we don't book it for her." Rachel, Iris' middle child agreed. "That's true, after all, she's never been anywhere before without Daddy." And they knew she would protest going this time.

However; they were at their wit's end as to how to help her, and so, after much discussion and more than a little arguing among themselves, they agreed it was worth a shot. They carefully planned all the details, including her flight from Nashville to Miami, the cruise line and itinerary, even making her hair and nail appointments for the week before she was to travel. Now all they had to do was convince her to go.

When the week of Iris' birthday arrived, she knew she had to snap out of it, if only for a few days. Sarah, Rachel and Jake, along with their families, were all coming for supper on Friday night. Counting herself, that was thirteen people. She hadn't cooked for that many since last Thanksgiving. Here it was, the end of August.

At first, they had wanted to take her out to a nice restaurant, but Iris had lost her desire to fix up and go out, so she'd offered to cook for all of them instead. Besides, even though her grandchildren were well behaved, six of them in a crowded, noisy restaurant, might be a strain on her already frayed nerves.

Not to mention, the last time she had gone to a nice restaurant was Valentine's Day, a little more than six months ago and she'd been with her husband. She thought they would come home and make love, but instead David delivered his departure speech, packed his clothes and left. My, how quickly things can change. One thing she felt would never change; she'd always hate fucking Valentine's Day.

No, she just wasn't ready for a night out on the town. She was afraid she would feel too self conscious and ruin everyone's evening. It would be much easier for her to at least act normal in her own home, even though she no longer had a clear cut vision of what normal was. But for the sake of her children and precious grandchildren, she was willing to try.

So, when she got up on Thursday afternoon, she had toast and coffee instead of her customary pitcher of margaritas. She hadn't thoroughly cleaned house in months, but then, she didn't really mess up much either. All evening long she dusted, vacuumed, scrubbed the bathrooms and kitchen, and finally sat down at the kitchen table to make out her grocery list.

As soon as the grocery opened on Friday morning, she called in her list and by nine thirty a.m. she had received everything she needed for her evening meal. And, for the first time in a long while, she went to bed and fell asleep without the help of her new best friend, Jose Cuervo.

When Iris woke up at four o'clock that same afternoon, she got her supper started, made a birthday cake for herself, then jumped in the shower. By seven that evening, her house was presentable, supper was ready and to look at Iris, anyone would think she was fine. At least that was the image that she was desperately trying to portray to her children. She was afraid if they saw her the way she had been looking when she was alone, they would either try to have her committed, or at least insist she see a therapist.

When she showered earlier, she remembered to shave her legs for the first time in weeks. She conditioned her hair after shampooing, and blew it dry and styled it with a round brush. She had just been washing it and letting it dry while wrapped up in a towel, and only taking the towel off her head when she went to bed. She was surprised to notice how much her hair had grown and that she liked the new, longer length. Not that it mattered, it was simply an observation. She even put on a little mascara and lip gloss. "What the hell," she said to her reflection in the mirror, "it is my birthday."

The real shocker came when she got dressed. She had been wearing pajamas and housecoats for months, so when she went to slip on some jeans, she realized she had lost weight. A lot of weight. "Dear Mother of God," she muttered out loud. Iris had worn a size eight for as long as she could remember. She enjoyed going for long walks and doing step aerobics. She had continued to stay in shape after her kids were grown and gone from home. As a matter of fact, she had had more time to work out in recent years than ever before. But, when she fastened her jeans, she was surprised when they fell, and if it hadn't been for her bony hips, they would have fallen all the way to her ankles.

"There must be some mistake," she reasoned with herself. "Peggy wears a size ten; I bet these are hers." She had come over a few months ago and dried a couple of loads of clothes in her dryer because hers had gone out. Maybe a pair of Peggy's jeans had been left in the dryer and gotten mixed in with hers and hung in her closet by mistake. She pulled them off and checked the tag. They were a size eight. She pulled them back on, and even though it was August, pulled a heavy sweater on over her head and tucked it in the jeans, cinching them with a belt. Then she hurried into the dining room to set the table. The kids would be there any minute.

All in all, Iris thought the evening went well. It was her first birthday as a single woman, and she was spending it with those she loved best. Her children were very attentive to her and she bet they had agreed before they came, not to mention their father, because nobody brought him up at all.

Her grandchildren were lively and funny and were full of stories about their new teachers and the kids in their classes. School had just started the week before. Four of them were in elementary school and the other two went to preschool. Iris couldn't believe how fast they were growing up.

Everything seemed almost normal until they presented her with her gifts. At first, it was just a certificate at the salon for a hair color and cut, a brow and lip wax and then a manicure and pedicure. Iris just laughed and said, "I didn't realize that y'all had noticed my lack of self maintenance. I promise I'll use your gifts very soon."

And then her grandchildren offered her their gifts. Iris was amazed when she opened the airline ticket to Miami. "Why in the world would I want to go to Miami?" she asked. Her children knew she loved the beach and probably just thought she needed to get away from the house she had shared with her husband and had practically boarded herself up in for the last six months.

She didn't think she would ever use the ticket but thanked them anyway and thought it was a sweet and thoughtful gesture. Then she opened the last envelope containing yet a bigger surprise. Inside was a cruise line ticket. Now the airline ticket made sense.

She and David had been on a few cruises before that had left out of Miami. She didn't want to act ungrateful, but her insides were quivering suddenly and her stomach was cramping. "Please God," she whispered under her breath, "give me the strength to keep it together for just a little while longer." Her children saw the shock register on her face and looked anxiously at each other.

But then her mask fell back into place. She laughed and joked and told them they had spent way too much money. She then said, "Y'all should put the airline and cruise tickets in a hat and let the kids have a drawing to see who wins it. I'll babysit for whichever couple wins the trip and pay for the additional ticket you'll need."

They knew she was trying to get out of going herself, but they weren't playing along. They offered to help clean the kitchen, which Iris declined, gathered up their children, hugged and kissed her goodnight, and amidst many cries of "happy birthday, Mama," and "we love you," they loaded up in their vehicles and were gone.

Just like that. In one day she had turned fifty and now evidently, that meant her family thought she was mature enough to go on a cruise by herself. She had never even been out of Tennessee by herself. "Holy shit," she said as she locked up the house, "I was wondering how I was going to gather up enough courage to leave home just to use the salon certificates;

now this." At least the trip was scheduled for November. That gave her a couple of months to decide how to get out of it.

She went back to the kitchen and made herself a pitcher of margaritas. She wouldn't let her daughters help her clean up, but she would gratefully accept Jose's help. She was considering giving up her married name and was thinking that Iris Cuervo had an exotic ring to it. "Why not?" she asked the bottle. "I've spent more time with you in the past six months than I have any other man."

She finished the kitchen, then sat at the kitchen table staring at the tickets. She finally got up and undressed, put on her oldest pair of pajamas and fell exhausted into bed. The pitcher of margaritas was empty and the sun was just coming up. She must have sat in the darkened kitchen longer than she thought.

When Iris awoke the afternoon following her birthday party, she sensed something was more wrong than usual. Normal wrong, she had gotten used to, but different wrong, must mean something else had happened. Then she remembered the airline and cruise tickets. She got up, went into the bathroom, and like she did almost every day now, had diarrhea.

At least that was better than throwing up, which she had done a lot of in the first weeks following David's hasty departure. She took that as a clear sign of improvement. Her nerves were definitely getting better. When she went to the sink to wash her hands, she was momentarily startled at her reflection in the mirror above the sink. "What the hell, now?" she asked herself in a worried tone. She had black smudges under her eyes and tiny rivers of black running down her cheeks.

Not being accustomed to wearing mascara, she had forgotten to wash her face before going to bed. She accepted the smudges under her eyes, but seeing the streaks running down, made her flinch. That meant that she was still crying in her sleep; something she thought she no longer did. At least her sobs hadn't woken her up in a long time. It must have been all the emotions of the night before.

She thoroughly cleaned her face, applied moisturizer, and brushed her teeth and then brushed her hair. She pulled her hair back and up in a neat ponytail and secured it with a scrunchy. Iris wouldn't have believed it if someone had told her, but she looked a good ten years younger than her fifty years. She had always had the fresh faced, bright eyed look of youth, and had never needed or worn much makeup.

Digging through her closet, she found a jogging suit, that because of it's clingy fabric, fit her a little better than the jeans had. Putting on a well worn pair of sneakers she vowed that tonight, after dark of course, she would go for a walk through the neighborhood. It was something she used to do each morning, but she didn't want to run into any of her neighbors yet, so she'd wait until their houses were dark. Then there wouldn't be much of a chance of anybody else being out and about.

After seeing the concerned and slightly frightened look in her children's eyes last night, when they first looked at her, and then glanced at each other, Iris was determined to ease herself back into the land of the living.

Before dressing, she located her scales under the bathroom sink, dusted them off, and stepped tentatively up on them. Iris couldn't believe she'd lost right at twenty pounds. Having been a rather voluptuous size eight, with curves in all the right places, she now thought she looked like a girl who had not quite reached puberty. Not quite a skeleton with skin stretched over it, but a little too Peter Pan-nish for her liking.

No wonder her family had exchanged furtive glances among themselves. They'd probably been a little freaked out. They had seen her plenty of times lately, but she'd always had on her pajamas and robe and had kept her diminishing figure hidden.

The first thing she would do is boil herself two eggs to eat with her toast. Then, she would use real sugar in her coffee instead of artificial sweetener. Real sugar was better for you anyway, as she reminded herself of how health conscious she was.

For the next couple of months, after her birthday and before the prospective cruise, Iris reinstated herself as a mother and grandmother. She'd missed the friendships she shared with her daughters and son and the sheer joy of her grandbabies. Her birthday party had reminded her of all that she had been missing out on.

She attended some of their soccer games on Saturdays, if they weren't too early. She slowly made herself stop sleeping all day and being up all night, and was now going to bed about two or three in the morning instead of waiting for daylight. She got up about ten or eleven now and was showered and dressed by noon. Definitely a sign that she was getting better, in her opinion.

Eventually, she even went to a mall in Nashville, about an hour's drive away, and bought some new jeans, blouses and underwear. She didn't want to shop at the mall in nearby Franklin, where she knew most of the sales people. She didn't want anyone she knew to know she was now wearing a size four.

Iris knew a lot of the parents and grandparents she ran into at the soccer fields, and she could feel their stares once they realized who she was, but at least nobody had been rude enough to comment on her weight loss or mention her asshole of an ex-husband. It was quite obvious by her standoffish behavior, that she didn't want to be approached. She was only there to support her grandsons' teams, and brag on them profusely after each game.

As time always does, it went by quickly. Autumn in Tennessee is a spectacular display of leaf color, and with warm days and cool nights, comes as a welcome relief to most people, after the hot, humid, long summer. But personally, Iris liked it hot.

Fall always made her feel a little sad, but this year, it had really done a number on her. She fluctuated back and forth between feeling suicidal and homicidal. She was still going for walks late at night, but now she had to wear a jacket, and sometimes when a cold front dipped down far enough to include middle Tennessee, she even needed gloves and a hat.

When she would get back home, she'd only make a half pitcher of margaritas, which was only about two really, maybe two and a half. It was too cold now to sit on her porch at night in her swing, so she piled up on a chaise lounge in the sunroom, where she could still sort of feel like she was outdoors. "All things considered," Iris complimented herself, with a toast of her glass, as Halloween drew near, "I'm making great progress."

The only thing disturbing her thoughts now, well not the only thing, but it was beginning to take precedence, was the fact that the kids still expected her to go on that damn cruise. And, what was so bad, was that it was scheduled for just a few weeks away.

There was one other demon that had reared it's ugly head as well. She was beginning to feel like someone had made a voodoo doll in her likeness and was sticking a pin in a new area just as soon as the old wounds from previous pin sticks would heal. Most of the pains, up until now anyway, had been of the emotional kind. But lately, when she went to bed at night, now that she and Senor Cuervo weren't spending quite as much time together, some feelings were creeping in that she wasn't ready to deal with.

Instead of going to bed and passing out, she only felt a slight buzz after only having a couple of shots of courage.Consequently, Iris now found herself lying awake for some time before finally going to sleep. She didn't believe in taking drugs of any kind, to help go to sleep, or for any other reason. She personally took no medications at all, and hoped it would be many more years before she would be forced to. She was sure, if she asked him, her doctor would write her a prescription for a sleep aid; however, as health conscious as she was, she preferred to treat herself the old fashioned way.

By getting shit-faced on margaritas, she felt that at least the lime offered up some nutritional value, the tequila probably helped keep her blood thinned and free of clots, and God only knew how many other benefits there were, such as mind numbing and body relaxing and nerve soothing. Yes, it was quite the little tonic, and besides, it tasted good.

But, now that she was getting better in so many ways, there was one thing that was getting worse. She was absolutely, positively, beyond a shadow of a doubt, achingly, mind-blowingly, unmistakably and undeniably, horny beyond all description. There, she had admitted it, if only to herself.

She tried not to think of her asshole of an ex-husband during the times that this curse visited her. But, it was hard not to. Sex had been the best part of their marriage; by far. It was the backbone of their relationship, the glue that had kept them together throughout the years, even more so than the children.

They had never had a problem or argument between them that couldn't be solved in bed. In the early years of their marriage they had been like rabbits, and with three babies in three years, they had proof.

Sarah was born nine months to the day after their wedding, Rachel came along eleven months after Sarah, and Jake eleven months after Rachel.

Through all the ups and downs that came with raising a family, running a business, and just a man and a woman living under the same roof, neither of them had ever used sex as either reward or punishment for the other. It had always been a natural, spontaneous celebration of their love and passion and attraction for each other.

But, the bastard had ruined all of that. At least for her. She couldn't help but hope the slut had used sex to lure him and lock him in with a pregnancy, and would now turn cold in bed. And, if that didn't happen, she prayed that his pecker would just rot and fall off.

At least she was able to be mad as hell at the asshole now and didn't think nearly as little of herself any more. She really felt herself coming around to normal, even though she detected a new version of what that would be.

Iris had always loved Halloween. She especially had made a big deal of it when her own kids were young enough to go trick-or-treating. And now, her grandkids were the perfect ages to make it exciting for her, once again. The older ones just cared about the candy, but with the littler ones, it was still all about the costumes. God, the innocence and excitement of childhood was a beautiful thing to behold.

She carved pumpkins, strung orange lights around the porch, hung ghosts from the trees and bought a black, plastic, witch's kettle to serve candy from. She couldn't wait for the little spooks to start ringing the doorbell.

All of her grandmonsters stopped by before going to her son's home to dump their treasures in the den floor. There they began trading things they didn't like for things they did like with their cousins, as their parents thoroughly inspected each piece. Iris had left candy on the porch for any late stragglers and had gone to be with her family until it was time for them to go to their respective homes. It was not yet nine when they finished trading candy, but it was a school night, so Rachel and Sarah rounded up their broods as Iris prepared to leave too.

As he was walking her to her car, Jake asked, "Mama, are you getting excited about your trip?" He seemed so happy for her and proud of the gift he and his sisters had given her that she didn't have the heart to tell him that the prospect of going on a cruise alone, made her physically ill.

She smiled warmly, reached up to give him a hug and a kiss on the cheek and told him, "I can hardly wait." On the drive home she realized she was supposed to leave Saturday after next.

After being at Jake's house among the giggles and squabbles and pleasant chaos, her house felt empty and cold and even lonelier than before. For the first time she began to think that the cruise she didn't want to take, and hadn't made any preparations towards yet, might not be the best thing that ever happened to her, but she knew damn well, it wouldn't be the worst.

Somehow, over the next several days, she managed to get her hair and nails done, and shopped for what she hoped would be the proper clothes for a single, fifty year old woman, traveling alone. She didn't want to appear promiscuous, but she always enjoyed dressing somewhat young and loved fun, stylish clothes. And, with her new size four body, she actually rather enjoyed putting together a cruise wardrobe.

She packed her new clothes, sandals, bathing suits, lingerie and all her toiletries the day before. She had already packed a carryon, with a new book, headphones, passport and tickets and a simple change of clothes in case her luggage got lost or delayed.

She went to the bank, had the post office hold her mail and arranged for a limousine to carry her to the airport early Saturday morning. There was only one flight from Nashville to Miami each day, and it left at the ungodly time of seven a.m. Iris didn't want any of her kids to have to get up at four in the morning like she would have to, to drive her to the airport and for what it would have cost her to park her car for a week, she could pay for the limo to take her. She would be getting back the following Saturday night about nine, and her whole family had promised to be there waiting for her when she got off the plane.

When Iris went to bed on Friday night, she didn't expect to get much sleep. She had to get up at about the time she'd been accustomed to going to bed. She lay there already missing her family and wondering if she was making a huge mistake by going after all.

Chapter 2

The captain's voice spoke through the speakers, bringing Iris back to the present moment. "We will now conduct our safety drill. Each of you are required to report to your cabin, where your steward will direct you to your assigned station. Life jackets are located in your rooms. Please wait to put them on when you get to your station, as the hallways and stairwells become too crowded otherwise. You will receive specific instructions from the safety director assigned to your station. This is a mandatory drill. Thank you for your cooperation."

"Oh, hell," Iris mumbled under her breath. She had completely forgot about these stupid drills. She knew it was in her best interest and the cruise line would be negligent if they didn't carry them out, but they were still a pain in the ass.

"May I take your glass?" a handsome young man asked her. His smile was like watching a live advertisement for teeth whitening. "Yes, thank you." She returned his smile automatically. It would have been hard not to.

Watching from just a few feet away, William was amazed at how her spontaneous gesture transformed her face. She had seemed stuck-up and cold to him as he'd been observing her by the railing. He thought now that perhaps she had just been lost in some unpleasant or painful thoughts. No one could be cold with a radiant smile like hers.

In the year since Rebecca's death, he had poured himself into his business and had not so much as thought about another woman. His company manufactured auto parts and he had an extremely profitable business, located in Franklin, Tennessee where he also lived. With both Saturn and Nissan plants close by, staying busy was easy. He had only taken Sundays off in almost a year.

But, his employees who were devoted to him and worried about him since his wife's death, had gone in together and given him this cruise for his sixtieth birthday. He and Rebecca had not been blessed with children so the employees felt that they were all he had. It gave them great pleasure to return the kindness and generosity he had always shown them.

William was stunned by the gift and at first, wished they hadn't given it to him. But, even he knew he'd been too much work and no play. Besides, the thought of turning sixty, at home, all alone, was less than appealing to him.

And now, finding himself on the same ship as this amazingly attractive woman, who clearly wasn't wearing a wedding band, he was more than a little glad to be here. As he headed toward his suite he noticed she was going in the same direction he was. Good, he thought, maybe I'll find out which room she's in. Then he smiled to himself. Yesterday he wouldn't have believed that he would care which room was hers. One day later, he was acting like a sixteen year old stalker.

They both chose the stairs instead of the elevator and when she stopped at the door directly next door to his and took her key card from her handbag, he couldn't believe his luck. But, as he started to take his own key card from his pocket, he heard her say, "Well, hell, mine's probably the only friggin' key on the whole ship that doesn't work."

"I'm sorry, did you say something?" William asked from directly behind her. Iris jumped like she'd been shot out of a cannon and dropped her key. As he bent to retrieve it for her, she stomped her foot down on top of it, barely missing his fingers.

"If I did, I wasn't talking to you," she replied a little sharper than she intended. But he had scared the living shit out of her. With the thick carpet in the hallway, she'd had no idea he was there.

But, when he straightened up and she really got a look at him for the first time, she fleetingly wished she hadn't almost maimed him. She checked him out covertly while scowling up at him. He was taller than David who was a little over six feet. This guy had him beat by at least three inches. That comparison made her blush slightly for some reason she pretended not to understand.

He had movie star good looks, with black hair turning white at the temples only. He was broad shouldered, muscular and appeared to be about her age. Then she saw it. The white cheat line on his left ring finger. The bastard had obviously removed his wedding band very recently. Probably, today when he had boarded the ship. She could barely resist slapping that stupid grin off his face.

"I'm sorry I startled you. I noticed you having a hard time with your card. My wife used to hate them. She never could get them to work either." He gave her what he hoped was a friendly but not too interested smile. She was obviously leery of him, and he suspected all men. He was curious as to what had made her that way. Couldn't have been good and must have been recent, because she wore her anger like a suit of armor.

"Is that right? So, what did she do, buy a "key card for dummies" book?" she asked, not quite as sharply as before. He had at least admitted to being married. He laughed a warm, low laugh, and she smiled despite her effort not to. He really did seem nice and was probably just trying to be helpful. She relaxed a little and bent down to retrieve her key from under her foot.

As she was about to hand it to him so he could try it, he said softly, "No, unfortunately I lost my wife in a car accident about a year ago. But, I think you may have something there with that book idea. I smell a best seller." He was still smiling, but now she saw there was a touch of sadness to it.

Iris felt like she'd been hit in the face with a wet squirrel. Here she had wanted to castrate him for having a white line on his ring finger and he obviously had been grieving the loss of his wife and had continued to wear his wedding band until just now. You know, she berated herself mentally, just because your husband turned out to be a scum sucking, slut fucking, spineless bastard, doesn't mean all men are. She would have to dwell on this new way of thinking carefully though. No need to jump to any hasty conclusions.

"I'm very sorry for your loss. If you wouldn't mind trying my key for me, I'd really appreciate it." She held it out to him and smiled apologetically. As he took the key, his fingers touched her hand slightly. She was shocked by the thought that other than her son Jake, she hadn't had even accidental contact with a man in months. How could that be? Maybe she just hadn't noticed before. She definitely noticed this time, however.

William inserted the key into the lock and the door opened on his first try. He made sure he wiped the grin off his face as he pushed the door open for her with one hand and held her key out to her with his other. "I'm sure you warmed it up for me. I normally don't get that lucky the first time, either," he said humbly.

Iris wasn't fooled though. She'd seen the corners of his mouth twitch and knew he was fighting back a testosterone driven smirk. He was probably just like the rest of them, she thought, as she practically snatched the key from him and brushed past him to enter her suite.

He wished the door hadn't opened quite so easily. He could tell her feathers were ruffled as she appeared to be about to slam the door in his face. God, he thought, she's even pretty when she's pissed. She tossed her purse in a chair and whirled around, making her blonde, shoulder length hair swirl around her.

Her light brown eyes flashed with shards of gold as she looked into his steel grey ones. "Well now that you've proven how incompetent I am and completed your good deed for the day, I'm sure you're quite worn out. It was great meeting you." And having said that, she pushed on the door to close it, but his foot was holding it open. She looked down and saw a very large cowboy boot. At least a size 13, maybe even a 14, she surmised. What the hell was wrong with her? What difference could it possibly make what size boot he wore? God, she needed a drink and as soon as she got rid of King Kong, she was going to have one, or four.

As she continued to stare as if she'd never seen a western boot before, he thrust his hand in her face and said, "Actually we haven't officially met. I'm William Pendleton. It's a real pleasure to meet you."

She wondered why it was a real pleasure for him when she'd done nothing to make it so. But, she shook his hand anyway, and remembering his recent loss, tried not to be a total bitch. "Iris Corrigan. Considering I'd still be standing on the other side of my cabin door if you hadn't come along, I'm glad to make your acquaintance as well."

"Well, I guess we'd better get our life jackets. Here comes the cabin steward with our instructions. I'm sure we'll be directed to the same station. I'll grab my jacket and meet you in the hallway." And, with that, he turned and went to the next suite over, opened his own door with the first try, of course, and left her standing there admiring the way his butt had looked in his Levi's.

He went in and his door shut and Iris could no longer see his butt, so she went to get her life jacket. At least she wasn't dreading the safety drill as much as she had been earlier, even if it did delay her happy hour.

Iris barely had time to pee, wash her hands and apply some lip gloss, when she heard a knock on her door. She grabbed the life jacket and her small handbag and opened the door to find William, along with evidently a few of their neighbors, waiting for her. The crewman who was in charge of their group was very polite, but businesslike too, and it was quite obvious he was taking the drill seriously and expected the passengers to also.

He hustled them up on deck and to their muster station near the life boat they would use, if necessary, and then had them put their life jackets on. While Iris slipped into hers, she watched William struggle into his. After putting one arm through, he was having a time getting the vest to accommodate his wide shoulders and broad chest, allowing him enough movement to put his other arm through.

Looking at him, she guessed him to be about six-four, at least two hundred pounds, maybe a little more, of pure hunk. Besides the shoulders that she thought a good pilot could land a small plane on and broad chest, he had an almost flat stomach, straight hips, one of the nicest butts she'd ever seen and thighs that looked like tree trunks, straining against his jeans. He was wearing a white, oxford shirt with the sleeves rolled up over powerful looking forearms. She could see a peek of salt and pepper chest hairs where the top button of his shirt was undone.

He was obviously still wearing his traveling clothes. Her luggage had been delivered to her room while she had been up on deck for the ship's departure, as his probably had, but she hadn't had the opportunity to change yet either.

In talking with him, she hadn't detected an accent, so she figured he was also from the south, as she was. Otherwise, she felt sure she would have noticed. That, along with his attire, made her wonder if he was from Texas. That would be appropriate she thought, since Tennesseans and Texans had always bonded famously. Remember the Alamo? Even though that had ended badly, their intentions had been good.

Good grief. Just when she had thought her mental stability was returning, here she was on a sun drenched ship deck, reflecting on a bloody massacre. Shows you what can happen when you only have one margarita in a twenty four hour period. She made a mental note to fix this oversight as soon as possible.

William felt like a grizzly bear attempting to squeeze into a girdle. He could see Iris checking him out from the corner of his eye, but pretended not to notice. After all, turnabout's fair play, as in the hallway earlier and on the way to their muster station, he'd taken in as much of her as he could without openly staring.

She came up to about his shoulders, almost the exact same height Rebecca had been. But there, the similarity stopped. While his wife had also been beautiful, she'd had raven hair and eyes so dark they appeared almost black. Her grandparents on her mother's side had been full blooded Cherokee. In contrast, she had inherited fair skin from her father's Irish ancestors. In a way, he was glad Iris looked nothing like her. It might have been too painful, otherwise.

He thought she was a knockout in her own right though. She had pale blonde hair, curling slightly on her shoulders, and the oddest yellow eyes he had ever seen. They were slightly almond shaped and fringed in thick, dark lashes. Her skin was honey colored with a golden glow to it. He wondered if she was tanned all over, or if there were paler places she kept hidden. He wondered what it would take to find out.

Her top lip was slightly thinner than her fuller, bottom lip, which made her mouth form a perpetual pout. He really couldn't focus on her mouth long, though. He felt he might become dangerous if he did. She had a pronounced dimple in one cheek, a small, perfectly shaped nose, and the cutest pixie chin. But then he didn't really remember noticing chins before. Maybe he noticed hers because she had tilted her head up at him rather defiantly earlier. But, if that was supposed to be her 'fuck off' look, she was going to have to do better than that to scare him away.

She was no bigger than a minute. A little too thin for his taste actually, but perfectly proportioned. He had seen the hint of cleavage above the scooped neckline of the black sheath she wore, when she had stooped previously to retrieve her key card. He was pretty sure his hands could almost encircle her waist completely, and her above the knee dress showed off her slim, tanned, shapely legs.

Her hips were narrow and her butt moved like two bearcats fightin' in a burlap bag, when she walked. He was glad she had a nice ass. He was definitely more of an ass man than a boob man. A woman with a butt that looked like it had been smacked flat with a two-by-four would never appeal to him.

As they finished fighting with their life vests, they turned towards one another and busted out laughing. On him, his looked like it had been made for a small child and there seemed to be enough room left over in hers for a small family of gypsies to move in.

"If we have to depend on these to save our lives in the open sea," William stated seriously, "we're screwed."

Iris giggled and answered, "When we get back to our rooms, I think you should tie two jackets together and I'll cut mine in half. Maybe then we'd have a fighting chance."

At that time, the safety director in charge of their drill, asked everyone to crowd around closer together, so that he could be heard by all. As people pressed in close from all sides, William and Iris became wedged tightly against each other, still wearing their life vests, so it was very claustrophobic and warm. If they hadn't both been pleased with being sandwiched against each other, they might have been somewhat annoyed. As it was, Iris hoped William couldn't hear the rush of blood flowing through her body, being forced more rapidly than usual by the fast pounding of her heart.

She could see the instructor's lips moving, but with all the noise her body was making in her ears, his words sounded like "blah, blah, blah," to her. It was a good thing she had heard all this several times before on other cruises, because she seemed to be deaf to what he was saying.

William was also familiar with the drill instructions and wasn't even pretending to be listening. He was turned just slightly towards Iris and could smell the scent of her shampoo and some kind of delicious perfume. It was obviously applied lightly because he hadn't noticed it until he was this close to her.

He had an uncontrollable desire to put his arm around her waist in a proprietary gesture, but didn't. He was just sensing her relax a little with him, but still had a vision of her gnawing his arm off at the shoulder if he tried it. Way too soon they were dismissed and like everybody else, stripped off their life jackets immediately.

As everyone scattered in various directions and in a unanimous hurry to their respective cabins, a lengthy announcement came over the loud speakers. "Those of you who signed up for early seating, have approximately an hour and a half before dinner is served at six thirty. Please check the instructions you were given upon boarding, to see which of the dining rooms you have been assigned to. The maitre d' will direct you to your assigned table. Second seating begins promptly at eight o'clock. Although tonight does not require formal attire, there will be no shorts, t-shirts or bare feet allowed in the dining rooms at any time. There are several restaurants on board which serve a variety of cuisine in a more casual environment, if you prefer. Please check the directory of the *Whimsical* that is located in your cabin and also is posted on each level of the ship, in numerous places. Should you require assistance, do not hesitate to ask any crew member. We consider it our privilege to serve our passengers aboard the *Whimsical.* Thank you for sailing with us this week. We will strive to provide you with a safe, fun and memorable cruise."

Most of the passengers had stopped where they were and listened intently to the announcement and now, began as one, to move again. William and Iris began to make their way to the level of balconied suites where they were both staying. "Did you sign up for early or late seating?" William felt nervous asking her for some reason, but decided it was an innocent enough question.

"Late. I'm rather a night owl and I was afraid to eat too early for fear

I'd be tempted to cruise the chocolate buffet they set out at midnight." She wondered which seating he had requested but didn't want to act as if she cared so didn't ask.

As they approached their cabins though, William said, "Since we both seem to have almost three hours before dinner would you like to have a drink with me about seven? That gives us a couple of hours to unpack and shower and dress for dinner."

Iris hesitated slightly before answering and then, with a small shrug of her shoulders said, "I only have the makings of a margarita, but if you want to bring whatever you like to drink, then I suppose you can come over at seven. We'll take our drinks out on my balcony. That way you can smoke if you choose to." Iris detested smoking, and wondered how he would answer. She hadn't smelled cigarettes or cigars on his clothing or breath so far, and sincerely hoped that was one bad habit he didn't have.

"That's very considerate, but I've never been a smoker. Growing up in a tobacco growing state, I was one of the few people around that didn't, though. I'm afraid I do however, enjoy another product of my home state. That's what I'll be bringing over to drink later on." He smiled then and asked, "Would you like me to unlock your door for you?"

She handed her key to him and said, "Why not? I'd rather practice opening it myself, when no one else is around. Less humiliating that way."

He slung his life jacket over one shoulder, unlocked her door, once again on the first attempt, and held it open for her. She stepped inside and turning to take her key said, "Thanks. See you at seven." She promptly shut the door and leaned against it.

Iris listened as his own door opened and closed. She was remembering what he had said about being from a tobacco growing state and was bringing a "back home" product to drink. Tennessee was a tobacco producing state and could he possibly mean Tennessee whiskey? "How ironic would that be?" she asked her reflection in the entryway mirror. "And, how convenient?" She walked into her bedroom, where her two suitcases and her cosmetic bag were waiting to be unpacked.

When William entered his own tiny foyer, he was momentarily startled by his own reflection in the mirror above the small table. At first glance he hadn't realized it was himself he was seeing. The man in the mirror was smiling and appeared to be about ten years younger than the man who had entered this suite for the first time, after boarding the ship, just a few hours ago.

He whistled without realizing it, as he threw his suitcases up on the bed and unzipped them. He hung his shirts, slacks, jacket and tuxedo in the closet. His socks, underwear, shorts and swim trunks, he stacked neatly in the drawers of his dresser. He laid the empty luggage on the floor of the closet and shut the doors. The outside of the sliding closet doors were mirrored, reflecting the king-sized bed and making the room look more spacious than it was.

Cruise ships in general aren't endowed with large rooms and with William's considerable stature, it was unthinkable that he could spend a week in anything other than a suite. The regular cabins weren't even as large as his walk-in closet at home, and had a ridiculously tiny shower.

At least his suite had a large bed, a sitting area with a full sized sofa and a reasonable bathroom with a regular tub/ shower. And, the most important feature that kept him from feeling claustrophobic was the wall of glass, with a door leading out to the balcony. He kept the drapes pulled all the way open to the remarkable view of the sea. Nature provided him with not only the sense of space he needed but the kind of spiritual beauty that man would never be able to duplicate.

He sat on the foot of the bed and pulled his cowboy boots off. He placed them on the shelf in the closet with his leather sandals, running shoes, loafers and black, shiny dress shoes he would wear with the tux.

He unbuttoned his shirt and took it off and opened the balcony door. He stepped outside and stood reflectively against the small balcony railing, wearing just his jeans and socks. He raised first one foot, then the other, pulling his socks off and tossing them back through the open door to land silently on the floor with his shirt.

William stretched and flexed and breathed deeply, totally unaware of what a striking picture he portrayed. Tall and bronze and muscled, he looked like a poster child for AARP. No one, including Iris, would have accurately guessed him to be turning sixty in just a few days. He appeared to be early fifties, at the very most.

But all William was thinking about at the moment was how good he suddenly felt. A five hundred pound weight seemed to have been lifted off his chest, allowing him to breathe deeply and fully for the first time in a year.

Had it really been only a year since Rebecca had died? It seemed as if he'd been walking zombie-like through life for centuries. If it hadn't been for his business, his friends and employees, he felt he might have possibly considered suicide. For months after her death the desire to join her had been so appealing. Life without her, life without anyone to love for that matter, had seemed so pointless.

Finally, he felt he had rounded the corner and he had no doubt as to why. As the last light of day painted the sky and the sun sizzled into the sea, he knew what he had to do. And, he only had a week to do it.

Whatever demons possessed Iris, he would exorcise, the dragons that would surely try to chase him away from her, he would slay. Nothing and nobody would keep them from the happiness he knew they could have together, and deserved. How he knew these things, he didn't waste a single moment questioning. All that mattered is that he knew.

Iris struggled to lift her luggage to the bed. They felt like someone had taken her clothes out and then filled them with concrete. God, but it had been a long, tiring day already. But then, she'd been up since four, having only had a few hours of restless sleep, in anticipation of her trip.

As she began to hang the pretty new wardrobe she had spent hours and hours shopping for, she was suddenly very glad she had splurged and chosen such nice things. She had been dressing more like a widow lately (when she bothered to dress at all) than a woman who had simply been dumped by her husband.

She chuckled slightly when she recalled those first six months after David had left. She would have preferred being a widow and could have killed him herself, if she had thought she'd get away with it. But now, she didn't want to waste time thinking about the past.

She found her thoughts were very much on the present, and very definitely on William Pendleton. She liked the sound of his name and grinned foolishly as she pictured herself as a teenager sitting in class, writing "Mrs. William Pendleton" over and over in her notebook. What young girl hadn't done that with each and every boyfriend's name?

Jesus, Joseph and Mary! She had only met this guy a little more than an hour ago. And, even though he had been friendly, polite and attentive to her, he was obviously lonely and just wanted to make a friend on the ship. It was quite obvious she was traveling alone and he was probably just being nice.

She secretly hoped he didn't turn out to be too nice though. She blushed, and feeling a little warm, walked over and opened the balcony door. The mild, gentle breeze felt refreshing on her skin and gently lifted her hair. She was going to have to stop thinking along those lines or she wouldn't be able to look him in the eyes when he came over for that drink.

Her sundresses, capris, tops and evening wear, filled the closet. The shelf was lined with her sandals, flip-flops, evening shoes and handbags and a pair of athletic shoes. The few dresser drawers provided, barely held all the lingerie, night gowns, swim suits, and shorts she had brought. Good grief, what had she been thinking? She had brought enough stuff to be gone a month.

Iris had been trying to get out of this one week cruise since her birthday in August. Why had she packed as if she never wanted to go back home? But she knew why. If it wasn't for her kids and grandkids, she wouldn't have anything or anyone to go home to. She took this enlightenment of her inner self as a sign of improvement. She felt a change was coming over her.

There was a twinge of optimism that had been absent for so long, she hardly recognized it, but there it was. Not feeling quite as tired suddenly, she turned to her closet with renewed energy and the desire to find the perfect outfit for this evening. Humming softly to herself, she removed each item and held it in front of her, critiquing herself in the mirror.

William had finished performing the age old rituals of man. He had "shit, showered and shaved" as the expression goes, and felt ready to tackle the world. Although he'd really rather tackle Iris, he mused. He brushed his teeth, used mouth wash and combed his damp hair back from his forehead, where it lay in loose curls at his collar. His hair had never turned grey and the white at his temples had only shown up recently. No wonder, he thought.

He had chosen a pair of grey slacks, a light blue shirt, navy sport coat and was wearing his well polished loafers without socks. He hated socks and only wore them with his boots and his tuxedo shoes. He wore his loafers, running shoes and of course sandals, without them. William thought that any man caught wearing socks with sandals in public, should be stood up against a wall and executed by a firing squad.

That was the first of two fashion mistakes southern men didn't make. The second one was to wear one of those panty looking, bikini swim suits. Surely no real man could possibly stuff all his equipment in one of those banana hammocks and live to tell about it. And back home, even if you survived such self inflicted torture, you'd still be ridden out of town on a rail. No decent, jealous husband or boyfriend wanted his wife or girlfriend having that much information about a perfect stranger. End of story.

He checked his appearance one last time, grabbed his bottle of Jack Daniels and just before leaving his room said, "Look out Iris. Ready or not, here I come."

Iris was as ready, she guessed, as she'd ever be. She was wearing a pair of black, crepe pants that fit smoothly over her hips and buttocks, then flowed more loosely, almost like a long skirt, to her ankles. You could only tell it was really pants when she walked or crossed her legs and the fabric separated. She wore a pink, silk blouse that buttoned up the front with tiny pearl-like buttons. Her silver, strappy sandals had a low but dressy heel to them and the pearl and diamond ring she wore on her right hand, and matching earrings, completed her ensemble.

Her hair was freshly shampooed and glowed in the soft lamp light. It was parted on one side and hung all one length, straight to her shoulders, then flipped up gently on the ends. She almost never wore foundation but she'd applied blush lightly, wore light brown eye shadow on her lids, accentuating the unique color of her eyes, put on a little mascara, showing off her beautiful lashes, and finished with a pink lip gloss.

"There, William," she warned him, even though he hadn't yet arrived, "that's more effort than I've put forth for anyone in nine months. Besides, this is about as good as I get, so take it or leave it."

Just at that moment there was a knock on her door and she jumped. She thought it was a good thing she'd finished putting on her mascara or she would have probably put an eye out. Thank God it was finally time for that drink. She couldn't believe she'd waited this long. She was a little nervous as she went to answer the door.

When Iris opened her door both she and William just stood there, drinking in each other's appearance as if they'd been parted for days, instead of only two hours. Neither of them spoke or moved, as if they were so out of practice, they were completely lost as to what to do next.

They finally spoke at the same time. "Good evening, Iris. May I come in?" was overlapped by "Hello, William. Please come in." They laughed and she stepped back, pulling the door open wider, so he would have room to enter. She barely had room to close the door, the foyer was so small with both of them in it.

With a dainty flourish of her adorned hand, she motioned him towards the sitting area and said, "Make yourself at home. I was about to prepare myself a margarita." As he moved towards the wet bar, she noticed the Jack Daniels. Her heart skipped a beat, but all she said was, "Please help yourself to whatever you need at the bar."

Her suite suddenly seemed a lot more compact with him in it. But, it wasn't just that he was a big man, she was thinking, it was his very aura that made everything else seem diminished. She had never known anyone with such a commanding presence about him.

William put a few pieces of ice from the full bucket into a glass and poured about three fingers of whiskey over it. Of course he had thick fingers, so the glass was about half full. He set his drink down then and looked at Iris. "I make a pretty mean margarita. Would you like me to mix it for you?"

Iris was afraid he'd see her hands shake if she made it herself, so she accepted his offer. "Yes, thank you. While you're doing that, I'll fix us a snack. There was a basket of goodies delivered just a little while ago from the travel agency my children used when they booked this trip for me. There's cheese, crackers, grapes, chips and chocolates."

"Excellent...all the major food groups. Now that you mention it, I'm starving." He didn't comment on any of the information she'd just unknowingly given him about herself. So, she had children, he reflected as he mixed her drink; as in more than one. And, they were old enough to give her this cruise. He had estimated her to be about forty, but now wondered if it was possible that she was a few years older than that. He secretly hoped so, for his sake. The fewer years between their ages, he felt, the better for him.

Iris found a couple of saucers in the bar and a serving tray. She took the grapes out and washed them, sliced some cheese and set the chips and crackers out on the coffee table in front of the sofa. She was pretty hungry herself.

William said, "Iris, I must just be overlooking it, but I don't see the salt anywhere." He was stirring her drink absentmindedly as he searched the bar with his eyes.

"No," she replied, "I forgot to tell you, I don't take my margaritas with salt. Sorry I wasted your time looking for it."

"No problem. Here, taste this and tell me what you think." He handed her the margarita and she drank thirstily from the glass. Damn, but it was good! If she hadn't been so aware of him watching her, she felt she could have downed the entire glass without stopping.

As she sank into one plush corner of the sofa, she said, "Wow! This is excellent. You're not a professional bartender, are you?"

Skirting the coffee table, his own drink in hand, he made a sound that was a mixture of low chuckle and sarcastic admission. "Humph. Hardly. Although, I'm not overly proud of the fact that I've tended my own personal bar at home a little too frequently over the past several months." He placed himself in the opposite sofa corner, his right arm laid across the low back and angled his body towards Iris, in a conversational pose.

As she handed him a saucer with cheese, crackers and grapes on it, she replied knowingly to his comment. "You're preaching to the choir, now. Just a few months back, I'd toyed with the idea of changing my name to Iris Cuervo."

She smiled guiltily up at him and he laughed heartily at her own admission.

Even though it was just a joke, he detected a touch of truth in what she'd said. His heart went out to her, but he didn't want to push too hard or too fast to get her to talk about the things she so obviously needed to.

They sipped their drinks, nibbled at their snacks and kept the conversation light and impersonal. In the beginning, they were both too afraid of hitting a raw nerve in one another and tiptoed through their dialogue as carefully as soldiers through a mine field.

Eventually, feeling more relaxed, William got up and got them both a fresh drink and reminding himself of his one week crusade, he was compelled to explore a little into what had made her bond so intimately with Jose Cuervo in the first place. But, perhaps he should offer up some insight into his own life, in order to allow her to trust him. One small step for mankind, but a giant leap, he felt, for her.

Therefore, like a child wanting to dive into the deep end of the pool, but knowing he'd better learn to swim first; he placed one foot in the shallow end of the water to test the temperature.

Chapter 3

Handing Iris her second margarita, William settled back comfortably into the couch, resuming his position; however, she noticed he wore a slightly more serious expression.

They had been chatting about only the present, both of them reluctant to touch on their more recent past. Having discussed the cruise ship's amenities, their pleasant suites, the itinerary that would take them to three different islands, other cruise lines they had tried and other islands visited, Iris felt a little more comfortable having a man she had only just met today, sitting within reach of her.

Of course, the margarita had certainly helped, but it was William's easy, genuine, laid-back personality that made her feel so comfortable with him. She'd always heard people talk about meeting someone new and feeling like they'd known them all their lives, or perhaps had met them in a previous life.

Personally, she'd always thought that was a load of horseshit. You know, just an excuse as to why they'd slept with someone on their first date. Even with his rugged good looks, impeccable manners and true gift for making margaritas, she knew there was no way in hell she was going to be that easy.

But, sitting in such close proximity to such a gorgeous male specimen, she knew her friend Peggy would have jumped his bones by now;

exceeding all her previous remarkable speed records. She had to admit after nine long, agonizing months of celibacy, she was beginning to understand Peggy's whoring ways. Perhaps when she got back home she'd make up with her and rekindle their friendship. After all, you never really knew someone until you'd walked a mile in their shoes or in this case, slept alone for nine months in their empty bed. She felt a stirring of kinship with Peggy in her heart and a stirring of pure lust for William in the lower regions of her belly. She stood up and opened the balcony door and invited William to take off his jacket.

As she reclaimed her corner of the couch, he stood, removed his sport coat and laid it carefully on the back of a nearby chair. Watching his body move and flex with an athletic confidence, she had to fight back the urge to invite him to remove his pants, as well. She hoped he would attribute her flushed cheeks to the margaritas and the warm night air.

Sitting back down, he made rolling up his shirt sleeves look like an art form. If sleeve rolling was an Olympic competition, he'd score a perfect ten. She had a feeling he'd score highly in the bedroom too. There was no way this guy could possibly fall into the category Peggy described as "heap big wind, no rain"…no fucking way.

William saw the admiring look in her eyes as she watched him get more comfortable. He was relieved she'd given him permission to remove his coat. He picked his drink up off the table and wondered how she would feel when she learned he was celebrating his sixtieth birthday this week.

At least he hoped it was going to qualify as a celebration. That would depend, he knew, on Iris. So he threw a few crumbs of information out in the open about himself, in hopes that she would reciprocate.

"I hope you don't think I've been too forward today, Iris. It's just that, other than the six days a week I've spent at work and the very few invitations to dinner I've accepted from a few close friends, I've rather become a recluse since Rebecca's death, a year ago this month."

"I too received this trip as a gift, from my employees, though. Unfortunately, I don't have any children. Or any close family left, for that matter. And, I made up my mind before leaving home yesterday, that I was going to make today the first day of the rest of my life. I know that's an old cliché, but I think it's appropriate in my case."

Iris listened intently, and understood the white line on his ring finger, all the more clearly. He'd probably taken it off just before leaving home as a commitment to himself to begin his life anew. She had personally removed her own wedding band the night David had left her. But that was different. He didn't deserve any sentimental consideration.

"I didn't even use the airline ticket I was given with the cruise," he continued. "I opted to drive down. It's only a day and a half drive from my home in Tennessee to Miami. I wanted to use that time as an adjustment period between the past and the future."

My God, she thought, as his words spilled forth. This man has been through so much more than I have and if he can pull himself together enough to start over, why shouldn't I make more of an effort to do the same?

His remark about living in Tennessee hadn't gone unnoticed either. She wondered where? Knoxville was northeast of her, Memphis southwest, Chattanooga southeast, or could he even possibly be from Nashville? That was a little less than an hour due north from Springhill! Surely not, she reasoned. The gods surely wouldn't be that kind to her. But then, perhaps the gods had bigger fish to fry than her with her piddly problems. Maybe there was a cupid, after all, and he had accepted this mission.

William continued, "I poured myself into my business, pushing the limits of my durability, and I'm afraid, demanding too much from some of my employees, as well. Roger, one of the foremen, who's also my best friend, thank God, had the balls to set me straight. He explained to me that there was nothing he could do if I chose to destroy my own life, but there was no way he was willing to go to an early grave with me. He said he still had too much to live for and that if I'd pull my head out of my ass, I could see that I did too. I credit him with saving me." He found he was more comfortable telling Iris all of this than he had thought he would be. "I had been too bitter, too grief stricken, too mad for far too long, to make it back on my own."

His story reminded Iris of those first months that she had shut herself off from even her children. She felt she knew a little about how he had suffered. There had been grief, bitterness and anger, oozing from her pores. Oh, and let's not forget self pity, she reminded herself. Let's give credit where credit is due. She had placed self pity on a pedestal. Except then, her children and grandchildren had saved her. Poor William had evidently had almost nobody. She didn't know the friend he spoke of, but she sent him a mental 'thank you'. She felt unshed tears in her eyes but didn't release them. She was afraid he would stop talking and she wanted desperately for him to continue.

"That's when I started back closing the business at the regular time and not asking people to come in on Saturdays. That very day, I called a meeting and apologized profusely for my selfish behavior and asked everyone to tell their families how sorry I was for monopolizing such an unfair amount of their time." He looked truly embarrassed with his next statement. "Rebecca had been killed the Friday after Thanksgiving Thursday and I'm ashamed to say, I worked my employees extra hours all the Christmas and New Year holidays when we are normally closed."

Iris couldn't help it. One tear after another rolled down her cheeks and she wiped them away with her napkin. William didn't see them, however. He was staring over her shoulder out to the dark sky and even darker sea. Ironically, it wasn't sadness that made the tears force themselves from her eyes finally. It was the remorse he felt for the treatment of others, the courage it took for him to accept the blame and apologize and most of all, the compassion she felt for this man, whom she thought had a bigger heart than any man she'd ever known.

No wonder his employees had gifted him this cruise. It must be because next week was Thanksgiving and the anniversary of Rebecca's death. How much he must have loved her and how happy they surely had been. Iris had not had the pleasure of knowing Rebecca, but knew that she would have liked to. William seemed like such a good man that she knew he would only love a good woman. How lucky Rebecca had been to have been loved by this man.

"The day Roger had put his foot down, was Valentine's Day. I had been even more demanding that day, than usual. When I'd sat at my desk that morning and looked at my schedule, I became irate, as I realized it was February the fourteenth. A day set aside to celebrate love. A woman I had loved for more than thirty years was dead, and she wasn't coming back. I think that morning was the first time it really sunk in. She was gone for good and forever." He let out a sigh and smiled weakly at Iris.

William had already said more than he had intended to, but was just working up to how he happened to be on this cruise at this particular time. "I was a real shit-ass all day. It was like I knew it, but couldn't control myself. I criticized perfect work. I raised my voice to an employee, which is something I had never done before and will never do again. The woman I had yelled at had been seen by a co-worker crying in the ladies' room, and told Roger, who was her supervisor. That was the last straw. He came unglued and let me have it with both barrels." William laughed with the memory, although it hadn't been funny at the time.

Iris was leaning forward slightly, hanging on every word of William's confession. It made her feel so much better about her own strange behavior these past months. Maybe there was hope for her, yet. "At lunch time, I called the meeting I spoke of earlier," William told her, looking a lot more relaxed than he had at the beginning of his story. "After apologizing, I told them to have a happy, loving Valentine's Day and gave everyone the rest of the day off, with pay. I'm really lucky nobody quit during those first few months. It seems they understood a lot more than I gave them credit for."

Suddenly, Iris spoke for the first time since William had handed her the second margarita and began talking about his experiences of the past year since his wife's death. "I hate fucking Valentine's Day." As soon as she realized she had spoken out loud, she slapped her hand over her mouth so hard she almost cut her lip on a tooth. She was so embarrassed, she felt as if her face was on fire.

William laughed and said, "Now it's your turn. This has got to be a story I want to hear. But, tell me over dinner." With that, he glanced at his watch and exclaimed, "Oh my God, Iris, I'm so sorry! I ran my mouth so long, we've completely missed dinner in the dining room."

"You're kidding," she said. "It sure doesn't seem like we've been talking that long. What time is it?"

"Five minutes until nine." He was glad he'd told Iris what he had, but sorry he'd made them miss dinner. He hoped he hadn't blown it. But she didn't seem to mind at all.

She got up and headed to the other room saying, "I noticed some restaurant menus on the dresser earlier. I'll get them and see which of them are still serving."

She came back to the sofa and they sat side by side talking about their options and finally decided on pizza. Not only did they both love it, it was made fresh until midnight.

William grabbed his jacket off the chair and Iris closed the balcony door. She ran water over the two saucers, glasses and knife they'd used and left them in the sink. He rolled his sleeves down, put his jacket back on and was ready to go by the time she was. Discussing pizza had made them both ravenous.

Slipping a light wrap on over her shoulders, Iris asked, "William, do you see my purse anywhere?"

He found it on the foyer table and handed it to her. "Why don't you just let me put your key in my pocket and then you won't have to carry a purse," he suggested.

"Great idea. I already have my wrap to keep up with. It would be just like me to leave one of them behind if I took my purse, too." She handed him the key and he slipped it in an inside jacket pocket. They walked out and William checked to make sure the door locked when he shut it.

It felt so natural to both of them, that neither of them realized how smoothly they had slipped into the familiar, comfortable habits of a couple. Iris did notice, however, when William placed his strong hand at the small of her back as they walked down the hall to the elevators.

When the door opened, a very young couple were just finishing a kiss and they laughed at getting caught. As they exited the elevator, they held hands and smiled, as only those in love do, at the older couple.

"Let me guess," William said to them. "Newlyweds on your honeymoon?" Iris just smiled back at them.

"Yes, sir." The young man spoke proudly and the young girl looked adoringly at her new husband. "How'd you guess?" he asked William.

William held the door open for Iris and laughed at the boy's question. "Believe it or not son, but I was a newlywed once."

The youngsters obviously assumed the older couple were married to each other, because as the elevator doors were closing, the groom winked at William, in the way of two equals sharing a manly moment and said, "Looks like you're still doing o.k. to me." He could still hear the old guy chuckle through the closed elevator as it started up. The newlyweds looked at each other, grinned, and raced down the hall towards their suite. The two old farts, no matter how nice they had been, were already forgotten.

William and Iris agreed on pepperoni with extra cheese and chose a corner booth, where they waited for it to be cooked and brought out to them. Neither of them minded the wait. At least it was being made to order, instead of precooked and kept warm under one of those heat lights that made everything taste like cardboard. He had a Miller Lite to drink and she had a Smirnoff Ice. They both declined a glass and preferred to drink straight from the bottle.

"So, you hate fucking Valentine's Day, huh?" William grinned mischievously as he questioned her. "I sure am glad I'm not the one who ruined it for you. You were breathing fire when you made that statement. Is the guy still living or did you just turn him from a rooster into a hen?"

"He's still living. But I'm pretty sure he's being turned into a hen, even as we speak. Henpecked, at least. The "one who ruined it for me" as you so understated, is my ex-husband." She spent the next couple of hours filling William in on the whole, sordid affair. How David had dumped her on Valentine's Day, was now remarried to a much younger woman and expecting a new baby. She told him about the new house he was building and how her so-called best friend, Peggy, had seemed to thrive on telling her all the juicy details. "Telegraph, telephone, tell Peggy," Iris explained to William.

She didn't hold anything back. He had been honest with her, so she described her own depression and withdrawal from life, the excessive drinking, not eating, the weight loss, all of it.

"Luckily for me though, I have three wonderful, grown kids and six perfect grandchildren who teamed together and reminded me of how much I still have worth living for. Like Roger did for you, just under different circumstances," she added.

"I'm still ashamed that it took me nine months to get a grip." Iris thought this was just as good a time as any to lay all her cards on the table, so she said, "I turned fifty in August and my family gave me this cruise as a birthday present. Right up until the last few days, I didn't know if I'd have the courage to do it alone."

"Well, I for one, am certainly glad you did." He knew better than to comment on a woman's age, but was vastly relieved that there was only a ten year difference between them. He had been afraid that she might be as many as fifteen or twenty years younger than him. She didn't just look great for fifty, she looked great, period. And the fact that she had three children made him doubly impressed. When the time was right, he would make sure she knew just how great he thought she looked, but tonight was too soon. He didn't want it to come out wrong and sound like a cheap attempt at panty removal.

They had long since finished their pizza and beers, and both felt they had revealed enough skeletons to fill several closets. It was time to have a little fun, in William's opinion and a thought came to him.

"Iris, would you like to go into one of the night clubs, check out the music and maybe dance?" He felt like he was asking a girl out on his very first date ever, as he held his breath, waiting to hear her reply.

Now, Iris really couldn't believe her good fortune! Evidently, William liked to dance or was at least willing to. She loved to dance and David had preferred to just listen to the music and get drunk. But, the few times she had said yes, when someone else had asked her to dance, he had gotten mad and acted like a jealous caveman. Thinking back to those times, she was pretty sure that David had always been an asshole. She had just refused to see the obvious.

William had seen her eyes light up like a little girl's at Christmas, when he mentioned dancing. Score one for me, he thought happily. Thank you, Rebecca, for those dance lessons you made me take twenty years ago. And thank you, God, for not giving me two left feet. He sent both thank yous silently up to heaven. He and Rebecca had gone dancing once a week, occasionally twice, after that, and he remembered those times as some of their happiest moments. He was looking forward to "tripping the light fantastic" with Iris. It would be the perfect way to make her feel comfortable in his arms. He was already smiling down at her when she answered with, "I can't think of anything I'd rather do."

They left the restaurant and he took her hand. They were on a mission to find some good "oldies" music. One disco was playing hard rock that was so loud it could undoubtedly jar the fillings out of your teeth. They kept going. The second one was just a piano bar with no dance floor. The third one was perfect. A little fifties and sixties rock and roll, some modern country, and it had a large dance floor. Several people were out there doing the electric slide. That was always an easy one that got people out on the floor and appealed to dancers of all ages. Iris felt like Goldilocks, who had just discovered baby bear's bed. It was just right.

It was around eleven o'clock by then, so the place was jumpin'. They wove between the tables looking for an empty one, but not having any luck. Finally, two couples next to them stood up. They had been sharing a small table next to the dance floor. "Excuse me," one of the guys motioned to William as he spoke. "You appear to be looking for a place to land and we happen to be taking off. You better grab this one, before somebody else does."

William and Iris thanked them profusely and pounced on two of the vacated chairs like chickens on a June bug. As soon as their butts hit the seats, someone was there to clear the table and take their drink orders. That was the one thing about service on a cruise ship. The service was impeccable.

They didn't dare to get up to dance until their drinks arrived. They needed them as evidence that the table was taken. Fortunately, it didn't take long. William hung his jacket on the back of his chair and Iris folded her wrap and left it in plain view on top of the table. Along with their napkins and drinks, their occupancy was sufficiently established.

The band struck the first chords of a Brooks and Dunn song called Neon Moon. "Do you know how to do the cowboy cha-cha?" William asked, as he noticed some couples about to begin the dance.

"I thought you'd never ask." Iris smiled radiantly as he stood, reached for her hand and practically raced her to the crowded floor. They didn't want to miss a minute of this dance.

No words were necessary as they dipped and turned, skipped and twirled, in perfect unison. People watching them, assumed they had been dancing as partners for years. They made an amazingly striking couple.

Him, with his muscular height and dark hair, playing leading man to her blonde petiteness. Men and women both, watched with a mixture of appreciation and jealousy. All the dancers and the band, received a loud round of applause at the song's conclusion.

As they made their way back to their table, they received a few nice compliments from people along the way, as did some of the other dancers. It was a fun dance for both participants and observers.

They sat the next couple of songs out, as they were line dances and they preferred to wait for the ones that would place them in each other's arms again. The band then announced they were taking a fifteen minute break and upon their return, would be switching gears and would be playing some oldies, both fast and slow. They wanted to give everyone the chance to dance to something. The band had seen it all and knew that some guys would only attempt a slow dance, not requiring too much skill or coordination, but would be just enough to satisfy their date.

William and Iris had been sitting side by side, facing the dance floor and giving their own appreciative applause to the musicians and dancers. During the much quieter break, they could now hear each other well enough for conversation.

"You said earlier that you drove from your home in Tennessee to Miami. Where in Tennessee do you live?" she asked casually.

"Both my business and home are in Franklin. That's in Williamson County. Have you ever been there?" William saw disbelief register on Iris' face as he asked.

"Been there? We're practically neighbors! I live in Williamson County too; in Springhill!" And then it hit her just exactly who he was. When he talked about owning a business earlier, she hadn't given much thought to it. But then, he'd only mentioned his last name once, when he'd introduced himself earlier in the day and she'd been focused on his boots. It had gone in one ear and out the other, at the time. And later, talking about his business, he hadn't mentioned the company name. He probably thought it would mean nothing to her. Besides, he didn't strike Iris as the type to brag.

He was the Pendleton in Pendleton Manufacturing, Inc. It was one of the largest makers of auto parts in the country, supplying parts to both foreign and domestic automobile manufacturers all over the world. This guy probably had more money than Trump, and was a hell of a lot better looking.

She fleetingly remembered reading in the newspaper about his wife's death, back when she still took the paper. No wonder he had been able to pour himself into his work. He had quite a company to pour himself into. Her heart went out to him once again, however.

Money not only didn't solve everything, she imagined, but had probably kept him more isolated and lonely than most men would have been after losing their wife. She could only imagine the number of casseroles that had been brought over by female neighbors wanting to "help him get over his grief" so to speak.

That explained becoming a recluse when he wasn't at work, she thought. Otherwise, this gorgeous, wealthy, single man would have been chased relentlessly by every eligible and several ineligible women in the area. Lesser men would envy him she knew. But, after just meeting him today, she also knew he was above that. Above pursuing casual sex or meaningless relationships just to fill the lonely days and the seemingly endless lonely nights.

She didn't yet know his exact age, but like herself, suspected he came from an era and upbringing that made him view such behavior as both undesirable and unacceptable.

But now, a year after his wife's death and nine months after her husband had deserted her, she knew she was ready to get on with her life and sensed that he was too.

His exclamation sounded as incredulous as her's had. "Springhill! You've got to be shittin' me! You're only twenty minutes away. I attend meetings there all the time at the Saturn plant. I don't freakin' believe this. How could I get this lucky? I thought I'd used up my quota just meeting you onboard a ship of five thousand people. This is more than coincidence, Iris. This is fate. It sure does simplify things."

She was about to ask him "what things?" but the band started playing at that exact moment. The song was Mustang Sally and there was no way she could sit still to that one.

"Do you swing?" she asked hopefully.

"Baby, I was born to bop." And, with that, he proceeded to prove it. He had great rhythm and lead her skillfully through every move she'd ever done and taught her a few new ones. She'd never had so much fun in all her fifty years. Whether it was fate, as he said, or a blessing or just pure luck, Iris didn't know or care. She only knew that he made her happy.

The next song was a deliciously romantic, slow one and William folded Iris into his arms. She wasn't tall enough to lay her head on his shoulder, so she leaned it against his chest instead. They were both slightly sweaty from the vigorous dance they'd just finished and she could smell his man scent through his shirt, along with his cologne.

He smelled clean and masculine and sexy, all at the same time. He spoke her name and she pulled away just enough to look up at him. He lowered his lips to hers in a brief but exquisite kiss. It felt both gentle and forceful, but not urgent. Like he was claiming her as his. And that was fine with Iris.

William kept the slightest bit of distance between them after that kiss, because he was feeling the stirrings of an erection. He wanted her so badly, he had visions of stripping them both naked and taking her on the band stage in full view of everyone. Now that would be a show stopper, he was thinking, as a tap on his shoulder brought him to his senses.

He turned as some guy asked, "May I cut in?" What the hell? He didn't know people actually cut in like that anymore. Not anybody smart, anyway. But, it surprised him so and being mannerly, he knew the thing to do would be to let this asshole finish the dance with Iris. He didn't want to, but he didn't want to embarrass her by telling him to fuck off, so he handed her over to him. Besides, the song was almost over.

He sat back down at their table and watched the jerk as he ran his mouth constantly during the last minute of the song. Iris was looking up at her new partner coolly, and answering his questions with one word replies.

William sized the guy up as he was beginning to think the song would never come to an end. He was much shorter than him, probably five foot ten inches or so, styled blonde hair, fortyish, nicely dressed and a fair dancer. He wanted to kill him and knew he could, with his bare hands. He couldn't stand seeing him hold Iris in his arms. At least she had put ample distance between their bodies. "That a girl," he silently praised her.

Just when he thought the band was playing the longest single song in history, they finally stopped. The asshole said something else to her and he saw Iris shake her head in the no direction. The jerk escorted her back to their table. William jumped up to hold her chair for her, and she resumed her seat by his side. At least the guy didn't ask to join them. He just thanked her for the dance and left. He had ignored William completely.

Iris apologized for the interruption even though it hadn't been her fault. She could tell William wasn't any happier about it than she had been. But, he tried to make light of it, for both their sakes.

"No apology necessary. It's not your fault that you're the prettiest girl in the room. Let me guess, he offered to buy you a drink. I saw you shake your head." He was smiling for her benefit, but seething inside.

"Yea, he did. I told him I was with you. I thanked him anyway though, just to be polite. He's probably not too many years older than my son, Jake." She smiled at that. "I guess I should feel flattered."

William excused himself and said he'd be back in a flash. He told her to spill her drink on any guy who tried to move in while he was gone. He noticed, when he said that, that both their glasses were almost empty. She laughed and promised to do just that, as he walked away. William had seen the guy who had cut in on them, go into the bathroom. He went in and sure enough, there he was, combing his hair in the mirror.

"Hey, you there, James Dean." The guy glanced at William's reflection in the mirror and kept combing his hair. "I don't appreciate you cutting in on me and my fiancé. I'd greatly appreciate it if you don't do it again." And, having said what he came to say, turned to leave.

"Dude, I looked first. She wasn't wearing a ring on her left hand. You think I'm stupid?" He stuck his comb in his pocket and proceeded to wash his hands.

"Yes. Obviously you are, or you wouldn't have talked back to me," William said, walking over to the sink. "You want to see a fucking ring? I'll show you two of them. One around both of your eyes if I see you near her again."

Close up, he was a formidable opponent, Matt concluded, as he tried to appear calmer than he felt. He figured the woman's date to be a good ten years older than he was, but the motherfucker was built like a brick shithouse. He would have to approach her sometime when Godzilla here wasn't around.

"Look man. I didn't know, o.k.? I'm not a mind reader. Didn't see a ring and, let's face it, she's hot. Just take it as a compliment." Matt was relieved as the door opened and a man made his way to one of the stalls.

William leaned to within a few inches of his face and lowered his voice. "I don't need your compliments. But, if I run into a dry spell, I'll be sure to look you up." He turned and walked out. Matt realized he had been holding his breath and let it out slowly.

Iris had finished her drink and as soon as he got back to the table, William downed the rest of his. He motioned for the waiter to bring them one more round. They had been there for over an hour and had been dancing more than drinking. One more wouldn't hurt them.

They danced until two in the morning. They laughed a lot and kissed a few more times and by the time the nightclub closed, felt as if they had been together for much longer than part of just one day. They strolled up on deck for a moment, delaying the time that they would have to say goodnight and go to their separate suites.

He stood at the railing with his arm around her and she leaned against his side. The jacket and wrap they had put back on was just enough between them and the early morning air. There were a few other couples strolling nearby, but they were oblivious to anyone except each other.

The waves slapped against the side of the ship far below. The moon was high in the sky and would be full in a few more nights. It reflected a wide strip on the water. Neither of them could remember a more perfect moment. It was as if the past had floated out to sea and the present had gently been ushered back in and belonged only to them. They had both had a long, tiring but eventually happy day. Exhaustion finally sent them below to their rooms.

William fished Iris' key from his jacket pocket, unlocked her door and held it open for her. She stepped inside and turned to thank him for such a wonderful evening. But, before she got the first word out, he swept her so hard against him, it took her breath away.

One arm was tightly around her waist and with his other hand, he held her head firmly, pressing his mouth hard against hers. For the first time, their tongues sought each other out.

William placed his back against the open door and moved his feet apart, allowing him to pull her into his groin. She clung to him as if she was afraid of drowning if she let go. Iris had one hand on the back of his neck and the other in the curls of his hair against his collar. She arched against him and felt him grow hard against her belly. In her mind she fantasized about releasing him from his pants and wrapping her legs around his buttocks, straddling him and forcing his pulsing hardness deep inside of her.

The door next to hers opened and shut and they could hear drunken laughter as the occupants returned to their room. William and Iris had been just inside the open door in her foyer and hadn't noticed them coming down the hall. They knew they hadn't been seen and really didn't care. Still, it had been like a splash of cold water, enveloping them in reality. They were both flushed and panting and William chuckled low in his throat.

"You were just saved by the bell, young lady," he said softly, creating a little space between them, and kissed her hair. He was both disappointed with the interruption and glad. He had promised himself that even if she did give him the green light, he was going to prove to her on their first night together, that he was of good intentions.

As frantic as he was to have her tonight, it was more important to William to have her forever. He didn't want any regrets or misunderstandings between them. He didn't want to use her, take advantage of her months of loneliness or make her feel guilt or shame.

He would have more time tomorrow to express the depths of his feelings for her. As quick as it seemed, he knew he was in love with her. And, he didn't want her to think it was only lust and a one night stand he was after. But, tomorrow night, he reflected, it would take two, wild horses to pull them apart. He was a gentleman after all, but not a saint.

Iris leaned her forehead against his chest. Her knees were shaking and her breath was coming in short little gasps. "What makes you think I wanted to be saved?" she asked brazenly. She knew she sounded cheap, but was in no mood to care. "I already hate my neighbors even though I haven't met them yet." Then she giggled and he laughed and they returned to a sense of normalcy.

It was almost three in the morning, he noted, when William glanced at his watch. "Iris, if I don't go to my own room right now, I never will. I can't begin to tell you how much this evening has meant to me. Thanks to you, I feel reborn. But, I don't want to overstay my welcome all in one day. I hope you'll allow me to monopolize much of your time tomorrow, though. Actually, it's already tomorrow and we both need some sleep." His mention of sleep made Iris yawn. "Can I come by and get you about ten, for a late breakfast? We'll be at sea all day today and I'd love to spend the day with you, if you have no objections."

"I can't think of a single one," Iris answered happily. "Ten will be fine. But, why don't we order room service and have breakfast on my balcony? After only six or seven hours of sleep though, I warn you, I'll look like hell. I'm not a morning person."

He kissed her lightly on the lips and while pulling her door shut, he said, "If you're what hell looks like, then I sure do hope I'm not held up in purgatory for long. You can make a man look forward to the trip." The last thing he heard as he unlocked his own cabin was the tinkling sound of her laughter.

Chapter 4

Five hours later, at eight a.m., William awoke to sunlight streaming in the balcony door. In that brief moment between sleeping and being fully awake he was conscious of smiling, but couldn't quite remember why he would be happy.

His first thoughts were usually about Rebecca, the loss of Rebecca. He would arise, already filled with emptiness, dread, sadness and grief. It was as if he stuffed them in a backpack and carried them around on his shoulders all day.

Today felt different. He woke smiling. Why? Think. And then, in his first full moment of wakefulness, he remembered. Iris. His smile grew wider.

Then he also remembered the early morning scene in her foyer, just before they parted to get some sleep. He was smiling so much now his jaws were hurting a little. But then he was out of practice. Along with the grin, those memories were creating a reaction of a different nature. A tent had formed in the bed sheet. It felt like he might just punch a hole right through the damn thing.

Time to get a shower and relieve himself of this pressure. If he didn't, he would have to pole vault across the hall to Iris' room. He certainly wouldn't be able to walk. Too bad he couldn't just knock on her door and announce room service. He knew it would be a service she would long remember. "Down boy," he chuckled as he made his way to the shower, opting for a more civilized remedy.

Iris had left a wake-up call for nine. There was no one, besides William, she would have done without sleep for, especially on vacation. But, as the call came through six hours later, she picked up the receiver and slammed it back down. What the hell had she been thinking? Iris glanced at the clock, turned over, put a pillow over her head and groaned.

Why hadn't she told him she would meet him at ten p.m. instead of a.m.? What's the rush? Where's the fire? Then, the thought of fire brought the heat rushing back, as she remembered what had taken place just a few hours earlier.

God, but she had been so hot with wanting him and knowing how much he had wanted her too. After he had left and she'd undressed for bed, she had seen the proof of her desire in the damp crotch of her panties. If she had thrown them against the wall they would have probably stuck.

With the interruption from next door, William's cooler head had prevailed. She had been willing to lie down, spread eagled and allow him to explore every opening in her body.

She hadn't even been that willing on her first date with David. But then, she had only been fifteen at the time. Now, she was fifty. Older, wiser and hornier. Well, older and hornier anyway. Two out of three ain't bad, she reasoned.

Like William, she knew it was going to happen. And the first official day of the cruise was over. Today was Sunday and they wouldn't reach San Juan, their first port of call, until tomorrow sometime.

They had the entire day to explore the ship, explore their entertainment options and hopefully...no definitely, she amended her thinking, explore each other. She felt as she had when she had been a virgin. So many emotions to deal with, anticipation, desire, curiosity, excitement, with just a little fear and guilt thrown in to really stir the pot.

At least this time it wouldn't hurt. Or would it? After nine months, hell, she might have grown together for all she knew. She had never been one to masturbate, so the territory had been unchartered all this time.

Even though she had been sexually active since fifteen, David was still the only one she had ever been with. She had heard enough of Peggy's sexual exploits however, to feel certain David had nothing to be ashamed of in the endowment department.

But, Iris was remembering the bulge in William's slacks, straining so hard against the fabric, it had literally been drumming against her belly. So what if the first time with him was uncomfortable? The next time would be better. And, the next and the next.

Good grief. And she had accused David's child bride of being a slut. Here she was, about to make a notch on her own bed post. She hadn't yet let William make love to her for the first time, and she was already mentally planning several more rolls in the hay with him, this week alone.

But then, she hadn't stolen someone else's husband either. Maybe, Iris was thinking, she shouldn't be so critical of either of them. Maybe Samantha had simply fallen in love with David, and been smart enough and determined enough to get him, no matter how many obstacles had stood in her way. Iris smiled when she realized she had thought of her as Samantha, instead of the slut. That was a first.

Iris was not going to let anything or anybody keep her from what she wanted either. And she wanted William. Now, often and in various ways. She looked to see what time it was and bolted out of bed. Her future would be knocking in forty five minutes.

William showered after taking care of his personal business and was thinking a little more clearly. He didn't shave or finish his morning routine yet, because he wanted to go up on deck and get his run in first. He quietly left his room and took the stairs to warm up.

He and Rebecca used to jog together most mornings before going to work. She had been his partner, not only in life, but in the business as well. After she died, he had stopped jogging through their neighborhood. The scenery, even while beautiful, was too familiar, too her, too them. So he had joined the YMCA and most nights after work, he went there to run and work out. Sometimes he swam laps in one of the pools; outdoors if the weather permitted, indoors if it didn't. He knew he was in better shape than a lot of guys half his age. William flexed and stretched, glanced at his watch and began to jog.

The workouts had not only given him a great body, it had been somewhere to go, something to do. Some nights he grabbed a bite to take home with him to eat and other times he just made himself soup or salad, with maybe a sandwich to have with it. He hated eating alone in a restaurant and only did it occasionally when traveling on business.

He was looking forward to having someone to share his meals with, his home with, his bed with, share his entire life with. Not just someone, though. Iris. Nobody else would do. Anticipating his day ahead with her, he slightly picked up his pace.

There were others on deck who were either walking, jogging or running to try and offset all the food they would indulge in on the cruise this week. Those who didn't exercise could stand to gain at least a pound a day. Or more, if they also didn't practice self control. It was easy to do. The food was well prepared, decorative, delicious and plentiful.

Iris had confessed her poor eating habits and weight loss during the past several months, to William, the night before. He fully intended to see to it that she did much better this week in that department. She could stand to gain a few pounds. Plus, he just wanted her to feel happy and be healthy.

It was wonderful to have someone to take care of again. And he could tell she was a loving and nurturing woman just in the way she talked about her family. Well, they would take excellent care of each other, he vowed silently.

He had slowed to a fast walk, letting his heart rate come down gradually. His breathing was almost normal already. In a couple more minutes he would head back to his suite to clean up properly.

He was wondering what Iris would want to do after breakfast. Perhaps they would lounge around the pool for a while. That way, they could talk and get to know details of each others lives.

He wanted very much to hear all about her children and the grandkids. William was looking forward to having an entire family, even one already made. If they were anything like Iris, they would be a pleasure. He imagined the sound of young kids laughing and playing in his sprawling Laurelwood mansion. That would definitely be something different. But then, he was looking forward to a lot of new things. William felt a surge of optimism and happiness. Life was once again good.

He made his way to the stairs. He was too hot, sweaty and probably smelly, to get on an elevator with other people. Of all the ones he'd seen on deck, he hadn't noticed any of them. But then, he'd been busy with thoughts of Iris.

But, just before going below, he caught a glimpse of the guy who had cut in on him while dancing last night. He was leaning against the railing, facing in William's direction. The guy didn't notice him though, because he was deep in conversation with a girl.

By the gesturing and the guy's expressions, they appeared to be arguing. William could only see the girl from the back, but he had a strong sense of having seen her before. Perhaps he had just seen her yesterday, somewhere else on the ship. Yea, that was probably it.

Her hair was dark and hung half way down her back, like Rebecca had worn hers. It was long and straight, shiny and healthy looking. That's probably why he had noticed.

But, seeing this girl he didn't know, with a jerk he didn't trust, gave William an uncomfortable feeling. If this guy had come on the cruise with a woman, why had he hit on Iris last night? Perhaps this was his girlfriend and saw him do it or heard about it and that's why they were arguing. Well, he deserved a good ass chewing and he sincerely hoped this woman was letting him have it with both barrels.

With a shrug, he started down the steps. It was no business of his after all, and he was anxious to hit the shower for the second time that morning. He stole a look at his watch. In forty five minutes he would knock on the door of his future.

Iris had put her bathing suit on under her shorts and top. She was hoping William would go to the pool with her. She just wanted to relax, get some sun and find out everything about William's life he was willing to fill her in on.

She loved hearing him talk, his expressions, the sound of his voice. They had talked in the early part of the evening last night, but then had just enjoyed being together. Dancing, eating, drinking, laughing, kissing; it had all been so perfect.

Now she hoped he liked the sun and water as much as she did. It would be a glorious backdrop for lighthearted conversation. Hopefully, they had both unloaded most of the bad and sad stuff. As much as they'd needed to anyway, to explain how they both came to be on this cruise alone.

How fortuitous that his employees and her children had chosen the same cruise line, same itinerary and same week. Perhaps it really was fate, as William had suggested last night. Thank God, she had gotten her shit together and come, after swearing she wouldn't. The thought that she could have missed meeting him, knowing him, loving him, was too much to bear thinking about. O.K., so she wouldn't. Nothing but happy thoughts from now on, she told herself.

It was almost ten. Iris appraised herself in the full length of the mirrored closet doors. Her hair was clean and shiny and pulled straight back in a pony tail with a pink scrunchy. Since she was planning on getting in the pool, the only makeup she had on, was some waterproof mascara. A couple of years ago, she had splurged and had had permanent eyeliner put on her lids, so she looked more made up than she actually was. Her pink lip gloss would have to be reapplied after breakfast.

Her shorts were white, denim Levi's and her lime green tank top said "Lucky" across her chest. It was actually the brand, but Iris thought it was an omen as well. Pink flip flops and a lime green beach bag would certainly keep William from losing her in a crowd, she thought. The halter straps of her black, two piece tankini, showed at her neck. She would have to remember to untie them later. She hated strap marks.

Before she had lost weight, she had been rather big busted. She was a little glad to have lost some of it. She had always been self conscious in a swim suit, but now her breasts, though still in greater proportion to the rest of her, looked a lot more normal.

Turning sideways, Iris still thought her butt was her greatest asset. Still right up there where it was supposed to be. David had called it a "shelf butt". He said it stuck straight out and had often teased her about letting him set his beer bottle on it. But then David was an idiot. Now that she wore a size four, it didn't stick out like it had when she was an eight. Now she thought it was just right. "So screw you, David," she said, as she went to answer the knock on her door.

Iris wondered if she would ever get used to the shock of seeing William for the first time each day. He managed to appear better looking each time she opened the door and saw him standing there.

Surely, when the new wore off, she wouldn't still feel this electric tingle that started in her nipples and ran down her belly and caused her vagina to contract in tiny spasms. Get a grip, Iris, she told herself. He's here for breakfast, and you're not on the menu. "Good morning, William," she said with a smile. She raised up on her tiptoes and gave him a harmless, little kiss on the lips. She didn't trust herself to do more.

She turned away before he could see her drooling and walked out on the balcony with him on her heels. The first time she noticed the bottle of champagne was when he set it on the table.

"Your good morning kiss was just a little lacking, sweetheart," he chastised her, while pulling her close to him. He kissed her soundly, but sweetly, with no tongue action. He knew if he did, the champagne cork wasn't going to be the only thing to explode before breakfast. He was determined to pace himself. But, he was just as sure that tonight was going to be the night. He couldn't stand not having her one day longer.

Iris blushed as she admitted the reason for the hasty kiss. "I'm sorry, but so you're not offended, I'll tell you the truth. After last night, I hardly trust myself to behave with you." She grew even more flushed as she explained herself.

"Ditto darlin'. I feel your pain. But, we're going to have a little champagne, a lot of breakfast, get some sun if that's agreeable with you, and spend the day getting to know each other better. If you're not sick and tired of me by then, we'll dress for dinner and eat in the dining room tonight, like a civilized couple. Then we can catch a show, go dancing, do a little gambling, whatever your heart desires. I will make you witness to all of my manners, I swear, right until the moment that I lose my dignity and ravish you. Does that meet with your approval?" William had been working with the champagne as he spoke and just as he finished, the cork flew out over the railing and the champagne bubbled over.

Iris, upon seeing the champagne, had grabbed a couple of glasses from the bar just inside the door. They caught the bubbling geyser in their glasses, the best they could, without losing too much of it.

"In answer to your question, if I had told you first how I wanted to spend today, it would have sounded exactly like what you came up with. You're beginning to scare me a little, though. Can you read my mind?" She sipped her champagne and looked up at him with raised eyebrows.

"Yes, I can. So stop it! I've already told you. That happens after dinner and a show." He laughed as she swatted him with a room service menu.

After ordering fruit, pancakes with syrup, bacon and coffee, they sat in two of the only four chairs that would fit on the balcony. They propped bare feet up on the rail and sipped the champagne.

"Do you remember when I said that if you look like hell in the mornings, then I would consider making the trip?" He didn't look at her and continued to gaze out to sea.

Iris wondered if William thought she looked lousy that morning and hesitated slightly before answering. "Yes. I'm not used to only six hours of sleep, though. Maybe today isn't the right moment to make that judgment." She meant to be funny, but he didn't laugh.

Instead, he turned his head, looked directly into her eyes and took her left hand in his right. They still held their champagne glasses in their other hands.

"Iris, you look more like heaven this morning to me. Like heaven on earth. When you told me last night that you were fifty, I was truly surprised. I had you figured roughly ten years younger than that." Her heart sank until he continued. Did he think she was too old?

"I wanted to tell you then how beautiful I think you are. Not just for fifty, just beautiful, period. For any age, at any age, you always will be. You have that special something. That perfect blend of beauty and grace, intelligence and humor, little girl playfulness and grown woman sexiness. You are my vision of heaven, Iris, and I already know I've fallen in love with you." Iris was stunned by William's opinion of her.

"I know that's a lot to absorb before breakfast," he said, smiling at her then. "But I really wanted to tell you last night. I was afraid, after knowing me for only a few hours, you wouldn't believe me. I assure you I am serious. Seriously in love with you."

A tear spilled down her cheek from one golden eye, unnoticed by Iris, but seen by William. "That was the most beautiful thing anyone has ever said to me. Ever. How can I begin to thank you, not only for your words, but for loving me? I don't know what to say, except I love you too. In addition to the obvious physical attraction I have for you, I'm also in love with everything you do, and say, and think. You're deeper, kinder, more thoughtful and romantic, than any man I've ever known."

She laughed softly. "Hell, you're just more man than I ever knew existed in the real world. I feel like Cinderella who has just met her prince." Then quietly she asked, "Are you real, William? Is this really happening?"

He knew she was afraid of what they were confessing to each other after so short a time. Her questions were almost a whisper. He felt them hang between them as fragile as a spider's web.

"I am real, Iris. We are real. And this is happening. I don't want to frighten you, though. We'll go as slow as you need to. I'm not going anywhere." He laughed and rose from his chair. "Except to let room service in. I'm starving."

She hadn't even heard the knock. She had been replaying his words in her head. The ones where he said he wasn't going anywhere. Were there really men like that? Ones who didn't leave? He was right. She was afraid. Scared shitless in fact.

She had just poured her heart out for only the second time in her life. The first time had been to David. He had said he loved her, too. But then he left. Granted, it was almost thirty three years later. But that didn't make him any less gone. Watching William help the guy from room service lay out their breakfast, she reminded herself that he wasn't David. He was nothing like David.

By the time they finished breakfast and got to the pool, it was after eleven. They couldn't find two empty chairs side by side, so Iris claimed one, while William scouted around for another one for himself.

She got busy arranging her towels, facing her chair towards the sun and manipulating enough room beside her for William's chair. From her beach bag, she got out two different sun screens. A 30 SPF cream for her face and neck and 15 SPF for the rest of her. Even though she was blond, she wasn't fair skinned, and tanned easily.

She dabbed a small amount of the cream on her fingers and began to rub it gently on her face. Maybe William would spray the other on her back and shoulders for her, she thought with a smile. That was something David would never do. He hated getting the oil on his hands, so she would have to twist like a pretzel to apply it herself.

Happily occupied, Iris didn't notice how long it had taken William to get back with his chair. She did notice his expression, though. He seemed just a hair distracted, as he set his chair down close to hers. She handed him a couple of towels to spread over it before he sat down.

"These damn things are as scarce as hen's teeth around here. I thought I was going to have to dump some little ole lady in the pool and steal hers. I had to go all the way over next to the railing to find this one. I was beginning to think I was going to have to set it down and rest a spell before carrying it all the way back here."

"Yeah, right." She grinned at him skeptically. "You could probably have carried the chair with the little ole lady still in it, and not even been out of breath when you got here." She was applying oil to her legs now.

A secret little smile played on her lips as William asked, "Do you want to turn over and let me rub oil on your back? It would be my pleasure, I assure you." He gave her a very comical, lecherous leer and she laughed so hard she almost peed on herself. He let the back of her chair down for her as she flipped over on her stomach.

He sprayed the oil a little at a time, massaging her neck, shoulders and back with his huge but gentle hands. She closed her eyes and gave in to the luxurious feel of his fingers on her body. He even made getting a tan feel like an erotic experience, she thought, as she drifted in and out of a light doze.

Now that Iris wasn't looking at him, William replayed the scene in his mind, that had taken place a few minutes ago, as he had searched for an empty chair. He'd been quite a distance away, on the far side of the pool, when at last he'd spotted one. He looked down at the young woman sitting closest to it and asked, "Excuse me, are you saving this chair for someone?" At first, he didn't recognize her. But when she spoke, he looked more closely.

"Why, Mr. Pendleton! What a pleasure to run into you. I was hoping our paths might cross. I knew this was the cruise you were booked on, since I helped make the arrangements, but with several thousand people onboard, and such a huge ship, I thought the chances might be slim. But now, here you are. Would you like to join me?" the girl asked excitedly.

As she spoke about making his arrangements, it came to him who she was. Her name was Allison something. She worked at Pendleton

Manufacturing in the human resources department, he remembered now. He knew she had been there ten years, because he had personally presented her, and several others, with a token of appreciation gift when they reached their tenth year of service.

He barely remembered that particular occasion, however; because it had taken place just a few months after Rebecca's death. During the entire gift presentation, all he had thought of was how he and Rebecca had always awarded the gifts together.

She was the one who remembered the personal details of their employee's lives. Names, marital status, children's ages and hobbies and interests. Even as the company doubled and then tripled in size, she still maintained an open door policy. And everyone, especially the female employees, considered her a friend and confidant.

Rebecca had unfortunately had to have a hysterectomy soon after they were married. That's why they had no children. His intuition had told him that their employees, no matter their ages, had filled that void somewhat, for Rebecca. She was very compassionate and caring. And while she kept the things they shared with her confidential, when asked to, he knew she had both rejoiced over their personal triumphs and sympathized when misfortune struck.

She never forgot a wedding gift, a baby present, or to send flowers and a personal note with the passing of a family member. There was no telling how many she had helped financially, off the record, when tragedy overtook their lives, such as a life changing illness.

The company provided excellent medical insurance. But, a couple of times there had been a single mother, receiving no child support from the long gone father and couldn't afford to miss even an hour of work. He knew Rebecca had paid rent, utilities and bought groceries, for more than one single parent who had missed work because of their own illness or that of their critically ill child. No wonder the entire staff had grieved right along with him, at her passing. He felt in their own way they had loved her, too.

Looking at this young woman now, he knew Rebecca would have remembered her last name. He had done well to remember her first name. She must have started working for them right out of high school he thought, as he guessed her to be about thirty. With already ten years employment with the company, he didn't think she would have time to have gone to college first.

But, that wasn't unusual and not a requirement for most of the positions held at his company. He would take effort, loyalty and natural intelligence, over some lazy, overeducated idiot, with no common sense, any day.

Nothing against a good education. He had gone to the University of Tennessee in Knoxville, after his four years in the Marines. It's just that he had a lot of really smart, well trained, dedicated employees who hadn't had that opportunity. He thought perhaps this girl fell into that category.

"Allison, right?" he asked, and held out his hand for her to shake. He noticed she wore no ring on her left hand and only a small, simple, pearl ring on her right. "And what's with the Mr. Pendleton stuff? Everyone at the company calls me William, as you well know."

Allison swung her legs gracefully to one side of the chair and sat up, at the same time reaching to clasp his hand. She had been lying with her long, slender legs stretched out before her. "I know at work we do, however; I didn't know about after hours." She looked up at him with cornflower blue eyes, batted her lashes and smiled seductively. "After all, I've never had the pleasure of your company while not at work, William."

She said "William" as if they were old lovers, instead of mere acquaintances. Using his hand she was still holding on to, she pulled herself up from the pool chair and stood tall and close. She had made sure, in doing so, that one breast had brushed against the hand he automatically helped her up with.

He let go as soon as she was on her feet and took a step backward. There wasn't much room to back away from her, though, since the empty chair he had come for, was touching the backs of his legs.

While still several inches shorter than him, he figured her to be at least five feet, nine or ten inches. Her long, dark hair was held back with a large clasp at the nape of her neck. Her ample breasts strained against the thin fabric of her miniscule, red bikini. It covered so little of her voluptuous body, he wondered why she'd bothered wearing it at all. Why not simply use two band aids up top and a stopper down below?

Her face was made up as if she was going to a party, with bright red lipstick and enough eye makeup to keep Maybelline in business for a while longer. He smiled as the image of Wonder Woman popped into his head.

She mistook his smile as an invitation, because she wanted to. Even though he had not responded to her comment concerning keeping his company after hours, she pursued it anyway.

"Perhaps we can get to know each other better in the next few days, and nights, of course," she added. As she spoke, one hand moved to the clasp and releasing her hair, she swung it, to where it fell loosely over her shoulders, almost covering her breasts. And that took some doing.

At first, William had been only amused at her obvious flirtation. Now he wasn't. Now he knew why she had seemed so familiar to him this morning. This was the woman he had seen on deck, arguing with the blonde guy from the club.

It felt like spiders were climbing up his spine. What was their connection? And, if they were together, why was she trying to seduce him and her boyfriend so hot for Iris?

"If my fiancé and I should run into you sometime during the week, then maybe we can have a drink together." He gave her a conspiratory smile and added, "You'll be the first person that I've introduced to the future Mrs. Pendleton. Have a great vacation and thanks for the chair."

He left her standing with wide eyes and her mouth slightly open. He felt those same eyes boring holes into his back as he walked away, holding the chair high, so as not to bump anyone with it.

Whatever game she was playing, he felt sure her blonde friend was in on it with her. There had been other women who had tried their best moves on him, both before and since Rebecca's death. But nobody had stood a chance.

He had never cheated on Rebecca. And until Iris, hadn't met a woman who could hold a candle to even her memory. He knew that Iris wasn't trying to replace Rebecca, just as he wasn't trying to replace David. They just deserved to start over, with their own brand of happiness.

He didn't have the time or the inclination to play games with that girl, Allison. Besides, she was just a child to him. There had to be thirty years difference in their ages.

William sincerely hoped she didn't say or do anything to embarrass him in front of Iris. Hopefully, they wouldn't run into her, while together. Trying to explain the presence of a young, attractive, female employee on the same cruise as himself, might prove difficult.

Though he had nothing to feel guilty about, instinctively he knew it would be an introduction he'd rather not have to make. Maybe if their paths did cross, her boyfriend would be with her. Those two seemed very well suited to each other.

But then, Iris would recognize the guy as the one she had danced with last night. And she would think it was more than coincidental, just as he, himself, did. After what she had just been through, he knew Iris would have difficulty trusting another man. He couldn't afford for her to think he wasn't being totally honest with her.

Still, he couldn't take the chance of spoiling this perfect day by telling her about running into Allison, so he wouldn't. It was a huge ship, with thousands of passengers and crew onboard. More than likely, he had no cause for concern.

While William had been massaging oil into her skin, Iris had dozed off. When he was finished, she woke up, stretched and turned over. She could have taken a nice, long nap, but didn't want to waste a moment of her time with him.

"How long was I out of it?" she asked. She felt a little embarrassed, like a teenager, who had fallen asleep in class.

"For hours. You probably have third degree burns on your back by now," he teased her. Actually, he'd been so deep in his own thoughts, he hadn't realized she was asleep. But it could have only been for a few minutes.

She quickly checked the backs of her legs to see how red they were. "You better not have let me lay here and burn," she said anxiously.

"Sweetheart, I'm only joking. Do you really think I'd allow you to burn and not be able to lie on your back? Oh no. You're not getting off the hook that easily. I've got big plans for you later, little lady."

For the next few hours, they talked, played in the pool, stole a few kisses and talked some more. Iris was thrilled when he urged her to tell him all about her children and grandchildren. It was like throwing a rabbit in a briar patch. There was no other topic she had rather discuss.

"I can't wait to meet them," he told her. "I hope they'll like me and allow me to become a real member of the family. My parents were in their forties when I was born. They had given up on ever having a child when I finally came along. They're both gone now and without kids of my own, I've missed out on the grandpa scene, as well."

"William, they'll be so thrilled that I'm happy again, they will probably grovel at your feet." She grinned a little sheepishly then. "I suspect their motive for sending me on this cruise, was the hope I might meet someone. But, they're going to be shocked when they learn I met somebody from back home."

He learned the names and ages of her kids and their kids, and asked about their hobbies and interests and which sports they played. She was amazed he remembered who belonged to which household, where everyone lived and where they worked and went to school.

He was such a good listener, she was beginning to believe he might actually care about her family. Surely, nobody worked so hard learning the details of somebody else's life, just to get laid. Or did they?

Shit, she hated not being able to trust him completely. That had been one of David's parting gifts to her. He had destroyed her trust in not only himself, but men in general. And William was definitely a man. If they look like a duck, walk like a duck and quack like a duck, they're usually a duck, she reminded herself.

William laughed heartily at the stories she told about her children when they were growing up. And, despite the normal teenaged escapades all kids put their parents through, it seemed to William that Iris had loved every moment that she'd spent raising them.

It was quite obvious that she was very proud of the adults they had become. And the one thing she praised them most for was their parenting skills.

"At first," she explained, "when my babies started having babies, I was scared to death. The thought of these people taking care of my precious grandbabies, kept me awake most nights. I had to keep reminding myself that I'd been a mother at seventeen, and yet my three had survived my ignorance and inexperience. Sure enough, they've done a magnificent job as parents."

"As obviously you have, Iris. You made it easy for them. They only had to follow your lead. Children who are nurtured and loved and cared for, usually grow up to nurture and love and care for their own children. It's just too sad that every child doesn't come into the world having an adoring mother like you." Iris flushed under William's praise, but also felt pride in both herself and her family. They had turned out so well, it was hard not to brag on them.

"It sounds like you're now reaping the rewards of your devotion and sacrifice," he added. "And when I meet them, I'm thanking them big time for forcing you to take this cruise."

Iris smiled, thinking about the possibility of him actually meeting her kids. "You've only known me one day. How do you know you'll be thanking them by the end of the week?" she asked. "You may be demanding they send you on another vacation because I ruined this one for you."

"The only way you could ruin it for me, is if you tried. And why would you want to? I'm at your beck and call, your wish is my command and very soon, I hope, I will become your love slave. I think you're gorgeous, I adore you, and I've already offered you my heart. And, I'm just warming up," he finished emphatically.

She laughed at his sales pitch. "I would be a fool to screw this up, wouldn't I? But, knowing me, if there's a way to do it, I'll find it. In the meantime, stick a fork in me, I'm done. I've got to get out of the sun." She glanced at the watch she kept in her beach bag. "No wonder I'm well done. It's going on four o'clock. I need a shower, a nap and a margarita. Not necessarily in that order."

Iris got busy packing up her stuff, folding the towels and putting her clothes on over her bathing suit. William stood to slip his t-shirt back on and glanced in the direction where Allison had been sitting.

He hadn't dared to look her way all afternoon, for fear Iris would follow his gaze. He wasn't hoping to see her, quite the opposite in fact. He desperately hoped he didn't see her again all week. He sighed with relief when he didn't see any sign of her. He felt as if he had successfully dodged a bullet.

"Let me carry that beach bag for you Iris," he offered. "It's got to be heavy with those wet towels in it." He casually slung it over his shoulder. William reached for Iris' hand as they headed to their suites.

She had to admit, so far it had been a perfect day, following what had been a wonderful evening the night before. Maybe, she admitted the possibility to herself, this guy is the real deal.

Her own self confidence had been so shattered, that it was difficult for her to understand what he saw in her. It was obvious what she saw in him. She went over all the positives in her mind.

Good lookin' as hell, nice, thoughtful, romantic, a gentleman, great dancer, perfect kisser, smart, funny, wealthy, and oh yea, available. Then why in the hell was she afraid a trap door would fall open and she would hang herself?

Get a grip, Iris, she told herself firmly. Any other woman on the planet would be offering up sacrifices to the gods for a blessing like him.

She wanted to hate David for making her so insecure, but she couldn't. Right now, she was feeling rather grateful to him for setting her free. Maybe time does take care of things after all, she thought philosophically.

Nine months ago, I could have gutted him like a fish and now I'm practically having warm and fuzzy feelings for the bastard. Iris smiled. Maybe she would pick up a little something for the baby and send it by her daughters to the baby shower.

She smiled again as she realized how much better she was feeling about everything. And there was no doubt that it was because of William. It felt wonderful to be wanted and cared for again. She squeezed his hand and looked up at him with a warm smile.

Chapter 5

They had almost reached their rooms when William said, "Iris, I have a confession to make before we go to dinner tonight. So I might as well get it over with now."

"Oh great," she responded, stopping at her door. "Just when I was thinking you're perfect, you go and do something you need to apologize for. Well, what is it?"

"It's a confession, not an apology. I'm not sorry I did it. Yesterday, after the safety drill, when I learned you chose late seating in the dining room, I phoned the maitre d'. I had him check and we weren't seated at the same table, which was no surprise, so I offered him a handsome tip to move me to your table." He stopped and tried to read Iris' expression, but so far, it was blank.

"I'd figured you'd smell a rat when we were shown to our table tonight, so I wanted to tell you beforehand. Since late seating had not yet begun, nobody would be the wiser," he explained. "They try to seat passengers traveling alone at the same tables anyway, so I may have done someone a favor. Maybe two more people will meet and fall in love, who might not have otherwise." He smiled innocently, as he waited for her to react.

"If it wasn't so sweet and romantic and thoughtful of you, to go to the trouble and expense of doing that, it might piss me off just a tad." But, William noticed she was grinning as she said it.

"After all, we had just met and you were acting rather presumptuous. As if you already felt sure I would want to spend my time at dinner with you. Quite the manipulator, aren't you?" she accused. William set her beach bag down in the hallway and wrapped his arms around her.

"I just couldn't take the chance of a half dozen other guys spending a couple of hours each evening trying to woo you away from me. You understand, don't you?"

He was holding her loosely since they were both sweaty, but he was looking her directly in the eyes as he spoke to her. Iris felt the tingling warmth spreading like lava throughout her body. She was secretly thrilled he had gone to such lengths to spend more time with her. She would have hated sitting alone at a table filled with strangers. So she cut him some slack.

"You're right. You have nothing to apologize for. It was a bold move, but smart too. Besides, I'm looking forward to having dinner with you in the dining room. It can be quite a festive event as you know, and there's nobody else I'd rather enjoy it with." Iris could feel William relax.

"Whew! No wonder they say confession is good for the soul. I feel much better now. However, I'm pretty sure I still don't smell any better. I'm hittin' the shower and then catching up on some e-mails from the office. Would you like to get together before we go to dinner, for a drink? I promise to get you there on time tonight."

"I'd love to. About seven? I think I'll call home and let them know what a wonderful time I'm having. The kids were feeling a little apprehensive about shipping me off by myself. Now I can put their minds at ease." She smiled thinking how happy they would be, to know she was having a good time.

Iris opened her own door for the first time since meeting William. She turned and gave him a triumphant smile. He gave her a high five hand slap but then frowned saying, "I hope this doesn't mean you don't need me anymore."

"Oh, I need you, believe me," she replied, blushing. She stood on tiptoe and kissed him. "See you at seven, my love." She closed the door with a happy sigh.

Iris pulled off her clothes, anxious to get her damp swim suit off and wrapped herself in a soft terry robe. Grabbing her cell phone from her purse, she turned it on to check for a signal.

Before she left home, she had checked with her provider to make sure her number was set up for international service. Not getting a signal from her bedroom, she strolled through the tiny sitting area to the balcony. Perhaps, she thought, outside there would be a better chance of getting service.

However, she stopped dead in her tracks when she saw the flowers. On the small coffee table, in front of the sofa, there was a beautiful arrangement of exotic flowers in a bright red vase. Surely, these were far too expensive to be provided by the cruise line, she assumed. But, who would have sent them? "William, of course!" she exclaimed excitedly, reaching for the card.

But they weren't from William or the cruise line, the travel agency or the kids. Iris had a crease between her eyebrows as she pondered the name. Matt. She didn't know anyone named Matt. They must have been delivered to the wrong suite.

Turning the card over, she read, "You move as beautifully as you look. Will these get me a second dance?" Then it dawned on her who Matt was. The handsome, young, blonde guy who had cut in and danced with her last night.

With a grin and a shrug, she returned the card to it's envelope. Go figure, she thought to herself. Being pursued by two handsome men was definitely better than being dumped by one. She had no interest in the life-sized Ken doll who had sent the flowers, but she was flattered just the same. She doubted if he was even forty yet.

Just then, she realized that William had never mentioned his own age, even though she had told him she was fifty. She figured him to be around her same age. Although, something in the article she had read in the paper, after his wife's death, lead her to believe he might be a few years older.

Not that it mattered, she was thinking. He's built like Tarzan, but a lot smarter, and was tall and strong and solid. A little shiver ran through her as she remembered how hard he had gotten as she was pressed against him last night. But, she didn't need to be thinking about that right now.

"Calm down, girl," she told herself, walking out onto the balcony. She was going to call Sarah's house and didn't need to be panting into the phone. It was Sunday, so she was hoping to catch them at home.

After punching in the number, she stood gazing out to sea as she waited for the connection. It was so hard to believe she had just come aboard the *Whimsical* yesterday. She already felt as if she was a different person than the one who had left her house Saturday morning.

"Hello?" Iris smiled, hearing the sound of Sarah's voice. She could hear her grandchildren in the background. It sounded like more than just Sarah's two boys, though. She wondered if they had company.

"Hi honey, it's Mama. I'm just checking in." The connection was pretty good but Iris spoke a little louder than normal, just in case. Her kids always teased her about yelling into the phone when she called someone long distance. It was just a habit she had picked up from her mother and grandmother before her.

Holding the phone away from her ear a little, Sarah smiled. Some things would never change. She motioned the kids out of the kitchen and replied, in a normal voice, "Hi, Mama. Mike just asked me a few minutes ago if I had heard from you yet." Mike was Sarah's husband of twelve years.

"Well tell him I said thanks for thinking about me. How did the game go, yesterday?" Sarah's and Rachel's oldest two, played on the same fall soccer team, and Saturday's game had been for the championship in their age group. She hated that she had missed it. Originally, it was scheduled for the previous weekend, but had been rained out.

"They won by only one goal! I thought I was going to have a nervous breakdown before the game was over. Maybe it's a good thing you weren't there. It was a real nail biter." Iris could hear the pride in Sarah's voice. Her nine year old was their leading scorer and Mike coached the team.

Rachel's husband, Danny, worked at the Saturn plant, as Jake did also, and couldn't be at every game, but assisted Mike at coaching when he could. Mike was David's right hand man in his construction company.

He and Sarah had met in college and married in their second year. Mike had been studying to be an architect, but quit when they got married, to work for his father-in-law. They were more like father and son than David and Jake were.

Jake had gone to work for Saturn right out of high school, and had never been interested in working for his daddy. Iris didn't blame him. David could be an asshole, as she well knew, although he and Mike got along well. But then David had always gotten along better with others, than he did his own family.

"Did Danny get to help coach?" Iris asked Sarah. She really hoped he had, because she knew how Rachel hated it when he had to work on Saturday.

"Yes, thank God. You know Rachel would have killed him if he had missed the most important game of the year. Even Jake and his family came to watch. Afterwards, we took all of our kids to Chuck E. Cheese. We had a great time, even though we all missed you being there," she added.

"I would have loved being with all of you, too," Iris said wistfully. "With everybody's busy schedules, we're not all together nearly often enough."

Sarah didn't want her mama getting homesick, so she changed the subject. "Well, you'll be back home before you know it. In the meantime, we want you to have fun and kick up your heels a little. How's it going so far?" she asked hopefully.

"Better than I imagined it would. I even danced a few times last night." She was testing Sarah's reaction, without divulging too much. "And, I've spent most of today at the pool. Please tell Rachel and Jake that I'm so glad y'all made me take this trip. I'm really feeling much better than when I left home."

"Mama, that's wonderful!" Sarah sounded both excited and relieved. They had all been so afraid that she would hole up in her cabin and drink too much. Thank goodness she was mingling with other people. Her eyes filled with tears as she heard how much better their mother sounded. The cruise had been a good idea, after all. She couldn't wait to tell her brother and sister. "Have you worn any of your pretty, new dresses, yet?"

"No, but tonight's schedule calls for semi-formal attire, so I'm going to wear the champagne colored one with the black lace overlay. It's sleeveless and pretty low cut, but I have a black, lace wrap to put over my shoulders. Do you think I should wear my hair up, or down?" she asked Sarah. They had always been more like best friends than mother and daughter. But then, they were only seventeen years apart.

"Why don't you wear it down tonight and up on the formal night?" Sarah advised her. "You look so young with it down and quite elegant with it up. It will make a bigger impression if you wear it up with your beautiful, new ball gown."

"Be sure you have your picture made on the formal night, Mama. I'm certain you'll be the prettiest woman at your table and probably in the entire dining room, for that matter." Sarah knew how attractive her mother was when she fixed up. She hadn't cared what she looked like lately, though. Who could blame her? In her mind, Sarah could picture how pretty Iris would be tonight at dinner and hoped she would have a wonderful evening. She deserved it.

"I think you're right, honey. I'll wear it down tonight and wear it up for the captain's dinner, later in the week. I guess I better get off of here. We've been talking quite a while. Is everything alright with all my babies? My big ones and my little ones?" she asked affectionately. They may be grown, but she still thought of her kids as babies too.

Sarah hesitated for only a second, but Iris picked up on it immediately. "All of us are fine, Mama. Don't you worry about a thing. Just have a great time and come home happy and tanned," she said lightheartedly.

"Sarah Elizabeth, don't insult my intelligence. What are you not telling me?" she asked worriedly. Her maternal sixth sense was on high alert.

"No, really. It has nothing to do with any of us. We're perfect, I promise." Shit, Sarah thought. She didn't want to mention her daddy and ruin her mama's good mood. But Iris sank her teeth in and wouldn't let go.

"What doesn't have anything to do with any of you? Who does it have something to do with? Is Peggy and her family alright?" Iris suddenly felt guilty about their estranged friendship and hoped Peggy was o.k.

"Samantha's in the hospital. Daddy took her this morning. She started cramping and spotting blood and they're afraid she might lose the baby. Her two kids are with me right now. I offered to keep them so daddy could stay at the hospital. I'm not crazy about Samantha, but daddy needed my help. You understand don't you, Mama?" Sarah asked hopefully.

"Of course, honey. You don't need to apologize for doing the right thing. But thank you for considering my feelings. Her children are certainly not at fault for anything that's happened, and your daddy knows you'll take good care of them. I mean, really, what else could you do?" Iris was sympathetic to Sarah's situation. She had barely spoken to her father since he had left home, but these were extenuating circumstances.

"Thank you, Mama. I feel a lot better now. You know I'd never take his side after what he did to you, what he did to all of us, actually. But, you're right. I had no choice. He just showed up on my doorstep with the kids, and they looked so little and afraid. And you know how softhearted I am towards kids. There really wasn't anything else my conscience would allow me to do."

"I understand completely. I would even have done the same thing if he had brought them to me. Right after I kicked him in the nuts, of course." She laughed, hoping to break the tension she knew Sarah was feeling.

Iris could hear the relief in Sarah's voice as she laughed too. "I can see you doing both of those things," she giggled. "Taking the kids in and racking his balls. Just maybe not in that order. You're a better woman than I am, Mama," she said. "I would cut Mike's off and wear them as earrings." They both laughed so hard, they cried.

It took a few minutes for them to say anything else. Each time they tried, they started laughing hysterically again. Finally, Iris knew she had to get off the phone and start getting ready. It was after five and William would be there by seven. She wanted to take her time getting dolled up for tonight. She knew it was going to be a special evening.

"Well at least I know nobody was listening in on this conversation," Iris said to Sarah. "Because if they were, the men in the white coats would have showed up by now and hauled us both off in straight jackets." That set off another fit of giggling on Sarah's end. Finally, they both calmed down.

"Sarah, I'll call you tomorrow to see how things are. If you talk to David, please tell him I hope both Samantha and the baby are fine. We'll be in San Juan tomorrow on our first stop, but I'll be thinking about all of you, and I'll leave my cell phone on in case you should need to reach me for any reason. Don't hesitate to call, o.k.?"

"O.k., Mama. But don't worry about anything. I'm sure everyone's going to be just fine, and besides, there's nothing you can do anyway. Your job, this week, is to enjoy yourself. Be careful in San Juan and don't go anywhere alone. Have you met someone you can hang out with?" Sarah asked.

"Oh, I won't be alone," Iris assured her. "I'll probably sign up for one of the group excursions." She felt Sarah had enough on her plate, without being told about William, just yet. And, she sure as hell didn't want David knowing her business.

There would be plenty of time after she got home for her children to be filled in on all the details. Well, maybe not "all" the details, she thought with a grin. Iris made Sarah promise to give the boys a hug and kiss from her, and to call Rachel and Jake. Which she did, the moment she got off the phone with Iris.

Coming in from the balcony, she walked back through the sitting room, stopping to smell the bouquet of flowers. They really were beautiful. Too bad they weren't from William, she thought. She hoped he would get at least a little jealous when he saw them.

She went into the bedroom to lay out her clothes for the evening. She emptied her thoughts of everyone else from her mind. Tonight was just about William, and her, of course. The two of them. And she wanted it to be perfect.

When William entered his suite, his ears were still ringing with Iris' words. She had called him 'my love'. It had been a year, and seemed even longer, since anyone had called him anything except William or Mr. Pendleton.

Even though he and Iris had only known each other for one day, it seemed perfectly normal somehow, for them to use terms of endearment when speaking to each other.

Besides, after tonight, he would be her love, he reminded himself. He changed out of his swim trunks into just a pair of clean running shorts and took his laptop out on the balcony. He was going to check his company e-mails and answer the most important ones. The balconies were separated by walls and designed for privacy, so William had no idea Iris was on hers talking on the phone.

There were almost fifty messages from suppliers, factories, a few friends and several from his office. A lot of them he forwarded to his personal assistant, some to the supervisors of various departments and a few, he answered himself. He noticed one from his foreman and friend, Roger, that was marked "urgent".

On the subject line, Roger had typed one word: Allison. That got that spider crawling up his spine again. Why in the hell would Roger be writing him an urgent e-mail about Allison? It didn't take him long to find out.

Evidently, Allison had spread the word, just before she left, that she was going to be on the same cruise as he was. She told a few close friends who also told a few close friends, and so on and so on. Roger had learned of it on Friday, but since William had opted to leave early Friday morning to drive to Miami, the gossip hadn't reached him before he left.

It wouldn't have changed things much anyway, he supposed. She was entitled to her vacation time and could choose to go wherever she wanted. If he had learned of her intentions, he might not have come on the cruise, and thus, wouldn't have met Iris. All in all, he was glad he had left a day early and missed having to make that decision.

The only part of the message that really annoyed him was, that evidently, she had led people to believe that he had invited her along. Well, he was definitely going to squash that rumor when he got back.

He wrote back to Roger, telling him that he'd already run into Allison at the pool today. And even though he had thought it odd that she was onboard the same ship, he hadn't thought much more about it, because she appeared to be with some guy. He didn't tell Roger that she had come on to him though. After all, it hadn't done her any good, and really didn't amount to anything. There was no point in adding fuel to the fire.

William then told Roger that he could offset the Allison rumor with a bit of the truth. He very simply told him that he'd met a beautiful woman and fallen ass over end in love with her. And he couldn't believe his good fortune, because she lived in Springhill which Roger knew was only a few minutes from Franklin.

In closing, he thanked Roger for the heads up about Allison and told him he hoped to have even better news about his new lady love, by the time he got back.

He replied to a few more e-mails and then signed off. "Enough of that crap," he said aloud, closing his laptop. "I'm on vacation, I'm in love and tonight's the night." He poured himself just a shot of Jack Daniels to celebrate how happy he was, then opened his closet.

He wondered what Iris was going to wear to dinner. He had no doubt that she would look great in whatever she chose. He wouldn't wear his tux, since it was only a semi-formal evening. So, he chose a dark grey suit that brought out the steel grey of his eyes, a crisp, white shirt, and navy blue tie and pocket handkerchief. Satisfied, he headed for the shower.

Waiting for the shower water to get hot, he picked up his hair brush, and holding it like a microphone, began to sing and dance in front of the mirror. "Do a little dance…make a little love…get down tonight…get down tonight." When the steam fogged up the mirror, he moved his performance to the shower, where he attempted to use the bar of soap as his mike, but it kept squirting out of his hand. He gave up and began to wash his hair, wondering how many other performers had experienced that very same problem.

At ten minutes until seven, William couldn't stand the wait any longer. It had been almost three hours since he'd seen Iris and he was having serious withdrawal symptoms. He had tried to nap after his shower, but had just laid there staring at the ceiling thinking of her. The pictures in the magazine he had thumbed through were boring compared to the images of her that he kept visiting in his head. No music was as melodious as the sound of her voice or her contagious laughter.

She really was everything he had told her she was, just that morning at breakfast. She was smart, funny, beautiful, sexy, loving, mature and yet innocent all at the same time. Her ex-husband must have gone blind, deaf and stupid to have left her for anyone else. But he was so glad that he had, even though he sensed it had almost destroyed her. Well, one man's trash really is another man's treasure and he intended to put Iris on the pedestal she deserved to be on.

He put on his suit coat and straightened his tie. He had checked his appearance so many times, he was sick of looking at himself. But, the evening he had been waiting for had finally arrived.

He had already gone over all the mental, emotional and sentimental data he carried in his head and heart. He had evaluated, dissected, categorized and departmentalized his life with, and memories of, Rebecca. Everything had been put in its proper place and finally, he was living again. He left his suite with a clear conscience, a light step and a broad smile.

Iris was just spraying on her favorite perfume. Just a touch, she thought, not too much. You can overdo even a good thing. There. It had been so long since she had dressed up, she had forgotten how well she cleaned up. "Not bad…not bad at all," she complimented the lady in the mirror.

Her recently curled, blonde hair hung loosely, almost covering one eye on one side and was tucked behind her ear on the other, held back with a rhinestone barrette. She had used hot rollers to give it a softer, sexier look. "Very Veronica Lake like," Peggy had once told her.

As usual, her makeup was sparingly, although attractively applied. She wore simple diamond studs in her ears and a diamond dinner ring on her right hand.

The dress fell to just below her knees in soft folds of champagne colored silk, was sleeveless with a low cut fitted bodice and belted in a pleated, cummerbund style, made of the same fabric. The entire dress was covered in black lace, making the silk beneath appear almost to be a slip.

Iris liked the way her breasts showed ever so slightly above the V shape of the neckline. And, the wide, tuxedo style belt, accentuated her tiny waist. The skirt would be just full enough to swirl gracefully while dancing. It had cost a little more than she was used to spending on a single dress, but tonight she was glad she had splurged.

Her black, fabric heels had a thin strap that showed off her dainty ankles and fastened with little rhinestone buckles. The matching clutch she carried, sported a rhinestone clasp.

She didn't know if it was the sun she got today, the stunning dress, or the fact that she was in love, but she positively glowed. She twirled around slowly so she could enjoy the feel of the skirt against her skin.

When William knocked at the door, she hurried to open it. She was anxious to see what his reaction would be when he saw her. Even though she had suffered with low self esteem when David had left her for a younger woman, she felt like her old self tonight. Confident, vibrant and happy. She rushed to greet the man who had made all that possible.

For a moment, neither of them spoke. They stood, she in her foyer and he in the hallway, as if they were made of stone. They each wanted to speak and knew they should, but all they seemed to be able to move were their eyes.

Iris took in everything at once, the entire package, while William burned to memory, every inch of her. Each detail of her hair, face, clothes, accessories, jewelry and body, would be forever etched in his memory. If someone asked him twenty years from now what she had looked like tonight, he knew he would be able to describe her to the nth degree.

She thought, no she knew, he was the most handsome, the most masculine, sexiest man she had ever laid eyes on. She no longer cared if anyone else saw her new dress, or about the time she had spent on her hair and makeup. She didn't care if they never left her suite, or her bed. In thirty three years, she had never wanted her husband the way she wanted this man she had only met yesterday.

Just as she opened her mouth to tell him exactly that, he took one, long step and suddenly there was no need for words. In one moment, he seemed to enter the room, reach for her, press his lips to hers and kick the door shut. He had done it all, leaving nothing for her to do, except melt into his body and return his kiss.

He picked her up in his arms, still without a spoken word between them and laid her gently on the bed, her head propped on the pillows. Moon-glow from the balcony door lit the bedroom, casting just enough light to see by and yet not enough to embarrass her, he hoped. The only other light came from a small lamp in the sitting area that was separated from the bedroom by a wall that didn't quite come all the way up to the ceiling. William knew Iris would feel a little awkward the first time he saw her naked. After all, she had only been with one man her entire life and he wanted to show her the respect she deserved.

Going back to the door, he hung the DO NOT DISTURB sign on the outside and then bolted it. He knew the cabin steward would have come in later to turn the bed down, if he hadn't. They would eventually turn this bed down themselves.

As he walked back to the bed, Iris watched him step out of his shoes, take off his jacket and remove his tie. She lay there thinking that he made the most out of every moment. He moved efficiently and precisely without showing any signs of hurrying. She simply lay there, content to watch what he would do next.

William placed his jacket and tie over the arm of the one bedroom chair and sat on the foot of the king sized bed. He unfastened first one rhinestone buckle, then the other, having no problem with them whatsoever, she noticed, even though his hands were huge and the buckles so small, they had even given her trouble. She made a mental note to add "nimble" to his list of attributes.

Letting her shoes fall gently to the floor, he ran one hand along her right leg as he crawled towards where she lay, her arms reaching to pull him down to her. As William felt her hands slide around his shoulders, he claimed her mouth with his and propped himself up slightly, to keep from crushing her.

At the same time, he moved his one free hand to her breast, rubbing his thumb gently over her nipple. Even through the dress he could feel it stiffen and protrude. Iris sucked her breath in slightly in response to his touch.

Sliding his hand down the length of her body, he found the hidden zipper on the side of her dress. And, in a movement she barely felt, since his tongue was now exploring the taste of hers, he slid the zipper down and began to pull her dress away from her upper body.

Iris arched towards him, allowing William room to maneuver his hand behind her back. He skillfully unclasped the black lace demi bra she was wearing and using one strong arm, pulled her to an upright position so he could slide her dress off her shoulders and remove the bra, leaving her naked from the waist up.

His mouth traveled to her neck and she began unbuttoning his shirt. He laid her back down on the pillows and lowered his head to her breasts. Removing his shirt, he tossed it to the floor. Taking turns with each, he played his tongue over her nipples, gently at first and then sucking harder, making Iris moan with almost forgotten pleasure.

As one hand cupped and kneaded her breasts, with his other he began to work the rest of the dress down over her hips. She raised her butt off the bed without even being aware she was doing so, in order for him to be able to slide the dress off completely. He blindly threw it behind him, where it landed on the chair with his jacket.

William felt Iris' hands in his hair when his mouth moved slowly from her breasts to her belly. She heard the erotic sounds of his belt buckle being undone and his zipper coming down.

Iris wasn't wearing stockings, which left only the barrier of her black lace panties. But not for long. She was propped up only a little by the pillows beneath her head, but she was able to see him stand and remove his slacks, socks and briefs. His massive frame cast an impressive shadow on the wall, getting help from the light of the moon.

Her eyes didn't dwell on his shadow long, though. After shedding his clothes, he turned once again towards where she lay watching him. Iris hoped, in the semi-darkness, William didn't see her stare at his erection, as it pointed towards her like a divining rod sensing water. He was only the second grown man she had ever seen completely naked, and she was mesmerized by his powerful physique.

As he had been undressing, she had pulled the top layer of bedclothes from beneath her and pushed them out of the way. She expected him to lie down beside her but instead, he knelt and returned his lips and tongue to her lower belly, using one hand to raise her bottom, while removing her panties with the other. Feeling them slide to her ankles, she helped remove them, using her feet.

She was glad there wasn't much light in the room because now she felt her entire body blush, when he gently but purposefully positioned her thighs on either side of him. David had only performed oral sex on her a couple of times and quite frankly, even though she couldn't be sure, she suspected he hadn't been very good at it. It had never really aroused her the way other foreplay did.

But, "Katie Bar the Door," her mind screamed when William began to lick and suck her clit, occasionally dipping his tongue into the moist, now hot, flesh of her vagina. He slid one, thick finger deep inside of her and feeling her groin arch in reflex, he gently inserted a second finger. She clutched the edges of the pillows on either side of her head and a sound, half pain and the other half pleasure, escaped her parted lips.

He stretched out beside her then and lowered his head to her breast while allowing his fingers to plunge deeper and then also faster. Iris' very first words of the evening were "Oh, God, William!" as he felt her warm, liquid release on his fingers and a tremor vibrate through her body.

She was ready now and it was a damn good thing, William thought, knowing he couldn't hold out much longer, without possessing her completely. She wrapped her arms tightly around him and spread her legs welcomingly as he raised his body over hers. Iris guided his swollen, throbbing penis towards the comfort she was offering him.

William had really meant to be more gentle, at least the first time, but as he found his target and felt her legs go around his back, he lost his mind temporarily and suddenly buried himself deep inside of her, making her cry out sharply. He felt her hands push against his shoulders, trying to force him away from her a little and he knew he had hurt her without meaning to.

Whispering in her ear he said, "I'm sorry baby, so sorry. I'll go easy now. I love you, Iris." He wasn't completely aware of his own words, but they had a calming effect on her and he felt her relax and move her hands to his hair again, as he kissed her.

Much more slowly now and not allowing himself to thrust his entire length into her this time, they fell into a natural rhythm, building to multiple crescendos and then backing off just in time. Neither of them wanted their first time making love to each other to ever come to an end.

But finally, after neither of them knew how long, they reached the point of no return and this time they cried out together, in the ecstasy of mutual orgasms that threatened to go on and on.

They were soaked and so were the sheets, and removing himself gently from inside of her, he lay on his side, his head resting on one hand, laughing down at her. Iris had covered her face with one of the pillows, to muffle her cries of pleasure. Now, he pried it out of her grasp and kissed her possessively on the lips. It wasn't like the desperate, passionate kisses they had exchanged during sex. This one was filled with tenderness, love and satisfaction, and said everything they were feeling for each other.

William lay on his back, cradling Iris in his arms, her head on his ample shoulder, one leg crooked over his as she casually stroked his broad chest with delicate fingers. She no longer felt any embarrassment lying naked with him. She belonged to him now, and he to her. Their souls had been branded with the mark of their love for each other.

"Sweetheart, you looked so beautiful when you answered the door tonight, that I knew there was no way I could possibly share you with anyone else. I had planned things so differently for our evening together. We were to wine and dine, see a show and dance, or maybe visit the casino. I'm not apologizing for my actions, but I am admitting to being a barbarian. Do you think you could learn to love a barbarian, Iris?"

She tilted her head to smile up at him. "I'm sure I could if I had to, however, I'm not putting you in that category yet. I choose to believe there's a difference between being overcome by emotion and desire, and acting barbaric. Although, we have been at sea for two nights and I've yet to have dinner in the dining room, so I can see your point."

William kissed the top of her head and said, "You know, the others seated at our table are going to hate it when we finally do show up. Think of all the extra elbow room they've been enjoying. They'll probably spill something on us, so we'll leave again. All this talk about dining is making me hungry. Do you want to get dressed and check out another restaurant or stay in and order room service?"

Iris grinned mischievously and answered, "That depends on what you have in mind for dessert." She giggled as he pulled her over on top of him.

He ran his hands over her round bottom, gently pressing her against him and she felt him stiffen beneath her. "Well, let's see," William considered. "We've already had a delightful appetizer and I'm thinking we could skip straight to dessert right now. Perhaps in a while, we'll order some food to give us enough strength for our very own private midnight buffet."

She raised up to her knees, straddling him, and took his hardness in her hands. Sinking slowly onto the full length of him took her breath away. Once again, she cried out with the mixture of both pain and pleasure. He placed his hands on each of her hips and rose to meet her each time she lowered herself to take him deep inside. He filled her body as completely as his love filled her heart and soul.

They would eventually take the time for food and a lengthy shower together and finally sleep like spoons in a drawer until the bright, morning Puerto Rican sun woke them a few hours later.

Chapter 6

Having slept alone for nine months, Iris was startled at first to feel someone in the bed with her. But, it didn't take long, after the memories of the past several hours flooded her mind, to bring her fully awake. She couldn't believe how well she had slept, and without even one margarita. She turned over to find William sitting up on his side of the bed, drinking a cup of coffee.

"How long have you been awake?" she asked him sleepily. "And, more importantly, where's my coffee?" She couldn't help but notice how great he looked with his hair tousled, his chest bare, covered only part way with a bed sheet.

"Long enough to make coffee and order breakfast. I took the phone out to the balcony so I wouldn't wake you. But it should be here in just a few minutes now, so unless you want the room service guy seeing you in all your glory, you might want to put your robe on." He got up and she noticed he had put his briefs on, and after handing her the robe he had found in the bathroom, he pulled his pants on, as well.

Iris sat on the side of the bed with her back to him and quite modestly, wrapped the robe around herself, before getting up. He came around and gave her a light kiss on the lips before handing her a cup of coffee. "Wait until you see the view we get to enjoy from the balcony, while eating breakfast. We arrived in San Juan sometime while we were too busy to notice." He smiled, kissed her lightly again and patted her behind teasingly.

She turned slightly pink at his familiar touch, remembering everything they had done and enjoyed all night long. William knew instinctively that she would feel just a bit awkward this morning so he was keeping everything lighthearted and easy going. He could have easily made love to her as soon as he awoke, but after the marathon he had already put her through, he thought it might be more considerate to wait awhile.

Taking their coffee cups with them, they strolled hand in hand through the sitting area, out to the balcony. The view was indeed breathtaking. There were other cruise ships and smaller boats of all kinds, anchored in the sparkling blue-green-purple of the Caribbean water. The sun glinted off the well maintained surfaces of the boats and reflected blindingly off the water itself. In the not so far away distance, the beautiful stone walls and turrets surrounding old San Juan stood watch over all the bustling activity on land and sea. Both Iris and William had seen it all before, but never with each other. They stood at the railing, her head leaning against his shoulder and his arm encircling her waist. They were comfortable in their silence and when room service arrived with breakfast, it was almost an unwelcome interruption.

But as soon as they smelled the pancakes and bacon, they quickly got over it, and hungrier than they had realized, devoured every last bite between the two of them. "Good grief, you'd think I hadn't eaten in a week," Iris laughed, a little shocked at all she had been able to consume. She didn't say anything, but she could tell that now that she wasn't drinking so much, her appetite was better. William was glad to see her eat more than usual. Of course, they had used up a lot of energy the night before and both of them had eaten heartily.

"Yea, I was getting worried that you might get through before me and want part of mine." She popped him with her napkin in protest. "Ouch!" He rubbed his arm and laughed. "I'm glad I saw this violent side of you early on. I'll be better prepared next time."

"Well, if it wasn't for you, I would have had a real dinner in the dining room instead of a room service peanut butter and jelly sandwich at midnight," she accused.

"Guilty as charged," he admitted. "But, was it not the best damn peanut butter and jelly sandwich you've ever had?" His eyebrows shot up in question, obviously expecting a reply.

Iris rose from the table, sat in his lap and whispered in his ear, "It was the best damn everything I've ever had, my love." William slid his hands inside her robe and began to fondle her breasts, bringing her nipples out, taut and hard. Leaning back in the crook of his arm, she bit her lip, as his mouth replaced his hand, and he teased and sucked until he heard her moan deep in her throat. Since they didn't have much room and only partial privacy, he picked her up and took her back to the love nest her bed had become.

Afterwards, William rose and put his shirt and pants on, and slipped his bare feet in his shoes. Gathering the remaining items of his clothing, he looked down at Iris still curled up in bed, holding his pillow against her body.

"I'm going next door to get ready. I don't trust myself to shower here with you again. You were a good sport about missing dinner, but I doubt very seriously if you want to miss the entire afternoon and evening in San Juan." He gazed lovingly at her and marveled at how quickly and completely he had grown to love this woman.

Iris returned his adoring look and then busted out laughing. "If I wasn't so sore from making love, I wouldn't care if we never left this bed." She wasn't embarrassed to admit it, because they both knew how long it had been for her until last night. "And I've changed my mind. You really are a barbarian. Good thing I've developed a fondness for them. I really don't know how I survived so long without one of my very own."

"As long as you don't try to get by without one again, we'll get along just fine. We will eventually make it to the dining room, sweetheart. I just can't promise you when, because I don't like breaking promises." He leaned down to kiss her, hating to leave her for even a moment. "How long will it take you to get ready? I can't wait to see San Juan with you. Everything seems brand new to me, as if all I see and do is for the very first time."

Beaming radiantly up at him, Iris said, "I feel the exact same way; like my life is just beginning. Give me an hour, and I'll be ready with bells on."

William walked toward the door saying, "You better have more than that on, or we'll never see San Juan." After he was gone, Iris stood in the middle of the bed, hugging herself and jumping up and down. She had never been this happy in her entire life, or felt so loved by anyone. She jumped off the bed, hung up the beautiful dress that had served it's purpose, and left the DO NOT DISTURB sign on the door, so she could shower without interruption.

Exactly an hour later, she was ready. She wore an above the knee, sleeveless, yellow sundress, that was scooped both at the neck and the back. It was a light airy fabric which should be perfect for the warm, breezy day. Iris had figured out that sundresses were cooler and more comfortable than either capris or shorts, as the air could circulate underneath. Besides, she was feeling very much a woman again, and wanted to look the part. White sandals showed off her toe polish and tanned feet and legs. Her only jewelry was a pair of large, silver hoop earrings. It was quite windy, so she pulled her hair back and fastened it at the nape of her neck with a beautiful, silver clasp.

The only things she needed to carry with her were her lipstick, room key and credit card, so her purse was as small as it was unique. It had been made from half of a coconut, sanded smooth and hand painted white, with bright yellow, red and green parrots painted on it. It had a small leather shoulder strap, and while the purse itself was rounded, the lid was flat and held shut with a strip of Velcro. She had bought it years ago in Barbados and had never seen another like it. It was the perfect size and decor for her leisurely day in San Juan. She had only applied mascara and lipstick and was ready and anxious to see William, and hit the historic, cobbled streets of the beautiful old city.

When he arrived, right on time as always, she was glad she had decided to wear a dress, because William looked so nice in his khaki slacks. His short sleeved, white shirt was open at the collar and he wore Rockport deck shoes without socks. His dark hair was still damp from the shower and was combed neatly away from his face. Iris reached up and touched the soft curls that lay on his shirt collar, as she kissed him tenderly.

When they walked down the ramp directly onto the pier, many pairs of eyes turned in their direction. What a handsome couple they made, him with his dark complexion and hair and formidable size and she with her golden skin and eyes and light blonde hair, petite and dainty, strolling hand in hand. They were so obviously in love, people couldn't help but smile when they saw them. And they knew what they had found in each other and wished that everyone could be as happy as they were today.

William had brought along a digital camera, which fit in his shirt pocket. They laughed as they discussed previous excursions carrying heavy, bulky cameras, and camera bags loaded with extra batteries and film. They photographed cathedrals, statues, the governor's mansion, a convent and each other, in front of amazingly scenic backgrounds. A few times, someone else offered to take a picture of them together, and they gratefully accepted.

They walked happily up and down the busy streets, sometimes just window shopping, but looking inside many of the stores as well, when something of interest caught their fancy. They admired the local arts and crafts consisting of paintings, sketches, pottery, religious artifacts, blankets, hats and accessories of all kinds.

In the afternoon, they sat under an awning at an outdoor restaurant, eating a late lunch, having a margarita each, and people watching. They were much more interested in the locals than in the other tourists. The children were so beautiful and often they spotted a particular man or woman who was incredibly handsome or enchantingly pretty. Both of them were very happy to be spending the day in this exotic place, on a gorgeous day, living in the exquisite bubble that their love had encased them in. They received many admiring glances themselves, as people passed by their table.

Iris bought each of her six grandchildren a gift, as she always did, from wherever she traveled. Having five grandsons and only one granddaughter, made it a little more difficult for her to choose, though. She could always find dozens of items for a girl, but often had trouble finding something other than t-shirts for the boys. But William proved to be a big help and quite resourceful in helping her buy the boys' stuff.

For themselves, he purchased a bottle of tequila and rum to have delivered to the ship. He would pick them up there upon their return, before going to his suite. Luckily he didn't have to carry them around or he would have had to wait to make his purchases much later, as they were returning to the *Whimsical.* This way, it was done, and he could carry Iris' bags for her. They wouldn't leave port until ten p.m. and didn't have to be back onboard before nine.

There was only one blip on William's radar all day. While taking a picture of Iris earlier, he had seen Allison walk behind her, only a short distance away. She had stopped and smiled at him as if posing for the camera. He had taken the picture before realizing she was there. Thankfully, Iris had been oblivious to her, and even if she had noticed her, would not have known who she was. He soon forgot about it, however, as the afternoon turned to evening and the moonlight worked it's magic on the old city that became even more alive with nightfall.

Sounds of music and laughter, smells of spicy food and sea air, made them heady with feelings of romance and excitement. People danced in the streets of the plaza, William and Iris among them. They bought tortillas and enchiladas from stands scattered about and sampled the local Puerto Rican rum, made in various flavors. Neither of them had felt so alive in what seemed like ages.

After watching a group of dancers wearing traditional costumes put on a breathtaking performance, they heard the ship's horn sound and reluctantly made their way to where the *Whimsical* was docked. They retrieved their packages from one of the shops where they had made a few purchases. The owner had gladly put them in his storage area so they could dance and party without having to worry about them.

William claimed his bottles of liquor that had been delivered with his name and cabin number on the boxes they were packed in and he and Iris quickly dumped their purchases in their respective suites and hurried up to the deck. They didn't want to miss out on the festive atmosphere the ship's crew created when leaving one of their ports of call.

Having only one day in each of the three stops never seemed like enough time for most passengers and often they reboarded the ship reluctantly because they had been having so much fun. So the crew successfully recreated the exotic party that their guests had been enjoying in San Juan. They were experts in entertaining onboard the ship. After all, they did it each week with thousands of new faces appreciating their efforts.

There were buffet tables set up in several locations, as well as bars, and a band was playing, while happy, sunburned, slightly drunk men and women of all ages, sizes, nationalities and backgrounds, danced, ate, drank and partied like there would be no tomorrow. There were many quieter, saner places where someone could enjoy their evening onboard the ship, but very few took advantage of them on this night.

Even if you didn't dance or was perfectly sober, it was still very entertaining to listen to the music, watch the dancing, and taste the various dishes offered on the buffets. Many people lined the railings just enjoying the balmy Caribbean evening and watching the lights of San Juan grow dimmer and more distant as the ship sailed towards Saint Thomas. They would already be there when they awoke in the morning and the prospect of simply enjoying life in a new place, under the best of circumstances, would drag even those with ample hangovers from their beds at an early hour.

Finally, at midnight, after one of the best days of their lives, William and Iris retired to her suite, where they enjoyed a taste of one of the rums William had bought. They sat on the balcony and talked excitedly about their day in San Juan, the party the crew had provided upon their return to the ship, and the small treasures they had purchased.

William had bought Iris a stunning pair of opal and diamond earrings that she had protested had cost too much. He had only laughed and said that he was going to spend all the money on her that he hadn't spent on anything or anyone in the past year, so she might as well accept his gifts gracefully and get used to it.

"But, if you really want to give me something in return," he added suggestively, "then there's no time like right now." Upon which they left a trail of clothing from the balcony, through the sitting area and the bedroom, arriving at the bed naked and starved now in a much different way. All of their needs had been provided by everyone else throughout the day, but what they desired most, could only be gotten from each other. So they gave and rested, and gave some more, finally sleeping the way only exhausted, satisfied lovers can.

Though they didn't fall asleep until about three in the morning, they were awake and having breakfast on the balcony a little before nine.

Yesterday they had walked for miles sightseeing and shopping, and today all they wanted to do was lie on the beach, swim and snorkel. They had each brought their own gear for snorkeling and were wanting to go over to the nearby island of Saint John for the day.

There was a lot to see and do and great beaches on Saint Thomas, but they both favored the more remote, relaxed environment of Saint John. After breakfast, they went their separate ways only long enough to shower and change. Not that they needed time away from each other, it was just quicker to utilize both bathrooms. They would have been thrilled to spend every minute of every day together.

Besides, Iris had told William about her conversation with Sarah on Sunday, and now it was Tuesday and she hadn't heard a word from any of her kids since. She had a feeling that they hadn't called her because the news wasn't good and they didn't want to worry her with things she couldn't change anyway. But she intended to call one of them this morning and at least make sure her own children and grandchildren were well. William respected her privacy and knew her conversations with her children were, not yet, any of his business. Besides, he knew she would tell him what she wanted him to know.

After he left to go to his own suite, Iris called Sarah's house, but got no answer. She didn't try Rachel or Jake because they would both be at work. Rachel taught second grade at an elementary school in Franklin and Jake had finally been transferred from the night shift to working days at Saturn. Sarah didn't work and her boys would be in school, so she was more than likely out running errands. Iris called her cell phone and she answered right away.

"Hi Sarah, it's me," she greeted her daughter cheerfully. "We're getting ready to go over to Saint John, but I wanted to check in and see how things are going with Samantha and the baby, and more importantly, with my own babies."

"Who's we?" Sarah had picked up on that real fast. "Are you going with a group from the ship, or have you met a friend to pal around with?" She hadn't heard her mother sound so happy and upbeat in a long time, if ever.

"Yes, actually, I have. Believe it or not, I was lucky enough to meet somebody from just up the road, in Franklin. I'm sure we'll remain close long after the cruise is over and we return home. But enough about me. I'm having the time of my life. I called to hear about all of y'all."

"Well it's been pretty eventful around here, I'll admit. Michael lost another tooth and Davis learned to tie his shoes. He got to move his name over on the board in his classroom from the list of kids who can't yet tie to the list of kids who can. Needless to say, he's been struttin' around here like he's the only rooster in the hen house. Unfortunately, he's going around untying all of our shoes just so he can tie them back, and Michael's getting real tired of it. We have to remind him that Davis is only five, and the new will soon wear off. He'll be focused on some new activity by next week."

"Tell Davis that Nanny is so proud of him, and I'll let him come to my house and tie every pair of shoes in my closet that have shoestrings, just as soon as I get home!" Iris exclaimed happily. "Is Samantha home from the hospital yet?" She was asking more to be polite than for any other reason. But, she was truly shocked by Sarah's answer.

"Yes, she came home late yesterday afternoon. But Mama, she lost the baby. Her kids stayed with me for a couple of days, but they're at Jake's now, since he lives closest to their school. Daddy said he would come and get them tomorrow but that Samantha was so distraught, he didn't think she was up to caring for them yet. I'm at the grocery store now, picking up some things to carry to their house, so that when the kids get home, Samantha will have enough stuff for them for a few days. She's not supposed to drive because the doctor prescribed something for her to take for a while at least until she calms down."

Iris had sat quietly listening to her, not knowing what to say, or whether to say anything at all. But, when Sarah stopped talking, she knew she had to fill the silence. "I have mixed emotions about Samantha, as you well know, but I truly am sorry to hear she lost the baby. I was always so grateful that I never had a miscarriage. I can only imagine what she's going through. How is David holding up?" It was the very first time she had been able to feel the least bit sorry for him, and knew that she had come a long ways towards healing her own emotional scars by actually caring how he felt.

"To tell you the truth, Mama, he's a mess. I just didn't want to spoil your vacation by calling you and dragging you into all of this. After all, none of it was your doing. Half of me feels that Daddy is just having to lie in the bed he's made for himself, but the daughter side of me feels so sorry for him, I can barely stand to see him this way. We wish the whole damn thing had never happened, but now that Daddy's dug this hole for himself, we feel obligated to at least not kick dirt in on top of him. What a fuckin' mess, pardon my French."

Sarah usually didn't say the F word, even as much as Iris did herself, so that told her a lot about how frustrated her children were with the entire episode. She couldn't blame them. You expect your parents to set a good example, not complicate your life with this kind of bullshit. She was so sorry they had been hurt and was pissed at David for using them to bail him out now. She wondered if he would have been as helpful if it was one of the kids who had messed their life up so badly. Thank God, so far they hadn't, and after witnessing David's screw up, hopefully they had at least learned a very valuable lesson.

"That's alright, honey. I speak French sometimes myself and you've earned the right to say whatever you choose, under the circumstances. What do you mean when you say he's a mess? Is he more upset about the loss of the baby or more worried about Samantha?" She assumed it was some of both, so was completely surprised by Sarah's explanation.

"That's just it, Mama. He told Jake some things he would have never divulged to me or Rachel. I guess he thought being a man, Jake would sympathize with him, but he doesn't. It seems he regrets having his vasectomy reversed and getting Samantha pregnant in the first place. He had the nerve to say he was secretly relieved she had miscarried. He said living in the house with two young children was nerve racking enough at his age, but starting all over with a newborn might be more than he could handle. Can you believe it?"

"Yes. Remember who you're talking to? I'm the one who raised the three of you practically by myself. He did financially support all of us, but when it came to physically and emotionally being there, he was nowhere to be found. He's never even changed a diaper to my knowledge or cleaned up puke, or changed bed sheets in the middle of the night when they mysteriously became wet. In this day and age, when fathers are expected to actually participate in caring for their offspring, he would have been at a total loss. And you're asking me if I can believe he's secretly glad she miscarried? I'm horrified he admitted it to Jake, but other than that, not the least bit surprised." His confession to their son embarrassed Iris, but there was nothing she could do about his attitude. She no longer felt she knew David and was beginning to wonder if she ever had.

"Well, we're only helping out because of Samantha's kids. Somebody's got to. But, I swear to God, if he's not man enough to be honest with her and allows her to get pregnant with another baby he doesn't want, then he's on his own next time. I mean, just how many mistakes can one man make?" Iris got the impression that Sarah was actually expecting an answer from her.

"Evidently an infinite number, Sarah. I'm pretty sure there's no limit, like the number of fish they can catch or deer they can kill. Perhaps if there was a fee to pay or license to acquire, men would think before they dive into shallow water. Personally, I feel they should have to wear their bright orange hunting vests when out in public, so that us women can detect them from a safe distance and run like hell in the opposite direction." Sarah was giggling now and sounded to Iris like a little girl.

"I can always count on you to make me see the lighter side of things, Mama. And, to tell you the truth, none of us were too crazy about having a brother or sister years younger than our own kids. But if it happens, it happens. I'm sure we would all be crazy about the little shit, no matter how we feel about it right now. As long as Mike and I aren't having any more, then it's really none of my concern anyway. I wouldn't take a billion dollars for my boys, but I wouldn't give a nickel for another one," she admitted.

"Oh hell, I've got to go. I'm supposed to be ready in twenty minutes. At least I don't have much preparation for just a day at the beach, but I haven't even showered yet. Love up my babies real good for me, and tell everyone I miss them. Y'all are doing a great job holding down the fort there, but personally kiddo, I'd rather be here. I'll think about you though, while I'm lying on the beach and snorkeling and drinking margaritas. It's a tough life, but somebody's got to do it." She laughed at the string of expletives her daughter rattled off. "My goodness, Sarah, I do believe your French is improving. Pretty soon you'll be as fluent as Rachel. Love you, bye." Iris hung up and bolted for the shower.

Her hair was pulled up in a pony tail and still damp when William came to get her. She was fresh faced with no makeup and wore a short, denim skirt and Jose Cuervo t-shirt over her bathing suit that was a two piece leopard print. On her feet she wore a simple pair of white Keds. She wanted a sensible pair of shoes for getting on and off the water taxi and walking down to the beach on Saint John.

William wore his deck shoes, khaki shorts and a pullover shirt with his company logo on the front pocket. He picked up Iris' snorkel bag and she carried her beach bag. When he turned to close the door behind them, Iris giggled when she read what was printed on the back of his shirt. It read "You Gotta Try My Parts."

"I have tried your parts, honey, and I agree, they can't be beat." As soon as she said it, she knew it had come out wrong. She blushed and punched his arm when he laughed. "Don't say a word. I stand corrected."

They left the ship and hailed a taxi which took them to the area where a boat carried them from Saint Thomas over to Saint John. It was a pleasant, short ride, with all of the passengers in high spirits. And, why not? The sky was brilliant and the sun hot and the scenery heavenly.

There was a short trek from where the boat let them off, to the beach and it was noticeably different here on this island from Saint Thomas. Iris had been to Saint John several years before, and true, it was more populated now than then, but it still gave off a small town atmosphere. There were a few resorts and residences, some of which could be considered palatial, however a lot of the island was a nature reserve.

And when they reached the beach, they didn't step onto the sand so much, instead they sank into it. She loved the quality of the beaches here and on Anguilla and Aruba, better than on almost two dozen other islands she had visited in the Caribbean. But they each had their own special charm and attributes and Iris could honestly say some of the best times of her life had been spent visiting the islands of the Caribbean.

Being here with William made everything even more special to her. She didn't know why exactly, but she felt a twinge of guilt when she compared the perfect day she was having to what David was going through back home. Even though he was in a mess of his own making, the memories of other times here with him, made her a trifle nostalgic, and she was no longer angry with him, only saddened by how things had turned out for him.

William had taken care of renting a couple of beach chairs for them and after pulling off their clothes, they grabbed their snorkel gear and headed for the water. They swam out to a coral reef that wasn't too far off shore. On the way out, they pointed out starfish and beds of conch to each other. The water was warm and calm and when they returned to the beach, they were both surprised to discover they had been out for almost two hours.

Sinking gratefully onto the chairs, they drank bottles of water Iris had brought in her beach bag, and ate a banana and apple she had packed for each of them. The water had been so buoyant and pleasant and they had been so enthralled with the colorful fish and coral, they hadn't felt tired or hungry until they came back to shore. For the next hour they just rested and talked about what they had seen while snorkeling, and let the sun bake their already tanned skin. Iris' thoughts of David were long forgotten.

After a while, William walked back up to the road to a shack-like restaurant where they cooked burgers, ribs and jerk chicken. There were picnic tables to sit at if one preferred, but Iris hadn't wanted to leave the beach, so William ordered their's to go. He placed an order of ribs for him and the jerk chicken for Iris and sat down on the edge of a table to wait.

"You know," a sultry voice purred from just behind him, "I could get real used to seeing you in swim trunks instead of office attire." William knew without turning his head it was Allison, and he was glad Iris had chosen to stay on the beach with their stuff.

After receiving the e-mail from Roger about Allison running her mouth at work, he was inclined to be rude to her. However, she was just a kid and still an employee of his company, so he was determined to be polite, but firm. Without even turning to look at her he said, "Hello, Allison."

She walked around the picnic table and sat beside him, her left thigh and shoulder touching his. "You know," she smiled seductively and crossed one mile long leg over the other, "it's already Tuesday and we still haven't even had a drink together. The cruise is half over with and I had thought by now, we would have become much better friends."

"Then obviously, you thought wrong. I don't mix business with pleasure, Allison, and even if I did, I'm at least twice your age. Besides, I told you the other day, I'm happily involved with the woman I plan to marry." William prayed his food order would soon be ready, so he could get the hell away from this manipulative Amazon. Although not his type, she was quite obviously beautiful, and he felt it would cause trouble if Iris saw them together.

Little did he know, she had decided to take her beach bag and go to the restroom, which was located about half way between the beach and the restaurant. Besides needing to use the bathroom, she wanted to take her hair down and comb the tangles out, before putting it back in a pony tail. Coming out of the restroom, she decided to walk on up and help William carry their lunch back down to the beach. But, she froze as her eyes scanned the tables and she saw the two of them together.

Their faces were only inches apart and their bodies were touching. True, there were only a few tables and they were jam packed with people either eating or waiting for their orders. But, why was that girl practically sitting in William's lap, she wondered? She didn't know whether to continue on up the hill or go back to the beach, but she did neither. She just stood still as William turned to the woman and was replying to whatever she had just said to him.

She got the uncanny feeling they knew each other, but from where? She didn't remember seeing the girl on the cruise ship, but then, she had been so wrapped up in William, she had hardly noticed anyone else. They had been on the *Whimsical* for three nights and had not even gone to the dining room, casino or to any of the live shows. And there had been thousands of people present at the party last night as they were leaving San Juan. She didn't think she would recognize more than just a few, if she saw them again.

And she was pretty sure she would have remembered seeing this girl before, if she had. She was tall and had long, dark hair, way past her shoulders. The bikini she was wearing left nothing to the imagination and even from this distance, Iris could see she had a voluptuous, shapely body. Her legs looked to be twice as long as Iris' and when she tossed her hair and laughed up into William's face, she felt fingers of fear grip her heart.

Who is she and what does she want with William? If they did know each other and she was on the same cruise as them, did that mean that William knew her intimately? Was he supposed to be on vacation with her, even though they obviously weren't sharing his suite? If they were only friends or acquaintances, then why hadn't he mentioned her or introduced them to each other? And, if they were more than friends, why had William bothered hooking up with her and telling her he loved her? Was it all a lie? Had he been playing her?

Allison ran a finger down William's arm, laughing up at him and tossed her hair back, revealing her ample breasts. "Planning to marry and actually getting married are two entirely different situations, William. Don't you want someone to compare her to, before taking such a drastic step? I could put some lovin' on you that would have you throwing rocks at her." As she spoke, much to William's amazement, she reached over and slid her hand to the inside of his thigh, just high enough to brush against his testicles.

Iris had seen enough. She turned and fled back to the beach, shaking on the inside with the combination of fear and anger and jealousy. Tears were burning her eyes by the time she got to her chair and she practically collapsed into it and stared out to sea, fighting the impulse to cry. The girl had confirmed what she suspected. They definitely knew each other. Why would William want to be with her if he could have a young, beautiful, sex machine like the girl she had just seen him with?

The previously perfect day still looked the same, but was now ruined by what she had witnessed. If only she hadn't gone to the restroom, she'd still be happy and the day still perfect. Now, she was oblivious to everything except her own pain. Why did men have to be such bastards, liars and cheaters, everyone? How could she have been so stupid as to believe a man like William was really in love with a woman like herself? She was divorced, the mother of three grown children, six grandchildren, fifty years old, not ever having accomplished anything except raising a family and being a housewife.

He was a huge success, wealthy, handsome and a widower. Nobody had left him for someone younger or because he was a loser, like her, she thought. She was a loser, and now she was losing William, or maybe had never had him to begin with. Maybe that woman was his girlfriend and he had only been trying to make her jealous with her. Maybe they had an argument and split up and now she was trying to make up with him. Her thoughts were running rampant with various scenarios, none of them good.

William grabbed Allison's hand, and none too gently, removed it from his leg, getting off the table at the same time. He was shocked at her brazen speech and behavior and was embarrassed that someone from the ship might have seen or overheard. Had he known they had been seen by Iris, he would have been sick, just as she was. But he had no idea she was anywhere within sight.

"I'm going to forget this little display of yours, Allison, since as of right now anyway, you're still employed by my company. I don't want you to lose your job over an obvious misunderstanding on your part. I'm telling you point blank, to back off. I'm not now, nor will I ever be, interested in whatever it is you have in mind. Now, if you'll excuse me." And with that, he went to pay for the lunch that was finally ready and hurried to the beach.

Allison watched his retreat with a small smile playing at the corners of her mouth. Well, at least now he knew what she wanted in no uncertain terms, and unlike William, she had seen Iris watching them from the area near the restrooms. She had only to sit back and wait, knowing shit was about to hit the fan, and when it did, Matt would move in to console the old broad and she would gladly lick William's wounds herself. And, anything else he wanted licked, she thought, as her tongue moved over her lips, as if to prove her point.

Chapter 7

While eating lunch, William and Iris were both unusually quiet. Part of the reason was that they were famished and both of them were busy devouring the delicious food. He brought each of them a bottle of water to down it with and other than comments about the ribs and chicken, neither of them spoke. The main reason, however, they chose to be quiet, was that neither of them was quite sure what to say to each other. They had been like two Chatty Kathy's ever since they had met, but now each of them, without the other being aware of it, was trying to decide whether or not to mention what had just taken place.

Knowing that honesty was always the best policy, William thought he should tell Iris about Allison. He didn't want to make a big deal of it, but if Iris was to witness some future antic of Allison's, at least maybe she wouldn't blame him for it.

Iris was thinking if only William would come clean about who the girl was, and his past or present relationship with her, then maybe she could go on as if she hadn't seen them together. Of course, he didn't know she had, but Iris was tempted to tell him, just to watch his reaction. If she caught him off guard, would he try to lie his way out of the situation? She sincerely hoped not. She wanted so very badly to be able to trust him. Surely fate had not allowed her to fall in love with yet another liar and cheater.

Just then, the words that William's mother had said to him so many times in his youth, came back to him, and he had no more doubts as to what to do. When he had been a little boy and even later, as a teenager, he had been guilty, as all kids are, of trying to pull the wool over his mother's eyes with stupid lies she could always detect. Her only punishment was to make him feel so guilty that he would eventually confess to the truth. She would look directly in his eyes and say, "Oh what a tangled web we weave, when first we practice to deceive." Then she would look so hurt and betrayed, not by whatever mischief he had been trying to cover up, but by his lies, that he could never go to sleep that night until he had confessed to the truth. He smiled and sent her a silent thank you for the guidance she was still giving him, even though she had been dead now, almost half his life.

William looked at Iris and said, "Sweetheart, let's get in the water for a while and cool off. I have something to tell you and it could take some time. We might as well be comfortable." He trashed their empty lunch containers and reached to pull her up from her chair.

Her heart was pounding but she wasn't sure if she felt more worried or more relieved. Either way, she gladly let him lead her out into the refreshing, clear water. They swam and floated for a few minutes and then William pulled her into his arms, and kissed her.

She relaxed in the water and let him hold her loosely, while she wrapped her legs around his waist for support. He could easily stand at this depth, but it would have been over her head if she had put her feet down.

Brushing a stray lock of hair away from her face, that had escaped her pony tail, he looked at her so lovingly that she knew that whatever he was about to tell her was going to be the truth.

William proceeded to explain that he had run into one of his employees on Sunday, by the pool, and while he admitted thinking it a little odd, hadn't considered it worth mentioning to her.

"Then that same day," he continued carefully, watching her eyes closely for her reaction to what he was telling her, "I received an e-mail from Roger." Iris nodded slightly, acknowledging that she remembered who Roger was, and silently urging him to continue.

"He warned me that this employee might have plans to pursue me, as ridiculous as that seems." Iris saw his face redden even more than it already was from the sun he had gotten today. However, he didn't look away, and continued to gaze steadily into her eyes. At least he's not a coward, Iris credited him silently, and if he was lying he would probably be glancing down or sideways, she knew. "I mean," he blushed a shade deeper still, "if I had a daughter, she would probably be older than Allison."

So, Iris cringed inwardly, her name was Allison. She hated even hearing him speak her name. She felt childish, being so jealous, but she reminded herself that she wanted the truth, whatever the cost. Be careful what you wish for, you just might get it, her conscience was telling her. Now, she knew they worked together as well and her heart sank further still.

Damn, her mind was screaming, as she focused on the meaning of this latest news, the sexpot had probably had the hots for William for a long time, and after his wife's death, had set herself up for the perfect opportunity to seduce him. It sounded so close to a scheme Peggy would have come up with, it made Iris mad at her neighbor all over again. That was unreasonable, she knew, but so what. If the shoe fits.

Iris couldn't help but wonder that if she and William hadn't met each other the very first day onboard the *Whimsical*, would this little gold digger have been successful? The thought of that made her queasy, so she tried to keep her imagination from running wild and just pay attention to what he was saying.

"I glimpsed her briefly a couple of other times, but we never spoke again." Until today you mean, Iris almost interjected, but with an effort, bit her tongue. Make him tell me, she warned herself. It's the only way I'll know if he's telling me everything.

"Once was in San Juan yesterday, when I was taking your picture. Still, I had no cause for alarm. But then, I saw her here today on Saint John, while I was waiting for our lunch to be ready." Iris braced herself for what was coming next, because if he was completely truthful and didn't whitewash over anything, it was going to be painful to hear. Of course, not as painful as seeing it had been.

Of course, he didn't know that she had seen them, so she felt she was at an advantage here. She dreaded hearing him elaborate on this girl touching him, that is, if he was completely honest. Did she still want him to be, or not? She was no longer sure. It was like reliving a nightmare, except his telling of it, made it all too real.

But, Iris was relieved when William gave his version of how it had happened and pleased at his response to Allison's forwardness. "Anyway," he went on, after explaining how quickly it had happened and how hastily he had removed her hand from his upper thigh, "I let her know in no uncertain terms, that I'm happy with you and I will never become involved with her. I also strongly hinted that if she didn't back off her nonsense, it could affect her job with my company. She's been there just a little over ten years, so if she has a brain in her head at all, that should have gotten her attention."

Little by little, William felt Iris relax in his arms and took that as a positive sign. "To tell you the truth Iris, I was embarrassed and a trifle shocked by her aggression." He laughed and gave her a little wink. "I'm no prude, as you well know, however, I can't help but feel there's a major difference between a woman being playful, romantic and sexy," he said in reference to Iris, making her smile finally, "and just coming on like a slutty whore, in public. I don't believe all young women behave the way she does, even though times have changed drastically; at least I hope they don't."

William laid Iris back in the water, allowing her to float along effortlessly, while he and the calm and buoyant water supported her. "The last thing I need is for this to turn into some sort of fatal attraction scenario." He laughed when he said it but they both knew it could be a real concern.

Iris never told him that she had seen most of what he had described had happened. There was no point. He had been truthful with her and even while she didn't like what had happened, at least he hadn't liked it either. They continued to relax in the water and she confessed to William that unfortunately the situation with Allison had reminded her once again of how Samantha had stolen David from her. Iris told him sternly that she had had enough of young women stealing her men, to last a lifetime.

"I don't think I could go through it again, William," she said seriously. "If I had known then that everything I was going through at that time would lead me to you, then, obviously, I would have coped a great deal better." He smiled and kissed her for the compliment. "But, I didn't know, and there were times I truly didn't think I would survive it." Genuine pain and suffering showed even now in her face as Iris was regretfully reminded of those dark days in her life.

"If not for the love and support of my family, I know now that I wouldn't have even tried to. I finally pulled myself together as much as I could for their sakes, not my own. They were the only thing left for me to care about, and I couldn't bear to see them worry about me."

Iris noted the genuine compassion in William's eyes and loved him all the more for it. His suffering had been even greater than her own and yet she knew he understood what she was saying as much as he possibly could.

"I will never hurt you that way, sweetheart. And, I'm very sorry that this fiasco today has brought all that unpleasantness back to you on a day that should have been perfect for the two of us." He pulled her to him and kissed her deeply while she clung to him, happy in the reassurance that he was still hers.

They went back to the beach to lay in the sun long enough for their swim suits to get dry, and Iris told him about her conversation with Sarah that morning. William was very relieved to have the topic of conversation changed to something that took the spotlight off of him for a while. "Talk about a fiasco," she said, "David's little playhouse is falling down around his head. Both of them, in fact," she giggled. "The one he used too often and the one he hasn't been using at all."

Filling him in on David's confession to Jake, William only whistled. Never having been in that situation he didn't want to say too much, but he couldn't imagine a man not wanting his own child. Perhaps if David had been childless like he himself was, he might feel differently.

"I'm ashamed to say," Iris admitted, "but there was a time I would have been glad she lost the baby and thrilled at his dilemma. I was so angry and bitter at first, I think I actually hated them both. Now I only feel sorry for them and only regret what they are putting the kids through; hers and mine." She looked meaningfully at William and said, "I only know I wouldn't want to trade places with Samantha right now."

William looked serious as he questioned her. "Are you sure, Iris? What if David decides leaving you was the biggest mistake of his life and comes begging your forgiveness? You have three children and a lifetime of history together. How would I ever be able to compete with that? I've lost before too, sweetheart, although under much different circumstances. You've given me my life back and I warn you, I'll not give you up without a fight. No, let me rephrase that," he said, reaching over and taking Iris' hand in his, "I'll not be giving you up at all." Iris was both surprised and touched at the turn the conversation had taken.

"Are you prepared for the possibility that he may try to win you back? Do you promise to tell me if he does? I want to know what I'm up against, if that should happen, so please be honest with me." This was the first time William had even considered this possibility and it scared the living hell out of him.

How quickly the tables had turned she thought. Only a couple of hours ago, she had been devastated at the thought of losing William to Allison and here he was now, seeking reassurance from her that he wouldn't lose her to David. What they both had been through had left them vulnerable, she knew, and afraid of losing the miracle they had found in each other. Her own jealousy and fears still fresh in her mind, she was quick to offer William reassurance.

"My love," she said tenderly, bringing his hand to her lips and kissing his fingers, "of all the stupid things in the world I might be capable of doing, taking David back would not be one of them. Even if I hadn't fallen in love with you, which I assure you I have, I fell out of love with him on Valentine's Day, the same moment he walked out my door."

"I gave him my heart at the age of fifteen and for almost thirty five years, it belonged to only him. When he so carelessly tossed it aside, I reclaimed it for my own. I have offered it to you now, and that's something I don't give away easily." The gentleness and sincerity with which Iris spoke, lifted an uncomfortable weight off William's heart.

"My heart can only belong to one man at a time," Iris continued, happy to see the relief in William's eyes. "And," she smiled at him and placed his giant hand over her heart, "I prefer it to belong to someone who deserves it. I'm not sure now that David ever did, but I am sure that you do. The difference is, I know you won't take my love for granted the way he did."

Iris released his hand, but he kept it on her thigh. It seemed he was happiest when touching her. "Just as I won't take you for granted, William. Neither of us are capable of inflicting that kind of pain on each other, because we know all too well how it feels to lose the only person we ever loved."

There were tears shining brightly in her eyes as she spoke, and William had to first swallow the lump in his throat before he could say anything. "It's settled then," he said, wiping her tears with the corner of her towel. "The rest of the world can go to hell in a hand basket as long as we have each other. Other than your family of course," he quickly amended. "I think this calls for a celebration. I'm going to get us something cold to drink. Margarita?" he asked, standing up.

"Like you even have to ask after the day we've had!" she laughed. "But, this time," she added, grabbing her beach bag and standing up also, "I'm going with you. If that she-cat in heat is anywhere around, I'll show her I have claws of my own!"

The day had been salvaged, and they climbed the little slope to the restaurant hand in hand. Late in the afternoon, they reluctantly left Saint John, vowing to return sometime for a week's stay. On the water taxi ride back to Saint Thomas, they laughed and teased and William swore that tonight, they would have a real dinner in the dining room.

"Yea, yea, promises, promises; I've heard it all before soooo many times," Iris teased him. Her yellow eyes were once again twinkling and her bright smile shining, in a face that was almost sunburned. William thought she was even more beautiful than she had been just four days ago, when they had first met.

Upon arriving at her suite, back onboard the *Whimsical*, Iris asked him if he would, for the time being, just set her snorkel bag out on the balcony. "Just until I have the time to rinse off my gear," she explained. "The bottom of the bag is sandy and I don't want to track it around on the carpet."

"Yes, your highness. Are there any other chores you would have me do? Say, for instance, a full body massage or maybe a back wash in the shower for starters?" Coming back through the sitting room from the balcony, he once again noticed the gorgeous bouquet of flowers. He had meant to tell her for a couple of days now, how pretty he thought they were. He was too much of a gentleman to read the card, and he had assumed, anyway, that her kids had sent them to her. Now, suddenly, a gut feeling made him ask her, as he came into the bathroom where she was combing out her wet hair, who they were from.

Iris had been laughing in the mirror as he teased her about his chores, but when he asked her who the flowers were from, he saw her glance furtively at his reflection and then look away again quickly. For a split second, he wondered if David had sent them. But, why wouldn't she have told him? Maybe for the same reason he hadn't told her about Allison from the very beginning, he admonished himself.

She continued detangling her hair and tried to sound matter-of-fact when she answered. Damn, she should have told him before now, but there really hadn't been any reason to. He hadn't mentioned them, so she hadn't even been sure he had noticed them.

For some reason she felt guilt, even though she hadn't done anything wrong. Now, she understood a little better why he hadn't mentioned Allison until today. It was just so much easier to avoid confrontation than to deal with it. Why hadn't she just thrown them away? Because they were beautiful, that's why, and she had actually enjoyed looking at them. And, she blushed a little, she had wanted William to get a little jealous. But, having a fit of jealousy herself today, she knew now that trying to make him jealous had been a foolish and selfish thing to do.

Iris hoped the abundant sun she had gotten today would mask the heat that flushed her face now, but William saw it and had an uneasy feeling.

"Well, it's about time you noticed them," she answered innocently. "You're not going to believe who sent them."

"Try me." His gaze locked onto hers as she checked the mirror for his reaction. His tone and expression told her that he smelled a rat. Her hair was as good as it was going to get until she showered, so she put the comb down and sat on the closed toilet lid. Her legs suddenly felt too weak to hold her. She was tired from being in the water and getting nearly too much sun in one day, but it was also her nerves that made her sit while she answered him. Even though she hadn't tried to deceive him in any way, she was afraid he would think so.

"Do you remember the guy that cut in on you the first night we met, when we were dancing? The one who looked like a life-sized Ken doll?" Shit! Why had she said that? There had been only one guy who had cut in. Of course he would remember. Who cared what he looked like? Was she still hoping to make him jealous, she wondered? Maybe to pay him back for Allison, on some subconscious level, she had wanted to remind him how nice looking the guy was. Shit-fire-fuzzy, as her mother used to say. Iris had never understood the exact meaning of that expression, but it seemed totally appropriate in this situation.

"Yea, I remember." Iris thought William looked like he was about to blow a gasket. "But, I associated him more with Barbie than Ken. That's an expensive flower arrangement," he explained, like she didn't already know that. What? Did he think these were the very first and only flowers that had ever been sent to her? Iris' guilt was beginning to fade and threatened to be replaced by anger.

"I didn't know you two were so chummy. Has he been calling you? Did he deliver the flowers himself? How did he know which suite was yours?" He fired one question after another, in quick succession, his voice getting a little louder with each inquiry.

"No, he hasn't called. No, he didn't deliver them. I found the bouquet in my room already, on Sunday when I came back from the pool. And, last but not least, I have no fucking idea how he knows which cabin I'm in, or if he even does!" Her voice had also grown a trifle louder with each answer, and by now she was standing with both hands on her hips, almost shouting at him.

Iris' head was held high and her chin was pointed at William like a weapon. "And, I can assure you of another thing, Mister Inquisitor, Ken and I are not nearly as "chummy" as you and your Amazon bimbo, Allison. So put that in your pipe and smoke it!"

When she flew past him out the bathroom door, he tried to reach for her. He hadn't meant to sound so angry, but his shock in finding out who had sent the bouquet had made him lash out uncharacteristically. He wanted to hold her and apologize, but she shrugged him off, so he followed after her.

"Iris, please. I don't know what came over me. I'm not accusing you of anything. I just need to know if I should beat this guy's ass. I just wanted to make sure he hasn't been bothering you."

Iris snatched up the entire vase as she passed hurriedly through the sitting room, and without slowing down a bit, stomped out onto the balcony and flung vase, flowers and all, overboard. It was about six o'clock and the ship had left Saint Thomas only a few minutes earlier. William reached her side at the railing and made a half hearted attempt at catching the vase, but she had tossed it out as well as over, and it was just out of his lengthy reach. They watched as it quickly disappeared.

"There, oh ye of little faith, happy now?" She stood looking up at him with her eyes blazing and her pixie chin held defiantly high. William fought back a snicker successfully, but couldn't completely suppress a grin.

"Do you know, that's the exact same look you gave me Saturday, the very first time we met? The very same threatening, defiant, fuck-off look that made my heart melt? But I have to warn you," he said, moving towards her, "it turns me on too." He scooped her off her feet and briefly she attempted to fight him off. Very briefly.

They were both too greasy and sweaty for the bed, so he stood her in the shower and while kissing her passionately, undressed her with one hand and held her tightly to him with the other.

They were both still wearing what they had worn to the beach over their swim suits and after a moment, he let go of her and focused completely on pulling off her t-shirt, skirt and bathing suit. He flung his clothes on the floor after hers and turned the water on, making sure it was neither too hot nor too cold.

They embraced and caressed and kissed, lathering each other with soap at the same time, and then rinsed each other off. He shampooed her hair for her and when they were clean, they toweled one another dry.

Iris knelt onto the towel that had been used to step out of the shower on, and took William's pronounced erection in her mouth. The shower had barely been big enough for them to both stand in, much less to have sex in. Even now, William could place both hands on each of the two walls on either side of him in the tiny bathroom and brace himself as she teased and stroked and sucked until he thought his knees would buckle. When he had, at last, all he could stand, he pulled her quickly to her feet, and taking her to the bed that was only a few feet from where they had been standing, he ripped the covers back and laid her on the sheet, with one of the pillows supporting her head.

The other pillow he placed underneath her hips, raising her just enough to help him access her with his practiced and knowing tongue. He felt her clitoris stiffen and swell slightly, like a female version of a penis. Her vagina was moist and hot when he explored there, but she didn't want to come just yet.

When she coaxed him up on top of her, he entered her hard and deep, leaving her completely breathless. It seemed forever until she remembered to breathe again. They kissed and spoke words of love that neither of them would remember later. All that mattered was their need to give of themselves and claim each other for their own.

This day had been a test they had passed, at least for now. They had suffered through jealousy and anger and both had bared previously held secrets they were relieved to finally have out in the open.

Making love healed the suffering their doubts and fears had inflicted upon them. When they exploded together, the flood of their passion washed away the worries of the day and anointed them with renewed love.

Lying together afterwards, entwined like pretzels, they would have been surprised if they had known their thoughts were quite similar at that moment. Ironically, they were each thinking of Allison, and feeling triumphant.

As difficult as it had been, William was glad he had been completely honest about her, with Iris. However, the one thing he hadn't told her was something he had forgotten about until he had found out who the flowers were from.

Unintentionally, he hadn't told her about seeing the two troublemakers together that morning he was jogging up on deck. It had never crossed his mind again until just then. He certainly wasn't about to break the mood by telling her about it now.

At that same moment, a smile of satisfaction was on Iris' lips. Not only was she sexually sated, but she felt victorious as she recalled the attempt Allison had made to seduce her man. Because that's how she thought of William now. Her man.

That bitch didn't have time to learn what she already knew about life. And, Iris felt certain that she had forgotten more than that child had probably ever experienced when it came to pleasing a man. But, it was all coming back to her, she admitted with a sigh of pleasure. She snuggled even closer to William's body as confirmation.

"As much as I hate to leave you," he said, kissing her clean smelling hair and squeezing her gently, "we've got just enough time to get ready for the eight o'clock dinner seating. It's our fourth night onboard, for Pete's sake. We should make a public appearance before people begin to think we've been quarantined because of some contagious disease. Besides, I'm absolutely starving."

Iris giggled and reluctantly untangled herself from him so he could get out of bed. "If being addicted to your love is a disease," she said, stretching luxuriously out on the bed, "then I confess I'm eat up with it. And, you're not the only one who's starved, by the way. I'm weak with hunger."

William had slipped his shorts and t-shirt on and gathered up his remaining stuff, including his snorkel gear. "Sweetheart, you're weak from more than hunger, I suspect." He gave her a knowing wink and patted her behind. She lay curled on her side, holding his pillow as she always did when he left her bed. It helped fill the void and she could smell his man scent where his head had rested briefly.

Iris could have easily taken a nap, but there wasn't time. It was already a few minutes after seven and she had less than an hour to get ready for dinner. "Give me until five minutes before eight," she mumbled sleepily into the pillow. "And take some fruit from that basket to tide you over until supper."

"Gladly," he responded, plucking an apple and a tiny box of raisins from the fruit basket that had already come in handy more than once. "See ya in less than an hour. So don't you dare fall asleep," he threatened, leaving to go get himself ready.

The tiny suite felt way too large and empty to Iris as soon as the door shut behind William. And as he entered his own rooms, he chuckled at how little time he'd spent there in almost four days. He had only slept the very first night onboard the ship in his own bed. He bet his cabin steward was grateful, though. It meant far less work for him.

William felt sure the guy had grown accustomed to finding many beds still neatly made in the mornings. There probably wasn't much that would shock a seasoned crew member anymore, he supposed. They had more than likely seen and heard it all before, many times.

Before he undressed and showered again, there was one thing he wanted to take care of. Calling the ship's operator and asking to be connected to the onboard florist, he ordered the largest, most extravagant arrangement of exotic and varied flowers they had available. He had the girl describe to him all the varieties of flowers and types of vases there was to choose from. He was emphatic that they be delivered before eight o'clock. At the price he was paying, she assured him she would get right on it. The florist hung up the telephone, glancing hurriedly at the clock on the wall. There would barely be enough time, but if he was sincere about the tip he had promised her, she was determined to make it a masterpiece.

Iris dressed in a pair of white flowing slacks and a bright, red, sheer blouse. It was so thin in fact, she had brought a red camisole to wear beneath it. On her feet, were her favorite pair of sandals. They were a butter soft, red leather, open toe number, with a wedge heel just high enough to keep her slacks off the floor. She wore ruby earrings and a ruby and diamond cluster on her finger that had belonged to her mother.

There hadn't been enough time to get creative with her hair, so she wore it down and loose, barely flipped up on the ends, in her usual, casual style. It was neatly tucked behind her ear on one side so her earring would show, but hung over her ear on the opposite side. Just as she finished applying her lipstick, there was a knock at the door. He's as steady as the sun, she thought, looking at her bedside clock. It was seven fifty five on the dot.

Grabbing a red leather clutch purse and tossing her lipstick into it, she flung the door open and gasped in surprise. Iris could barely see William behind the humongous vase of the most fragrant, exquisite flowers she had ever seen, much less received.

It looked like something you would see on display in the lobby of a five star hotel. She didn't think she could carry them, so she held the door wide, allowing him barely enough room to come through the door with his burden. Hurrying to move the fruit basket off the chair side table in the bedroom, she guided him through the room and around the chair, knowing there was no possible way he could see over or around the incredible arrangement. Iris was oohing and aahing and little squealing sounds of delight escaped her as he carefully set it on the table.

The abundant flowers stood full and tall and colorful in a stunning, hand painted, oriental vase. Iris sniffed them and pointed, naming the flowers she knew and wondering what some of the others were. "I'll have to stop in and ask about some of these," she babbled on, with William pulling her by the arm, gently but firmly, urging her towards the door.

"It's closed for the day, Iris. The lady who put this arrangement together, stayed late to do this as a favor to me. And, if you don't move your ass, the dining room will be closed too." But he was laughing, and very pleased with her reaction. She was still craning her neck, looking back over her shoulder, when he finally managed to get her out of the suite and into the hallway. Only when the door was firmly between her and the flowers, did she finally look at him.

And then, she flung herself at him, hugging him as tightly as she could and standing on her tiptoes, kissed him hard on the mouth. "Thank you, thank you, thank you." She emphasized each thank you with another kiss. An ancient couple emerged from a few doors down and shuffling towards them at the speed of sludge, witnessed Iris' display of gratitude.

"Young man," the old gentleman advised with a look of wisdom, "I don't know what you did, but I'll go out on a limb and suggest you do it on a regular basis!" His wife of more years than either of them had been born, playfully swatted his backside with her evening bag.

"Stay out of it, Casanova. You've got all you can handle right here and don't you go forgetting it." Her husband looked at her with weak, watery eyes filled with adoration.

"I haven't forgotten it in almost seventy years, precious, and if you'll model that little see-through number when we get back from dinner, I'll prove it to you."

William threw back his head and giving the old codger a high five, laughed until tears rolled down his face. Iris giggled so hard, she was afraid she would pee her pants and leaned against the wall with her legs crossed, until her fit passed.

Even with the time it took to compose themselves, they were still able to catch up to them as they waited for the elevator. William held the door back, and he and Iris both, waited patiently while their new, elderly friends imitated the Slowsky's in boarding it.

The four of them made small talk on the way up and when the elevator came to a jolting halt, both William and Iris placed a protective hand at the elbow of the fragile looking love-birds. Even though it was almost ten minutes after eight, they continued casually supporting them all the way to the dining room, where each of them was delighted to discover they were assigned to the same table. The third couple who made up their party of six, were young newlyweds from France.

It was the fourth night of the cruise, and yet the first time that all six of them were present for dinner at the same time. It was a very enjoyable event for each of them, so much so in fact, that William and Iris almost regretted not being present the previous three nights. Almost, but not quite.

As it turned out, they discovered the youngsters had missed dinner in the dining room their first night onboard, which, being newlyweds, was completely understandable. The old couple had been satisfied to spend their first evening of the cruise alone.

Nobody would ever have guessed that couples ranging from their twenties to their eighties, would mesh so perfectly, but they did. William ordered an expensive bottle of wine for the table to share before ordering their meals, toasting both the newlyweds and the couple who would be celebrating seventy years of marriage on Friday. He was eighty nine and his wife, eighty six.

Spending almost two hours together, they talked and laughed and even became misty eyed, sharing both highlights and lowlights of their lives. When they first introduced themselves all around, Iris called the old man's bluff when he said his name was Fred and introduced his bride as Wilma.

"Let me guess," she teased, "your last name is Flintstone." The French couple exchanged a knowing look because they had already questioned his sincerity in this matter, the first time they had met them. And when Fred brandished his wallet, showing Iris both his and his wife's driver's licenses, he feigned outrage that she hadn't believed him.

Fred had been at Normandy during World War II as a young soldier. One of his duties had been to retrieve the bodies of other soldiers, some alive but mostly dead, from the beach. He didn't go into great detail as it wasn't a topic to discuss at the dinner table, but he and Wilma had visited France under much more pleasant circumstances, many times over the years, and kept the others in stitches with tales of their experiences while there.

William touched briefly on the fact that he had done two tours in Viet Nam as a Marine, and he and Fred toasted one another with mutual respect. This was something Iris was hearing from William for the first time, but then she had only met him four days ago and Viet Nam, she knew, was a subject some men discussed reluctantly, if ever, depending on their experiences there. She felt that even though she already loved William passionately, she would grow to love him in deeper, more meaningful ways, the more she got to know him.

Julie and Julian, the French newlyweds, spoke about their beloved France with such descriptive zest and romantic passion, that Iris had William promising to take her there. She had never been to Europe at all, since her travels had been centered around the Caribbean, which she never grew tired of. But, listening to the two couples, old and young, talk about London and Paris, Venice and Rome, she grew starry eyed with desire to see and do everything they described.

William had taken Rebecca to Europe for their honeymoon and again for their tenth and twentieth wedding anniversaries, but he remained quiet about that, not wanting to spoil their prospective trip together, for Iris.

That was then and this was now and he had no problem separating his past from his future. There were many things he and Iris had yet to learn about each other's lives, and he looked forward to many happy hours talking and listening, teaching and learning.

After dinner, Fred and Wilma retired to their cabin, assuring both younger couples they could make it just fine without any assistance. Julie and Julian loved American music, both country and rock and roll, and happily accepted William's and Iris' invitation to share a table with them at the night club they had visited the first night they had met.

Even though the kids were roughly thirty years younger than the older couple, they thought they were fun and found it interesting that they had met onboard the *Whimsical* just a few days ago. The two of them seemed so perfectly suited for each other and as comfortable together as their parents were, after many years of marriage.

William danced once with Julie, as did Julian with Iris, and they became fast friends over the next few hours. They all left the club at one however, because they wanted to be rested for the full day in Sint Maarten. It was both Iris' and William's favorite island in the Caribbean and they couldn't wait to see their familiar haunts together.

Julie and Julian had signed up for the excursion that would spend the day at the clothing optional beach on the French side of the island, but William and Iris wanted to stay in Phillipsburg, on the Dutch side of Sint Maarten, visiting friends and shopping. They both had gotten plenty of sun on Saint John that day, and would have two days at sea on Thursday and Friday, to lay by the pool.

After hugs and kisses and promising to see each other at dinner again, they went their separate ways. Julian's parents had booked the honeymoon suite for them as a generous wedding present, since Julie's parents had paid for an elaborate wedding, inviting more than a hundred and fifty guests. Julie promised to give Iris a grand tour of the suite later that week. William was anxious to see it as well, thinking ahead to what he hoped would take place in their near future.

It had been an incredible, exhausting, and for the most part, wonderful day. Even with the emotional roller coaster rides Iris and William had both taken at each other's expense, they felt closer and more in love than ever, as they welcomed the new day in the same way they had welcomed the day before.

Later, William set the alarm for seven, giving them a little more than four hours to sleep. The following two days they would be at sea and could sleep as late as they wanted, but for now, they were willing to get by with one more night of very little rest, relying on the adrenaline rush their new love gave them.

Chapter 8

When the clock radio came on at seven, Iris was dead to the world. William smiled down at her, turning off the alarm. She hadn't heard it at all and was sleeping on her side, facing him, and he could see her eyes moving beneath her lids. Obviously dreaming, he thought, as a slow smile transformed her features even in sleep. He eased out of bed and got a pot of coffee going after a quick trip to the bathroom. Slipping on the pair of pants he had worn the night before, he walked out onto the balcony.

The sun was bathing the water, the white sand beach, and the pastel colored buildings that were located just a short distance from the ship, with soft morning light. He could see there were at least three other cruise ships in. There could be that many more as well, that weren't visible to him from this side of the *Whimsical*, he knew. Sint Maarten was one of the most popular cruise ship destinations in the Caribbean and he had been there when as many as six ships had been visiting there on the same day.

He went back inside and poured two cups of coffee, fixing Iris' just the way he knew she liked it. He drank his black, which she thought was disgusting. She took hers with both cream and sugar, and he had teased her, claiming she only used the coffee for color since there was no way she could possibly taste it.

He didn't say it to Iris, but she liked hers exactly the same way Rebecca had, so it was easy for him to remember. But he wasn't thinking of

Rebecca that morning, only Iris, and how happy and blessed he was feeling.

Setting her cup down on the bedside table, he took a sip of his coffee, gently brushing, with a massive hand, a long strand of her hair off her face. His gentleness and agility were in direct contrast to his bulk and overall size. After a minute, she became aware of his fingers in her hair and even though she was awake, she chose to keep her eyes closed, relishing his touch, just a moment longer. He lay her hair back on the pillow where it shone like spun gold in the sunlight that had crept in to cast an angelic glow on her face.

When he stopped smoothing her hair back, she opened her eyes and looked at the miracle God had sent her. She recalled one of her favorite sayings that she had consoled her children with over the years, when they had suffered one episode of adolescent heartbreak after another. "When one door closes to you, another one will open," ran through her memory. William was living testament to that fact.

"I see the wheels turning in that pretty head of yours," he said after giving her a good morning kiss. "What are you up to so early in the morning? I didn't know you had coherent thoughts before nine," he teased her. He fluffed both of the pillows behind her as she sat up and then handed her the cup of coffee he hoped was still warm.

Iris took an appreciative sip from her cup before answering. Following his gaze, she pulled the sheet up to cover her naked breasts. "I'll have you know smart aleck, that I have plenty of coherent thoughts before nine every day. It's just usually p.m. instead of a.m.," she declared haughtily, tossing her hair and pointing her chin in the "how dare you" gesture he knew well by now.

"Stop looking so sexy, hot stuff," he warned her. "Here, put this on." Plucking her robe off the bathroom door knob, he held it out to her. "Come out on the balcony while I order breakfast. I have trouble controlling myself with you sitting there in the nude," and he added with a jerk of his head toward the balcony, "there's a gorgeous day beckoning from Sint Maarten."

"Oh, yea!" she exclaimed, almost knocking him down as she jumped out of bed, throwing her robe on as she sprinted outside. "I had forgotten we would wake up here. I was still half brain dead," she admitted.

William thought Iris looked like a young girl as she threw her arms wide and then squeezed herself as if embracing the sun and sea, Sint Maarten and life in general. "God, I love this place!" She breathed deeply of the already warm morning air and smiled happily up at William, knowing today was going to be wonderful with him by her side in her favorite place in all the world.

Picking up the phone, he ordered breakfast and then wrapped her in his arms as they took in the much loved and familiar view.

Each of them had been coming to Sint Maarten for years, both on cruises and sometimes to stay a week or two at a time. It didn't matter who they had been with before, they were together now and thrilled with having such a beautiful day to spend here.

The conversation was lively over breakfast as they talked excitedly about their plans for the day, and as soon as they were finished eating, William left her alone to get ready. It was already eight and most of the shops would open at nine. Iris loved the fact that William enjoyed shopping. William, himself, had something very special in mind to look for today, but never hinted to Iris what it was.

After she had watered the flowers she had once again thanked him for, she chose a pair of Lucky brand denim capris and a white eyelet, button front, cap sleeved blouse that would be easy to get off and on while shopping for clothes.

She wore her favorite red sandals again because they were both comfortable and looked cute with the capris length jeans. Plus, her stuff was already in the red leather clutch that easily converted to a shoulder bag with an attachable chain strap. Saving time by not having to unlock the safe and lock it back again, she also wore the same ruby and diamond jewelry she had worn to dinner last night. It was convenient and looked just fine with her outfit.

After showering and applying only mascara and lipstick, she blew her hair dry, rolling the ends under slightly, instead of flipping it up and wore it loose, held back by a wide, red hair band.

Her tan and clothes and simple hair style made her look the early forty something years old that William had first mistaken her for. All she knew was that it was too hot for further makeup and she was too familiar with the Caribbean weather to waste too much time on her hair.

William whistled appreciatively when he saw her and she laughed when she noticed how well matched they were dressed, without having planned it. He wore denim cargo shorts that showed off his well muscled calves and a red, short sleeved, golf shirt that had a navy blue contrasting collar and navy logo on the chest pocket. He was wearing his brown, Rockport deck shoes, without socks, of course.

After all, he was still only fifty nine, not eighty nine. William would turn sixty on Friday, the same date as Fred and Wilma's seventieth anniversary. He still hadn't told anyone, but now that he had someone to share it with, it didn't seem like such a big deal, anyway.

Times before, arriving at Sint Maarten by cruise ship, they both remembered being able to walk right off the ship, onto the dock, but now, they were boarded onto a tender and deposited at the dock just a couple of minutes later.

There were so many beautiful new changes in this area of Phillipsburg, which was the capitol of the Dutch side of the island. Not so long ago, the beach had come right up to the rear of the buildings along Front Street. Now, a spacious, curvy shaped, concrete and brick boardwalk flowed between the wide, white sand beach and the rear entrances of the shops, restaurants and hotels, and even a few homes. The owners of these establishments had really spruced up this beach side of their properties which was what tourists saw when arriving by water. In addition to looking much cleaner and more inviting, it also took some of the crowded foot traffic from the sidewalks of Front Street and redirected it along the beach.

Iris had only been here once since the boardwalk had transformed the waterfront and William hadn't yet seen it, so they strolled along it for awhile, taking a few pictures and enjoying their view of paradise.

Standing on the boardwalk, the scene was spectacular in all directions. The beach was perfect here, cruise ships resided majestically just offshore and many, smaller boats dotted the water that was sparkling so, it couldn't be gazed upon without sunglasses.

The green hills that rose gently from the sea, were scattered with impressive homes that had views most would envy. On both the Dutch and French sides of Sint Maarten there was evidence of both the haves and have-nots, cohabitating peacefully side by side. You could often see a house that was obviously worth millions, within a rock's throw distance from one that you felt certain was not going to survive the next strong wind gust.

There were many nationalities and races of people living here who, through time, had blended to the point that people as familiar with the island as Iris and William were, saw neither class nor color, religion nor nationality, only the place and the people they had grown to love.

Walking back to the center of town, they crossed over from the boardwalk to the hectic, bustling activity that was Front Street. With thousands of people storming the area from the five cruise ships that were in port today, it was both exciting and extremely interesting.

There were many languages being spoken by both tourists and residents, and attire varied from swim suit tops being worn with shorts, to business dress that was worn by the shop owners and employees, to everything in between.

"That's one of the things I love about this place," Iris said to William, as they discussed all of it from their vantage point on a bench set beneath a palm tree. "The variety of people, the products being offered, the sights, sounds, smells and scenery. All of it fills me with the feeling of being so alive, like today is a gift I can't unwrap fast enough." Iris seemed to be looking everywhere and at everything at once, while she spoke, but William only had eyes for her. You are, he thought, listening to her explain her feelings, the only gift I can't unwrap fast enough.

"And, the remarkable thing is," she continued, unaware of his scrutiny, "I have felt this way every day that I have ever spent here, be it only a single day visit like now, or if I was staying on the island for two weeks straight. As much as I love Tennessee, I really do believe that if not for missing my kids and grandkids so much, I could live here happily, just going back home on holidays and to visit for short periods of time."

"But perhaps, if you lived here, it would lose some of the magic it holds for you," William sensibly pointed out. "I feel that way about Saint John, and here too, to a certain extent. And then, I get to thinking that there are so many places in the world that I haven't been to yet, that might appeal to my senses just as much, if I only took the time to travel more. I think that's something that we should do together, Iris." He looked at her meaningfully as he spoke.

The sincerity of his tone made Iris give him her full attention, and his next words made her pulse quicken. "I think if we planned it right, we could explore new horizons together and still be home enough to run a business and be a family."

When William talked about being a family, she knew he meant hers, since he had no family left. It gave her butterflies in her stomach to think that he could be serious about them having a future together, and she was so proud of both him and her children, that she could hardly wait for them to meet. As a matter of fact, she had an idea.

"Speaking of family, my love, Thanksgiving is next week and I was wondering if you would consider spending it with mine? But I warn you, there are twelve of those suckers in all, and whoever said it's easier by the dozen, lied!"

"I thought the saying was cheaper by the dozen," he corrected her. He loved the light that came on in Iris' eyes when they talked about her family. They must be as special as she is, he thought, and was both anxious about meeting them and excited. He had waited so long to have a family, that he could barely imagine getting twelve children, children-in-law and grandchildren all at once. But, to love her was to love them, he felt certain of that.

"But then, cheaper by the dozen makes absolutely no sense either, in this day and age, does it?" He stood and pulled her to her feet, kissing her lightly on the forehead. They began winding their way through the crowds of people on the sidewalks. They were in no particular hurry, although William did have a destination in mind.

"Iris, if you're absolutely positive that your kids won't mind me being there, I would love to have Thanksgiving with y'all. I mean, it would be the perfect opportunity for me to meet them all at the same time. I practically feel like I know them already anyway. Besides, the holidays really sucked for me last year, and sharing your family with me, would be the best gift you could possibly give me."

"Oh, they won't mind," she reassured him as they window shopped along Front street. "Nobody in my family has ever met a stranger." She laughed up at him and shrugged. "Not only that, but it's my house, my guest and my turkey."

He pinched her playfully on her butt and tried to look insulted. "Are you calling me a turkey?" Just then they came upon the jewelry store he had casually been steering her towards.

William had done business with Splash Jewelers for at least a decade and he and Rebecca had become good friends with them over the years. He knew they had truly been saddened when he had e-mailed them of her death a year ago.

Greg, the young man that they had known since he joined the family business here about twelve years ago, from India, was the one he primarily dealt with, although he was fond of them all. Greg had come over to Sint Maarten at the age of eighteen or nineteen and was about thirty now. He had married a few years ago and they now had a son. Greg e-mailed him pictures of the baby every now and then, and William smiled to himself, remembering the latest one he had received of Greg's wife and baby at the beach.

He had written him back, telling him how blessed he was to have such a beautiful family. Most of the guys here at the store were either brothers or brothers-in-law and William thought a great deal of all of them. Ironically, besides their employees, they had been the closest thing to family that he and Rebecca had known.

Greg and William saw each other at the exact same moment, and even though he was currently working with a customer, Greg flew around the counter as William stepped into the welcoming coolness of the store, and they embraced warmly. No words were spoken or necessary, but there were tears in both men's eyes. It was the first time they had seen one another without Rebecca being there, but Greg had seen the woman with William, and being the discreet professional he was, he simply gave him a look that said everything that was necessary. William understood that Greg's tears were for Rebecca, but his smile was congratulating him for finding yet another beautiful woman.

Iris had entered the jewelry store with William, however had remained a few steps behind him while the two men greeted each other. She understood immediately that they were more than jeweler and customer and knew instinctively that these people were accustomed to seeing William with his wife. She knew there were bound to be many more times she would find herself in this situation, but she wasn't jealous of a dead woman, only saddened to think of how William must feel, seeing someone he obviously cared about, for the first time since her death.

But, William had had a year to prepare himself for this type of situation, and recovered quickly, turning toward Iris and reaching for her hand. She gave him a tender look of understanding, and first shook hands with and then returned a hug from his handsome, young friend.

Greg smiled warmly at her and said, "Any friend of William's is also a friend to me and my family." His English was excellent and Iris had no trouble with his accent whatsoever. Iris returned his smile with one of her own. He seemed so genuinely glad to meet her that it was hard not to warm up to him instantly.

Almost all of the shops and businesses were owned or operated by people other than Americans, so she had long been accustomed to English being spoken here with a wide variety of accents. It was just part of the charm as far as she was concerned. If she only wanted to meet people who looked and sounded like her, she would have stayed home.

William urged Greg to return to the business he had been conducting and apologized to the patiently waiting couple for interrupting them. They assured him they understood, having done business with Splash for many years as well and felt the same way about all the guys there.

While Greg was busy with the older couple, William introduced Iris to all the others. Peter, Ray, Steven and Ricky, he had known for many years, but he also remembered Sam and Kevin from the last time he and Rebecca had been there. William asked about Gary, who was Steven's brother and Greg's brother-in-law, but was told he was off island with his family for a few days.

Ricky brought William a Carib beer and Iris a coke from a refrigerator they kept in the back office. "These guys have cost me a small fortune with their hospitality," William confessed to Iris, after taking a long drink from the ice cold beer. "They supply me with ample Caribs and I eventually fork over my credit card without even knowing what I spent until I get home and receive my statement."

He winked at Iris and smiled fondly at Greg who had joined them after completing a successful sale to the couple he had been working with when they came in. Iris had seen the spectacular sapphire and diamond necklace and earrings the woman had chosen and knew Greg must be feeling pretty good about the commission that would be coming to him from the sale.

Within minutes Iris felt she had known Greg as long as William had and could easily understand how they became so attached to one another. They seemed almost like father and son and it made Iris look even more forward to William meeting her family. His affectionate, easy way with the young man was an insight into his parental potential, and she was very pleased with this side of him.

She smiled as she imagined him playing with her grandchildren and becoming friends with her adult children. Her family didn't know it yet, she thought happily, but they were in for a real treat. No one could know William, she was convinced, without loving him. She looked at him adoringly and only laughed when he asked Greg to show them some diamond rings.

Iris spent the next hour trying on and oohing and aahing over, first one ring and then another. The rings were mostly made in the sample size of six, which lucky for her, was the size she wore. William insisted she try on every ring that struck her fancy, irregardless of the price.

"After all, we're just having fun," he assured her. "It doesn't cost anything to try them on and I'm not leaving while there are still Caribs in the fridge." Greg took the empty bottle from William and handed it to Sam who quickly replaced it with a full one. And, this time, he brought a Smirnoff Ice for Iris.

So, at the urging of both William and Greg, Iris tried on and admired tray after tray of exquisite diamond rings of all shapes and sizes in both yellow and white gold settings. After much debate, they agreed the pick of the litter was a two carat diamond solitaire, set in a white gold band, with a combination of channel set and round diamonds on either side of the raised solitaire. It looked spectacular on Iris' dainty, manicured hand. Anything bigger would have looked gaudy, she thought. Even this one was certainly more ring than she had ever owned. She gazed at it in awe, and wondered who could afford to buy such a ring for the woman he loved.

"O.k., o.k.," William laughed, tugging at the ring. "We were just having a little entertainment here. Remember, sweetheart?" Iris took one last, long, dreamy look at the beautiful piece before slipping it off and handing it back to Greg.

William heard a sigh escape her and felt a surge of guilt at the game he was playing. While Iris had gone around the shop looking in each glass case for rings she wanted to try on, he had used a combination of sign language and whispering to relay his intentions to Greg.

When she finally chose her favorite of them all, Greg was to take it back, putting it in the display case until they left the shop, then remove it, charge the amount to William's visa card the store kept on file, and have it delivered to the *Whimsical.* William gave him his suite number and Greg promised him he would find it waiting there for him, upon his return to his cabin.

William would have loved to offer it to her now, but he knew with a price tag of over sixteen thousand dollars, she wouldn't accept it. Even though that was a discounted price to William and a few thousand less than it would have cost back home in the states, he knew she would insist on swapping it for one of the others that had been priced far less.

But he had seen how it looked on her finger and watched her eyes grow big as she admired the ring's sparkle and clarity under the lights that were designed to emphasize the beauty of everything in Splash's vast inventory. And, of course, he had heard that sigh, as she had reluctantly given it up.

Just two more days, he reminded himself. He would give it to her on Friday, his birthday, when he would officially propose. Excitement made his pulse quicken, anticipating the moment.

"Iris, that ring costs almost as much as my first house. However, I do want you to look at some opals and choose something that would look nice with the earrings I got you in San Juan." Giving Greg a wink, he gestured towards a display that held opal pendants, rings and bracelets. Greg, pretending disappointment in losing the sale of the diamond ring, ushered Iris over to the opals.

"William, you've spent plenty on me already, and these pieces are all so beautiful. I don't know if I could choose only one. And, what if the piece I picked out was the most expensive? I can't let you do that!"

But the whole time she was protesting, Iris was staring at a necklace that had the same fiery colors as the earrings he had bought her, and the setting and diamond accents were almost a perfect match. The pendant was made to slide onto an omega necklace and fit close to the throat.

Greg zeroed in immediately on what had caught her attention and without her having said a single word or making a gesture, he quickly plucked the necklace from it's velvet bed and draped it around her neck, fastening it for her and producing a mirror like a magician, so she could see herself wearing the necklace.

Both men heard her intake of breath at the impact of seeing the piece laying like liquid fire against her tanned skin. They exchanged a smile and a nod over the top of her head to seal the deal. Greg punched in a price on a hand held calculator and flashed it behind her back, for William's eyes only. He gave Greg the o.k. sign with his fingers and while Iris was still turning this way and that in front of the mirror that was on the counter, Greg produced a tiny pair of scissors and snipped the price tag off, before she could glimpse the cost.

Seeing him remove the tag, Iris whirled toward William saying, "Oh no you don't! I was just trying it on. You know, for fun, like the ring." She reached behind her neck as if to unfasten the clasp, but William took both of her hands in his and placed them around his neck instead, silencing her with his lips on hers.

As usual, with him kissing her, Iris forgot all else and by the time he released her, all she could do was sink slowly onto one of the high stools placed along the glass counter and attempt to regain her composure. Greg pressed a plastic cup filled with cold water into her hand and she drank thirstily as if to drown the fire William had started in her belly. The amazement of his generosity and the excitement of his kiss had combined to leave her cheeks flushed and her protests snuffed out like a candle.

"Beautiful jewelry is meant to be worn, not argued about," William was saying, as he admired the way the fire in the opals and the flash of the diamonds emphasized the golden glow of her eyes. "And preferably," he continued, "by a beautiful woman such as yourself. Even though it's a gorgeous necklace, I'm convinced there's not another woman who could have done it proper justice."

Iris blushed a little deeper still at his compliment. "Thank you, my love," she said softly, and once again turned to face the mirror. She didn't say so, because it would sound too vain, but she did think the necklace looked as if it had been made for her. She couldn't wait to wear it with the earrings they had gotten in San Juan. She knew they would be stunning together and was already thinking ahead as to what she would wear to dinner that would best compliment her new jewelry.

They had been in Splash Jewelers for about an hour and a half and feeling they had monopolized enough of everyone's time and depleted a considerable amount of their Carib beers, William suggested they say their goodbyes and after many hugs and hand shakes and kissing of cheeks, they promised to return to Sint Maarten soon.

Greg had placed Iris' necklace in a satin jewelry bag that she had been able to fit in her handbag. It was much too nice to wear with what she had on and besides, it didn't go with the ruby jewelry she was already wearing.

They strolled along the sidewalk and occasionally went into a shop to look around. William found a new MP3 player he liked and after much protesting, finally allowed Iris to buy it for him. After all, it was like a drop of rain in a swimming pool compared to what he had spent on her, and she wanted to get him something so badly, he finally relented.

He smiled to himself as she paid for it, remembering the ring that would be delivered to his suite. He knew she would bust a gut when she found out he had bought it. She had looked like a little girl on Christmas morning when she had tried it on and he could hardly wait to see her expression when she realized it would be her engagement ring.

There was a great little hangout, right on the beach, that they were familiar with, and by the time they reached it, they were both hungry and thirsty and anxious to sit and relax. They grabbed a table right next to the boardwalk, practically running to claim it before someone else did. A couple was just leaving and the place was packed, as usual, with people waiting for a table. They were at the right place at the right time and grateful to snag one so quickly.

A server came by and took their drink orders. Iris shocked William by ordering a strawberry/banana daiquiri instead of her usual margarita, but she explained that this place made the best ones on the island. He kept with his Carib beer and they sat side by side, with their feet propped up on the two extra chairs at the table, watching the beach and boat activity, sipping their drinks, while waiting for their lunch.

"William, I've never been as happy in my entire life as I am at this very moment," Iris said, laying her head against his shoulder. He bent down and kissed the top of her head, tightening his grip on her with the arm he had around her shoulders. They sat that way for several minutes, content to just be there together, on a perfect day in Sint Maarten. They each stared out to sea, lost in their private thoughts of each other and the luck or fate or blessing that had brought them together less than five days ago.

When lunch arrived, they stirred as if from a nap and tore into the cheeseburgers, homemade potato chips and dill pickles, washing it down with bottles of water. "What is it about the sun and sea air that makes me ravenous?" Iris asked, staring at her empty plate in amazement that she had managed to eat every bite.

"I don't know, but I'm afraid that whatever it is makes my clothes shrink, as well," William teased, patting his rock hard stomach like he had gained a ton.

"I should have kept all my tags on my new clothes," Iris giggled, "and exchanged my new size fours for size sixes when I get back. It's probably a good thing I kept all my eights too, because after the holidays, I'll probably need them. You do like pleasantly fluffy ladies, don't you?" she asked playfully.

"Absolutely," William grinned mischievously. "That way, I can explore a new crevice every night." She punched him hard on the arm. "Damn, woman," he complained, rubbing his arm vigorously. "Exactly when did these violent streaks in you begin to surface?"

She thought for a moment and said, "I'm pretty sure it was Valentine's Day, but you're the first victim I've really been able to practice on. You do like your pleasantly fluffy ladies served up with a dash of mean streak, don't you?" She batted her long lashes at him, pretending all wide eyed innocence.

He surprised her by grabbing a handful of her hair and pressing his lips so hard against hers, they felt bruised, then released her suddenly. "Two can play the rough and ready game," he said huskily, and she watched his steel grey eyes turn smoky with desire. "And I happen to be ready." He rose quickly, throwing more than enough money on the table, then took her arm and pulled her to her feet. Grabbing the bag off the table that held his MP3 player in it, he practically dragged her out of the outdoor restaurant, back onto the sidewalk.

Neither of them spoke or window shopped, just kept up a steady pace during the fifteen minute walk to the tender that would get them to the *Whimsical* just a couple of minutes later. On the small, packed boat that taxied them to the ship, William gave Iris a deep, urgent kiss that would have been embarrassing if Iris had given a shit what anybody thought, but since she didn't, she practically pulled him down on top of her as her urgency matched, perhaps even surpassed his.

By unspoken mutual agreement, the other passengers held back, allowing William and Iris to debark the tender first. There were some raised eyebrows and looks of mock disgust from a few, but grins and giggles from the majority. For the most part, people are pretty understanding when it comes to love and lust and it was obvious the two hurrying onto the ship shared an abundance of both. After having both of their key cards swiped through a machine that registered their return to the ship, they hurried to the nearest elevator and punched the number for their floor of suites.

William backed Iris into a corner, praying the elevator wouldn't stop until it reached their floor. He almost mauled her breasts as she moaned against his lips. William was wondering what in the hell was taking the elevator so long, when it finally sprung open. Iris already had his shirt unbuttoned and they were both grateful that nobody was waiting to enter the elevator, because William had an enormous bulge in his shorts from his swollen member straining so hard against his zipper, it hurt to walk.

Fortunately, her suite was a short distance from the elevator. She already held her key card in her hand and she could hear William undoing his belt as she unlocked the door. By the time he closed it behind them, he had both unbuttoned and unzipped his shorts and letting them fall to the floor, he began to remove his briefs at the same time he stepped out of his shoes.

Iris almost tore his shirt from his back, kicking her sandals off while he quickly, but carefully maneuvered the buttons of her blouse. She undid her denim capris and William removed her bra so efficiently she wasn't even aware he had done it until he flung it onto the chair.

She felt the foot of the bed at the back of her legs before realizing they had moved across the floor to the bedroom. Dropping to his knees, pulling her panties down so roughly they ripped on one side, he almost flung her backwards onto the bed. Freeing her panties from her other foot, he grabbed her hips, pulled her forward, and thrust his head between her hot thighs.

Spreading her legs wider, he raised her butt up slightly off the bed so he could bury his tongue deeper into the slick recess that arched to meet his mouth. Iris' upper body writhed on the bed and she clutched handfuls of comforter for lack of anything else to hold on to. William moved to her clit and sucked hard while also inserting a finger into her. She screamed as she came, wrapping her legs around his shoulders and soaking his hand with the moisture she thought would never stop pouring from her.

Before her shudders had even subsided, he flipped her over like a rag doll and positioning her knees beneath her, he drove himself into her so hard and fast, she didn't have time to regain her breath before she came again and cried in pain that quickly converted to pleasure and back again.

She called his name, alternating between begging him to stop and pleading with him to never stop. She was mindless to what she wanted by now and deaf to her own rantings of both pain and desire. She reached back with one hand between her legs and clutched his swinging scrotum in her fingers firmly, squeezing and releasing gently and then harder.

Somewhere, from what sounded like a great distance away, she heard a bellow that sounded more animal like than human, but when he emptied what was surely a bucket full of sperm into her aching body, she knew it must be William making that noise.

When he finally released her hips, she fell exhausted, face down onto the bed, gasping to replace the air he had force fucked from her body. He lay over her, held up by his hands, dripping his final drops onto her buttocks. She felt his arms quiver to hold his weight off her and heard his ragged breath as he replenished his own lungs. He slowly dropped to one side of her body, onto the bed, with a thud and a grunt and she turned on her side and faced him.

He rolled onto his back and closed his eyes while she stroked his sweaty hair off his forehead and kissed his eyelids and nose and chin and at last, his mouth. She could faintly taste herself on his lips and knew she had never experienced a more erotic love making session in her life. She knew even if they were never able to duplicate it, she would remember this afternoon in Sint Maarten for the rest of her life.

When their breathing returned to normal, they showered and William put the shorts back on that he had been wearing and mixed them both a drink. Iris slipped on a pair of terry cloth shorts and a tank top. They had agreed to simply relax for the remainder of the afternoon, on Iris' verandah and enjoy the sun and the view. While he made her margarita, she watered the still beautiful arrangement of flowers and removed her exquisite new necklace from her purse and placed it in the safe with her other valuables. Then wetting a clean washcloth, she returned with it to the bedroom and wiped off the comforter at the foot of the bed that had been soiled by their lovemaking.

William, seeing her do this, laughed and asked, "What's wrong sweetheart? Afraid the comforter will get pregnant?" She turned and stuck her tongue out at him. "Well, now that was a mature answer, but lots better than bruising my arm again."

"It's just that we've been so careful to pull the bedclothes back," she explained, rubbing the damp spot vigorously. "There's no point in letting this pretty cover become permanently stained. Besides, I don't want our cabin steward to find any definite signs of my trashy ways. What he only suspects is one thing, what he knows for sure, is something else altogether." Laughing as she spoke, she stole a glance over her shoulder at William, but he didn't look amused.

"I know you're just joking, Iris, but please refrain from referring to our lovemaking as trashy behavior." He walked over to where she stood and placed his hands on either side of her face, fixing his steely eyes on her golden ones.

"A woman like you could never have trashy ways, as you put it. I love you and respect you and the physical love we share is a culmination of everything we feel for each other. There's nothing dirty about it, I assure you." He kissed her lightly and she smiled into his eyes. He saw the love there and a flicker of something else he couldn't quite identify.

She never spoke, just nodded in silent agreement with what he had said. Iris went to the bathroom to put the washcloth with the towels that needed to be replaced, and William returned to the tiny bar in the sitting area to put ice in their drinks. All at once it hit him. The emotion in her eyes had been relief. He realized that with his words, relief had momentarily washed over her, reflecting briefly in her eyes.

He glanced at her reflection in the bathroom mirror where she was at the sink washing her hands. She wore a gentle smile of contentment. Carrying their drinks onto the balcony and setting hers on the table, he stood at the railing sipping his Jack Daniels and looked over at the paradise that was Sint Maarten.

Soon, he reflected, very soon, she'll know just exactly how much she means to me. He raised his glass and silently toasted the island where Iris had chosen her own engagement ring, without having a clue as to the significance of her decision.

Chapter 9

For the next couple of hours Iris and William sat on the verandah watching the people on the beach and those running from shop to shop like busy little ants. Small boats motored and sailed past them and they waved and exchanged greetings with the happy occupants. One young man and woman actually pulled their bathing suits down and mooned them, as they sailed past, unconcerned because they knew they would never see them again, and both Iris and William clapped and whistled loudly in mock appreciation.

Pelicans swooped and dived from a bright blue sky into the clear Caribbean water, occasionally catching their prey, but seeming totally indifferent if they didn't. After all, how tough could life be for them here? If they came up empty, they just soared into the warm air and dived after the next fish that was all too visible beneath the beckoning water.

William and Iris were glad they had returned to the ship after their late lunch. Not only because of the passion that had driven them back with such urgency sooner than they had planned, but because they both agreed, this was so much nicer, being alone together, having a drink with their feet propped up, admiring their beautiful surroundings.

They knew thousands of people would rush to their respective cruise ships about five in the afternoon, when the horns and whistles would sound the warnings of their intentions to depart. And depart they would too, right on time, with or without all the passengers they had arrived with that morning.

The ship's captain held to a disciplined schedule and the cruise director, along with each day's news letter that was delivered directly to each cabin, constantly reminded passengers to keep their watches set on ship time. Invariably when ship time differed from a particular port of call's local time, a few people got left behind. When that happened, the individuals would have to pay, at their own additional expense, to meet up with their cruise ship at its next stop. Sometimes, like today, that would be in Miami, two days from now.

William and Iris were vastly entertained as they laughed at and sometimes even sympathized with, those hurrying towards the tenders. They could see as the ferrying boats got closer to the ship, the sunburned, or drunk, or simply happy people, sometimes struggling with all the packages that held from cheap to very expensive treasures acquired during their day in Sint Maarten.

Couples, they witnessed, were doing everything from kissing to arguing loudly, and children who were laughing and still wound up from their day at the beach, to those who were fast asleep in mama's or daddy's arms. All in all, they agreed, most everyone looked as if they had greatly enjoyed their time in Sint Maarten.

At six, the *Whimsical* departed, and even with the darkening sky, the island still looked beautiful as they sailed off shore, able to see the twinkling lights that signaled the beginning of evening life. "I wish we could have stayed overnight at least," Iris confessed to William, standing at the balcony railing, snuggling against him. "I love this island as much after dark as I do in the daytime. It's so alive with its great restaurants, bars, casinos and live music. I would have really enjoyed a night with you here."

"That sounds like an invitation to me," William said, and smiled down at her. "Don't look so forlorn, sweetheart," he teased, hooking a finger under her chin and raising her lips up to kiss them gently. "You act as though we'll never come back to Sint Maarten together. It's one of my favorite places too, you know, and it'll definitely be in our travel plans, so stop looking like your dog just ate your cat who just ate your canary."

"Yuck!" Iris said, laughing. "What an awful scenario you've conjured up in my mind, and just in time for dinner, too. I certainly hope they're not serving dog or cat or bird on tonight's menu or I won't be able to eat a bite," she admonished him. "And, the pelicans pretty much got me out of the notion for fish, so whatever you do, don't screw up my appetite for steak. I feel like it's my last remaining choice for supper."

William loved their shared sense of humor that kept them playfully bantering, constantly, back and forth. "Damn, and growing up on a farm, I have such a shocking number of really graphic cow stories, too. Perhaps you would rather hear about my experiences with my favorite sheep instead?" he asked her, making his comically lewd expression that always threw her into a fit of laughter.

It was hilarious to her, how he could transform his handsome aristocratic features into this image of an idiot pervert. She thought he would have been a successful movie star, had he ever had the desire. He was certainly more handsome than most of the current ones, she thought, wiping tears of laughter from her cheeks. The only one who could perhaps compete with his masculine good looks and sex appeal, would be Antonio Banderas, in her opinion.

"Go to your room!" Iris directed him, pointing toward her door. "Dinner is in an hour and a half and I smell like a French whore. Thank goodness the captain's formal dinner isn't until tomorrow night, or I would never be ready in time. Besides, I'm afraid I'm too jealous hearted to hear you reminisce about your adolescent sheep romances. Instead of counting them to fall asleep, I would probably lie awake with visions of shooting each one as they jumped the fence." It was William's turn to laugh at her expression and choice of words.

He gathered up his few belongings that were still laying about and looked at her with a shake of his head. "The two of us deserve each other, sweetheart, in more ways than one. Nobody else would put up with our insane jealousy and twisted humor. In the last few minutes of conversation, we have bumped off several species of domesticated animals and laughed about it, even though we profess to have loving and generous natures. But, what I find even worse, is your attitude towards French whores. You described smelling like one," he paused here for effect, "as if that's a bad thing." She giggled as he pretended to look affronted by her prejudice.

"I'm sorry, my love." Iris hung her head and managed to look genuinely ashamed. "As soon as I get home, I'll make a generous donation to both the local animal shelter and the FWU. Will that suffice as moral restitution?"

"That depends," he replied shrugging his shoulders. "What may I ask, is the FWU?" He had made his way to the door, and waited, with his hand on the latch, giving her both an inquisitive and expectant look over his shoulder. He was wondering, as he awaited her answer, which one of them was more full of horseshit, him or her. There I go again, he thought, as a smile twitched the corners of his mouth; another disparaging thought toward yet another innocent animal.

"Why," she arched her eyebrows at him, obviously surprised he even had to ask such a question; "the French Whore's Union, of course. You obviously have a hard spot for them, and I want to make up for my unkind remark."

"You mean soft spot for them, instead of hard spot?" he asked, laughing at her imagination. He knew, even before he asked though, that she had known exactly what she was saying. She was so beautiful standing there, with her hands on her slim hips and her breasts straining unrestricted against her tank top, it was all he could do to refrain from taking her again. He opened the door to remind himself he had been in the process of leaving.

"Not in your case, tiger," she said with a meaningful glance at his crotch. "Not in your case," she repeated softly for her ears only, when he had gone out, and closed the door behind him. Iris could hear his laughter as he unlocked his own suite and faintly still, when he had closed his door, as well.

Heat coursed through her when she turned to see the bed that was neat and clean once again, but still triggered the replay of their lovemaking in slow motion, searing her brain with unforgettable memories. A shiver ran through her lower belly and she leaned against the wall and closed her eyes, feeling the moisture between her legs and the dampness in her panties.

Iris took a much more leisurely shower this time, than the one she had shared with William earlier. She shaved her legs and under her arms like she did every day, shampooed and conditioned her hair and used one of the fresh scented, disposable douches she had brought with her, even though her insides were still tender from their most recent round of sexual aerobics. Finally, she felt clean, inside and out.

Dinner should be fun tonight, she was thinking, rubbing moisturizer into her golden brown skin. Her hair was wrapped in a towel and she wore only her panties. It was too warm to dress for dinner just yet and besides, she was still debating what to wear. She could hardly wait to wear her formal dress tomorrow night, to the captain's cocktail party and dinner. She wondered if William had brought a tux to wear. God, she thought, rummaging through her clothes choices in the closet, he really would look like a celebrity in a tux.

But tonight, everyone would be more casual and she was looking forward to hearing the stories the "Flintstones" as she called them, and the honeymooners from France, would tell about their day in Sint Maarten.

She and William would talk about their day as well, leaving out the best parts, of course. Iris smiled, thinking that Julie and Julian would probably omit some highlights from their day, too.

If only she and William had met when they were young, she daydreamed, now only staring into the closet, but not really seeing the clothes hanging there. Would they have fallen as quickly and deeply in love back then? Or, can you only feel this much, she wondered, after experiencing the many ups and downs, highs and lows, that life gives and then takes back?

Thinking of her children and grandchildren, Iris certainly felt no regrets for her thirty three years of marriage to David. Admittedly she had loved him; otherwise, it wouldn't have practically destroyed her when he had left. Actually, she believed that they had been happy for the most part, and knew that William had been happy with Rebecca, as well.

"Everything happens for a reason," her mother had always said to her. "Our lives unfold precisely as they are supposed to," she often told Iris. "We make things harder for ourselves sometimes, fighting the inevitable, but in the end, God's will shall be done."

Iris smiled to herself, hearing her mama's voice so clearly in her head that she could almost feel her presence. She knew her mother would be happy for her having found love again. She herself, had remarried after Iris' father had passed away. She and her second husband had spent almost twenty, wonderful years together before they died, less than a month apart.

Iris desperately hoped William was serious about continuing their relationship after the cruise came to an end, and prayed they would be blessed with many healthy, happy years together.

Once again, she focused on her wardrobe, but was reminded by her stroll down memory lane, that she still had yet to learn exactly how old William was. Knowing him intimately, it was hard to imagine him being a day older than she was and surely they were no more than just a few years apart, she suspected. As virile and fit as he was, he certainly didn't act or look any older than her, but still she couldn't help but wonder why he hadn't told his age when she had told him hers on the first day they had met. Maybe she would ask him tonight and have the mystery over with.

Finally making her decision as to what to wear, she returned to the bathroom to do her hair and her little bit of makeup. She had brought with her, an outfit she had bought in Sint Maarten a couple of years ago, but had only worn a few times. It wasn't the type of thing you would wear everyday, but was perfect for an occasion such as tonight. Not to mention, an appropriate tribute to the day spent on the island where she'd bought it.

It was a tan, black and white batik print tunic and pants, pajama style outfit that hung loose and flowing in a cool fabric that would be fitting for such a warm evening. The pants had a comfortable, elastic waist and the style was such that, even though she had been wearing a size eight when she bought the outfit, she could still wear it.

The long top had a Nehru style collar and sported wooden buttons in the shapes of exotic animals, all the way down the front. The top came almost to her knees. Looking at herself in the full length mirror, she thought it looked even better on her now than it had originally. The tunic wasn't as snug across her chest, nor the elastic the least bit tight on her waist.

The overall effect was very slimming and even though Iris could tell she had gained a few pounds in the last several days, the outfit camouflaged it beautifully. She guessed she had probably gained three or four pounds in the past five days on board the ship, but she knew when she returned home to her normal routine, she would shed them pretty quickly.

Even though William teased her about being too thin, she liked being a four, and after making a healthy investment in new clothes, had no desire to outgrow them any time soon.

She put on black, open toed slides that had a two inch heel, high enough so that her pants wouldn't drag, but low enough to be comfortable. Her hair was brushed back casually and hung in big, loose curls at her shoulders. Iris noticed her hair looked a little blonder against her tanned skin and the sun had undoubtedly lightened it some too.

Wearing no foundation on her face, she applied only a neutral color eye shadow to even the color of her lids, black mascara and a deep plum colored lipstick that plumped her lips slightly.

The jewelry she had chosen for tonight worked beautifully with the exotic looking outfit. There were large, gold hoops in her ears and several gold bangle bracelets clanged musically when she moved her right hand. A wide, gold ring was on the middle finger of her left hand.

The image in the mirror met with Iris' approval finally, and when she looked at the time, she saw she had almost twenty minutes until William would punctually arrive to escort her to dinner.

Since she had spoken to Sarah twice since she had left home, but not to Rachel or Jake, either one, she took her cell phone out onto the balcony, which seemed to be the only place she could get a signal, and called Rachel's house. It was not quite seven back home and there was no answer, so she hung up and called Jake.

He answered on the first ring, like he had been perched on the telephone, daring it to make a sound. His voice sounded pleasantly familiar to Iris, giving her a flutter of homesickness, but she detected anxiety or anger or perhaps both, she concluded, even though all he had said so far was hello.

"Jake, it's Mama. Did I call at a bad time? I called Rachel and nobody was home. Is everything o.k.?" Iris heard a loud sigh escape him, as if he had been told to hold his breath and had just been given permission to exhale.

"Oh, hi Mama. Rach and Danny are at basketball practice with the boys. You know how it is around here. We barely get done with soccer before we start basketball, and basketball playoffs are just over with when we begin baseball practice."

They both laughed, knowing what he said was true, and also knowing none of them would have it any other way. Her kids didn't force sports on their children, they simply supported them in whichever ones they wanted to play. But, ever since her grandkids were old enough to run, they had wanted to participate in pretty much all of them. Consequently, the children were healthy and strong, slim and muscular.

Iris and her own kids not only derived great pleasure from their games, but took pride in the fact that they excelled in both sports and academics. The children knew if their grades slipped, they would be benched until the next report card, and so far, not one of them had missed a single game. But, then again they were still in elementary school and the supply of hormones they would be gifted with by the time they reached junior high, perhaps even middle school, was not yet a factor. Iris remembered those days, and not too fondly, so pushed thoughts of her babies growing up, out of her mind.

"My boys have practice tomorrow night," Jake added. "Sarah says you've been having a real good time, Mama. You don't know how glad we are that one of our parents is happy. We were so afraid you would back out of going at the last minute, and at the same time, equally afraid you would go and be miserable. Me and Rach sure were relieved when Sarah said you sounded happier than ever before."

Iris smiled at hearing the familiar name he called Rachel. They had called each other Rach and Jake since they could talk. Iris had shortened Jacob to Jake as soon as he was born, but he was the one who had always called Rachel, Rach. It had stuck with her all the way through school and many of her friends and family members still called her Rach, but not Iris. She loved the name Rachel and had stubbornly refused to abbreviate it.

"So, obviously, you're not sounding so stressed out because of me, so is it your father who's got your nerves on edge?" Iris asked gently. Jake would always open up to her if nobody else was around. But, if his wife was within earshot, he would clam up, she knew.

"No, not really him," Jake smiled into the phone as he replied. His mama had radar when it came to her family, and no matter how far away she might be, he knew her signal was still strong. "It's his bimbo bride and her shenanigans." He laughed a little as he made his admission, and Iris thought he sounded like himself again.

"What's she done this time? Sarah told me Samantha's doctor had put her on an antidepressant. I assumed that would keep her on an even keel, for a while at least. What's her problem now?" Iris was getting a little tired of that woman being a worry to her children. She had felt sorry for her when she lost the baby, but knowing now that David really hadn't wanted it as badly as she had, Iris rather believed it may have been for the best.

"Well as it turns out, the happy pills created the latest crisis." Iris could almost see Jake run his hand through his hair as he spoke. Whenever he was excited or upset, the fingers of his right hand would run through his thick, sandy hair, brushing it straight back from his forehead. When he was a very little boy, she used to get him to go to sleep by running her fingers through his baby hair and gently massaging his scalp. Evidently the gesture still calmed him.

Thirty years old and a grown man with kids of his own, she was thinking. When in the world had that happened? Her mind returned to the present as he told her about Samantha's latest escapade.

"Evidently, she determined if one pill made her feel better, then two would make her feel great." Iris rolled her eyes in silence as he continued. "She started threatening suicide and swore she would do it if dad even thought about leaving her, now that she's lost the baby. I mean, he's not doing a very good job at hiding how miserable he is, after all. It's not like it's a secret." Iris wished David was there with her for just long enough for her to slap him so hard he might actually regain his senses.

"Anyway, he took the pills away from her, after counting them and figuring out she had taken more than the prescribed dose. He called her doctor and he said that dad should maintain possession of them, only giving her one a day. He told him they should calm her down when taken properly, but if they didn't, he would have to change the prescription to a different type. Different ones evidently affect people in different ways and sometimes can bring out thoughts of suicide or even homicide." Jake laughed so hard that Iris got tickled too.

"What you were saying didn't sound so funny, Jake. Why are we laughing?" Iris asked, between giggles. She dabbed at her eyes, hoping her mascara wasn't running. She waited until Jake finished composing himself.

"Sorry, Mama. You're right. What I told you isn't funny. It was remembering dad's reaction to what the doc told him and the look on his face when he was explaining it to me. He double checked the lock on his gun case and now carries the key in his pocket and he took his knife collection to his office at work. At the time I thought he was protecting her, but it only just now occurred to me, that he's looking out for his own skin. I just remembered the emphasis he put on the word homicide and the look on his face was much more serious than when he said suicide."

Iris didn't want to criticize Jake's father too much and knew it wasn't necessary, anyway. Her son saw the truth easily enough. "Well, I'm sure he did those things for everyone's safety," she graciously suggested. But then, she couldn't resist adding, "David wouldn't be David, however, if he didn't put himself first. He's always had a very strong survival instinct and I'm positive between him and Samantha, your daddy will come out the winner, somehow. Even though she's certainly not innocent, she is still young and if they get into a pissing contest, I'll put my money on David."

She could hear Jake's smile in his words. "Maybe so, Mama, but between the three of you, I'll place my bet on you. You were the best thing that ever happened to Daddy, and believe me when I say, he knows it now. I hope when you're ready and meet the right guy, he'll be the best thing that ever happens to you. After everything you've done for everybody else, you deserve to get more than you give, next time around."

Iris didn't have time for any details, but felt Jake had given her the perfect opportunity to at least throw out a hint about William. "Don't worry son, it's going to be way better for me the next time. Who knows, maybe better in some ways, for all of us." There was a knock at the door and Iris glanced at the clock. Five minutes before eight. She smiled.

"Aha!" Jake exclaimed loudly in her ear. "Sarah said you were sounding far happier than some sun and sea air could account for. You've met someone. Haven't you, Mama?" To Iris' relief, he even sounded glad for her.

If she carried her phone with her to open the door, she was afraid she would lose the signal and she didn't want Jake to think she had conveniently hung up on him, so she only laughed and gave him a cryptic reply.

"Gotta run Jake. I'll see you in a couple of days and tell y'all about him then. But, right now, my second chance is knocking at my door. Love you, bye," she quickly added, hanging up, and hurried to meet William.

After leaving Iris' suite, William was still chuckling over her French Whore's Union joke. He had a hard spot alright, he willingly agreed, but not for the FWU. He didn't know if it was because he was celibate for a year before meeting Iris, or if she would always have this effect on him, and didn't really care.

All he knew was that for whatever reason, he couldn't get enough of her. He felt like a horny, young Marine again, and knew he was acting like it too. It might have been a little embarrassing at his age, if it wasn't for the fact that Iris' sex drive was as strong as his.

He entered his own cabin and immediately saw the note that the cabin steward had slipped under the door. For security reasons, his package from Splash Jewelry was being held for him at the information desk located on the main level of the ship. He went immediately to retrieve it and once he returned to the privacy of his suite, he opened it and checked to make sure it was the right one. Not that there was much he could have done about it now, he knew.

But there it was, just as he remembered. Two beautiful carats of solitaire with a few more carats to either side of it. It wasn't as gorgeous in the box as it had been on Iris' delicate hand, but he hoped he would see it there again on Friday evening.

He smiled to himself, knowing how surprised she would be, and hoped she would be equally thrilled, when he placed the ring on her finger. William carefully locked the package in the safe in his closet and went to shower. He didn't allow himself many moments of doubt, because he couldn't even imagine what he would do if she didn't want to marry him.

He knew Iris hadn't even been divorced as long as he had been a widower. But, he didn't want to wait a minute longer than he had to. A year, rambling around his big house alone, had been excruciating. Although, he knew he wanted to marry her for many more reasons than just for companionship. She was not only everything he needed and wanted, but more than he had ever hoped to have again.

And, as an added bonus, he couldn't wait to have grown children and grandchildren that he had long since given up on ever having. William dried off and pulled on a pair of shorts, knowing he had an hour to check e-mail and relax before getting dressed.

After pouring just a splash of Jack over some ice, he carried his laptop to the balcony. He could still see a few twinkling lights from Sint Maarten in the distance. Grinning broadly, he thought about the fun he and Iris had had that day, both on the island and when they had returned to the ship. Feeling an erection in the making, he quickly changed his venue of thinking to more serious matters.

He had not yet mentioned the possibility to Iris and perhaps would just wait until he met her son, but he was very enthused about Jake's automotive background and experience with Saturn. Since the young man wasn't interested in working in his father's business, he was hoping to encourage him to consider learning and eventually running, Pendleton Parts, as he preferred to call it.

Turning sixty in two days and hopefully getting engaged, had him wanting to cut back on the time he spent at work. If Jake liked him, expressed genuine interest in his company, and turned out to be a competent assistant manager, then he and Iris could fulfill their dreams and spend much of their time traveling.

Thanksgiving was only a week away, and William was anxious to meet her family, and particularly her son. He wouldn't monopolize Jake's time, discussing business on a holiday, however, he hoped to put out a few feelers to see if he would be willing to meet with him at the factory and take a tour of the place, at least. First and foremost, William wanted to observe Jake and see how he interacted with his family, in his roles as son, husband, father and brother.

Jake's social skills would be as important to William, as his automotive experience. How his employees were treated mattered a great deal to him, and if Jake was anything like his mother, William thought everyone would warm up to him quickly.

William was planning to make Roger, General Manager, as soon as he got back to work on Monday. His buddy had supervised pretty much every department there at one time or another, and besides himself, knew more about the day to day operations than anyone else. It would be a well deserved promotion, and a financially welcome one, William knew.

Roger was in his late forties, married, with four kids. Two were in college, one on a full athletic scholarship, and the other on a partial academic scholarship. However; with their busy schedules at school, Roger didn't want them trying to work even part time, except in the summer, so he worked every available shift, to pay for all of their expenses that weren't covered.

And William knew there were a lot of them. Partial tuition, books, clothes, car insurance, etc. At least Roger's daughter, who went to MTSU in Murfreesboro, still lived at home and could easily drive to and from classes each day. Roger had told William in plain English, that there was no way he could afford even partial rent for her to live on campus.

Appointing Roger General Manager would then give William time to train Jake and hopefully, the two of them would become close personally, as well as professionally. He could be Roger's assistant and learn everything necessary, to someday take over the company in William's current position as President.

Many times over the years, he had wished for a son to share his business interests with. One who would love it and take care of it, long after he was dead and gone. He now had high hopes that Jake would be that son. And, even better still, Jake had two boys of his own.

Perhaps one day, the company would be called Pendleton, Corrigan and Sons, William daydreamed optimistically, and smiled contentedly at the thought. He knew Iris would be as pleased as he was with his plans.

But first things first, he reminded himself. They weren't married yet and Jake didn't even know he existed. "Next week might prove to be as interesting as this week has been," William said out loud, closing his laptop and going inside to get dressed.

He had answered an e-mail from Roger and forwarded him a few that he had received from other department supervisors, to take care of. He might as well start earning his new salary, in William's opinion.

Chapter 10

William was about to knock a second time, when Iris flung the door open. At first glance, he thought her eyes looked a little damp, and wondered if she had been crying. She was smiling, so he thought he must be mistaken.

"Where were you," he asked nonchalantly, "on the crapper?" Iris swung her small purse made from a coconut, and hit him in the gut with it. "Damn woman, what have you got in that thing? A box of rocks?" Grabbing his stomach, he doubled over in exaggerated pain.

"No, actually I've been picking up all the loose screws that you've lost from your head, Frankenstein," she teased, pulling the door shut and taking his hand. "That's no way to greet a lady; especially one you're supposed to be trying to impress."

"Ladies don't refer to the toilet as a crapper, you heathen. What were you thinkin?" she drawled. Her accent was even more pronounced than his. Not that either of them noticed.

"Please accept my apologies, your highness. Obviously, I'm not thinking clearly, so let me get this off my mind." He suddenly stopped in the hallway on the way to the elevator and pressed her against the wall. William kissed her lips hard, then claimed her tongue with his, then kissed her hard again.

He released her so suddenly, she almost slumped to the floor. Opening her eyes, she saw he was already walking away. "There. Now maybe that'll hold me over for a minute and allow me to think about something else, like supper. I'm starved," he said, pressing the elevator button.

"Apology accepted," Iris mumbled under her breath, as she hurried to catch up to him. Once inside the elevator, she checked her lipstick in one of the mirrored panels of the wall.

"Why do I try to wear lipstick around you? You end up with more on your lips than I do."

"You're just jealous because it looks better on me," William accused, pretending to primp alongside her. She stuck her tongue out at him.

"Now see," he scolded her. "It's shit such as that, that makes me do stuff such as this." He grabbed her as she squealed and tried to avoid him. "Just where in the hell do you think you're gonna run to in an elevator?" he asked, and pinned her to the wall.

Iris was giggling hysterically as he tickled her without mercy. The elevator door opened and a *Whimsical* crew member stood just outside the door, waiting to get on. "Is everything o.k., ma'am?" he asked her, with a look of concern. Evidently their frolicking had been heard through the elevator doors before they opened.

Iris composed herself, as William looked completely innocent. He offered her his arm in a gentlemanly fashion, and escorted her off the elevator, like royalty. Iris smiled at the concerned young man, and assuring him all was well, wished him a pleasant evening. When the crew member entered the elevator and the doors closed behind them, they glanced guiltily at each other and burst out laughing.

Dinner was a festive occasion, with all three couples often talking at once. Everyone was in great spirits after their all too brief, but beautiful stay in Sint Maarten. The two older couples laughed until they cried as Julie and Julian described their experiences at the clothing optional, Orient Beach. Their heavy accents and sometimes misused words, made their stories even more entertaining.

Wilma showed off a beautiful new sapphire, ruby and emerald bracelet, that Fred had bought her just that day, and it looked spectacular with a similar ring she was wearing, that he had gotten for her last year on another cruise.

"I'll never live long enough to wear the jewelry I already have," Wilma confided to the two younger women, in a whisper. "But, our daughters and granddaughters are finally letting me give them a few nice pieces every now and then that I don't wear any more. They fought me for a while, saying it made them feel funny, dividing up my jewelry, like I was about to kick the bucket. But, after I assured them that I fully intend to see my one hundredth birthday, they finally agreed to choose a piece at Christmas and on their birthdays."

Wilma looked lovingly at her eighty nine year old husband. "So Fred thinks every time one of the girls takes home a piece of jewelry, he has to replace it for me with something new."

The three guys had their heads together, looking very secretive, but refused to admit to anything, when questioned by the women. But, they all noticed the men looked even more pleased with themselves than usual. Fred motioned to the bar waitress and even Wilma was surprised when he ordered a bottle of wine that was even more costly than the one William had treated them with the night before.

She raised her eyebrows at him, but he only laughed and winked. She didn't care how much it cost, but was dying to know the secret. Fred leaned over and whispered that he couldn't tell her right now, but would, as soon as they were alone.

They ate and drank and talked until ten, when they noticed they were almost the last ones left in the dining room. Knowing the staff had put in a very long day, they agreed they should take their party elsewhere, and the two other couples were thrilled when Julian invited them all to the honeymoon suite to share one of the bottles of champagne they had on ice.

Everyone was properly impressed with their special suite, and told them so. It was twice the size of a normal suite, and the furnishings, linens, drapes and upholstery were upgraded, as well. The colors were soft and romantic in mostly white, with some pale aquas and dusty pinks, making it look like sunrise reflecting off a soft cloud.

"I feel like a fairytale princess when I'm in here," Julie said, in her carefully pronounced English, and positively glowed when her eyes met those of her new husband.

Julian spoke softly to her in French, making her blush, and the others felt perhaps they should leave them alone. But, the young lovers insisted they stay and enjoy the champagne with them. Their balcony was also at least twice the size of those that came with a regular suite, and there was room for all six of them to sit outside together and enjoy the warm late evening breeze.

The sky was crystal clear with what seemed like a million stars within reach. The moon wasn't quite full, but should be in another night or two. Looking at it, William was secretly hoping it would be full on Friday night and that the moon would reflect on the water as beautifully as it was right now, unencumbered by clouds.

Iris and Wilma urged Julie and Julian to relive their wedding for them. They wanted to know everything, they claimed; the dresses, the flowers, the guests, the reception, favorite gifts they received, all of it. Neither of them had been able to have big, fancy weddings.

Wilma had married at sixteen and Iris at seventeen and neither of their families had had the money for such things. All four of them listened intently, smiling to themselves and at each other, as the newlyweds remembered and described their big day.

Of course Julie's account consisted of a lot more detail about things that guys historically didn't pay much attention to, and she occasionally would roll her eyes at the other women when Julian would fail to recall some specific something or another.

"I'm sorry, ma cherie, but your beauty that day, blinded me to every other sight." He brought her hand to his lips and kissed it and looked meaningfully with his black eyes into her sky blue ones. Iris glanced at William and they stood up to leave. They both recognized, very well, the fiery depths of passion that smoldered in Julian's gaze.

Getting the signal from them, Wilma rose as quickly as they did, but between the wine and champagne and two eighty nine year old knees, Fred took a little longer to hoist himself up. Everyone thanked the kids, as they thought of them, for their hospitality and allowing them to see the tastefully done honeymoon suite.

Julie and Julian still stood on the balcony with their arms wrapped around each other's waists, since William assured them they could see themselves out, and waved their goodbyes. By the time the door had closed behind their guests, the newlyweds were entangled in each other's arms and locked in a kiss that wouldn't soon end.

William offered to assist Fred to his cabin since Wilma and Iris wanted to visit the casino for a while, but assured them he would join them there shortly. Fred wasn't exactly drunk, but at his age and having a little difficulty walking under perfect conditions, he was grateful for William's company.

It was already midnight and past his bedtime and he could never stay out late enough to accompany Wilma to the casino. So Fred was very happy that Iris had wanted to go too. He knew she wouldn't stay too late anyway, because it had been a long, busier than usual, day for them.

Their suite was just a ways down the hall from William's and Iris', so they popped into William's just long enough for him to show Fred the ring he had been telling him and Julian about that night at dinner. Fred was dutifully impressed and clapped William on the back in appreciation. It hurt his hand a little and he laughed and shook it. "Hell son, are you sure you're going to be sixty on Friday? I feel like I just slapped a brick wall."

William put the ring back in the safe and locked it, laughing at Fred's question. "Yes, sir, I'm sure. But let's not tell Iris until after she's accepted the ring and my proposal. I don't want to scare her away. She's ten years younger than me."

They left William's suite and headed on down the hall toward Fred and Wilma's cabin, with William holding Fred's arm for support. The ship was rolling a little bit and he didn't want his new friend to fall. At his age, any injury could be serious.

"Hells bells, boy!" Fred's voice was loud in the quiet of the empty hallway. "You couldn't scare that one off if you jumped out of the closet naked and yelled "boo!" William chuckled as he imagined himself doing just that.

"She's so in love with you, she can't remember when she wasn't," Fred further assured him, a little quieter this time. "Trust me, big man, I know a thing or two about women and Iris has got it bad for you."

They reached Fred's door and eventually he produced the key card and handed it to William. Why should he try to unlock it with his trembling hand, he reasoned, when William could probably do it in half the time.

"I hope you're right, Fred," William said, easily opening the door on the first try. Helping him across the threshold, he gave the card back to Fred and watched to make sure he placed it safely in his wallet.

"But, I've learned recently, not to take anything for granted, especially the good things." Fred saw a shadow of great sadness flash in William's eyes, but was too old and wise to acknowledge it. He had seen much in his many years as well, and knew firsthand, that it was much healthier to celebrate the happy and try not to dwell on the sad.

Fred offered his hand to William and thanked him for seeing him to his room and showing him the ring. "You will wait until Friday evening at dinner to propose, won't you? Me and the wife wouldn't want to miss it." He smiled, and William once again noticed that Fred still had a well maintained set of his own natural teeth. He saw a glimmer of the handsome, younger man that Fred had once been.

He returned the handshake, clasping the older man's hand and holding it briefly, before letting go. He and Iris were both growing very fond of the "Flintstones", as Iris called them in private.

"You betcha, Fred," he said, returning the smile. "I want y'all as witnesses if she says yes. That way, she can't back out as easily. I might even draw up something in writing that you and Wilma and the French kids can sign, as proof that she accepted. That way, I can show it to her later if she gets cold feet."

William left Fred then, making sure he didn't need him for anything before he did, and hurried up to meet the ladies. He had been gone longer than he thought, he noticed, after a look at his watch. It was just shy of twelve thirty and he and Fred had left them almost a half hour ago. Not that they had probably noticed though, he suspected. They were more than likely happily playing the slot machines and had momentarily forgotten about the men. And he was right.

When Iris and Wilma entered the casino, they walked around first, to see which of the quarter slots sent vibes their way. Wilma claimed she could get a feel for a winning machine, by just touching it briefly. If it seemed indifferent, she moved on. Finally, she touched one that felt friendly to her, she told Iris.

Wilma sat on the stool in front of her special one armed bandit, and asked Iris to go get her some quarters, holding a twenty dollar bill out to her. "I know I can just feed the money directly into the machine these days, my dear, but if you don't mind getting the quarters and a bucket for me, I still prefer playing the old fashioned way." She didn't want to leave the stool long enough to go get them herself, for fear someone would come along in her absence and steal the machine away from her.

Iris was amused at Wilma's system and didn't mind getting her quarters for her at all. In a few minutes she was back and Wilma was contentedly putting in a quarter at a time and pulling the handle.

Watching her briefly, but knowing that some people didn't like someone looking over their shoulder while gambling, Iris discreetly moved away to find a machine for herself. Wilma was so intent on the few quarters that she had just won that had fallen loudly into her tray, she didn't even notice when Iris left.

Iris didn't have a feel for any particular slot machine, but there was a certain type she liked to play, so she soon found one and, unlike Wilma, stuck a twenty dollar bill directly into the machine, and after seeing her eighty credits registered, began to press the spin button.

The quarters and the handle always left her hands filthy, so she preferred the more modern method of play. She also played the maximum on this machine with each spin, which was three quarters at a time. Chances were she wouldn't get to play as long, but if she did get lucky enough to win, she would at least win more money playing three, than one at a time. It was probably just a trade off, but then everybody had their own method.

Iris felt rather than saw, somebody at her shoulder and assuming William had found her, turned toward him with a welcoming smile. But, she was rather startled when she saw Matt standing close to her stool, instead of William. He returned her smile however, and not believing his luck, finding her alone, sat down uninvited, at the empty stool next to her.

At that moment, a server came around and asked them if they would like a drink. Iris had drank a glass of wine at dinner and a half glass of champagne in the honeymooner's suite, but at just past midnight, was no longer feeling the effects of either, so she decided to order herself a margarita on the rocks, no salt of course. Matt ordered himself a beer, much to Iris' dismay. She really didn't want him to still be around when William came in, but now she knew he would stay where he was, until the beer arrived.

Pressing the bet button again, she tried to ignore him. As of yet, neither of them had spoken to each other and Iris hoped he would get the drift that she wasn't interested in conversation. The machine hit for twenty quarters with that play, and Matt held his hand up to give her a high five. Iris didn't play along though, and sat quietly waiting for the machine to finish posting her credits.

"That's no way to treat a guy who sent you a hundred dollar bouquet, lady. The very least you could have done is say thank you." Iris could smell beer on his breath when he leaned close to her. Figuring at this hour, he might be drunk, and not wanting to cause a scene, she decided to be polite, but firm.

"You're right. Thank you," she replied, without looking at him. She continued to play the machine as if he wasn't there. The server came back with the drinks and Matt threw a twenty on her tray, and winking at the waitress, told her to keep the change. He had paid for both drinks before Iris had been able to open her handbag to get her money out. But now, she handed him a ten, even though she knew that was too much, but it was half of what he had given the girl. When he refused to take it, she reached to stick it in his shirt pocket.

Matt grabbed her wrist, hard, and leaned so close to her, their noses almost touched. "Don't insult me," he literally hissed at her, still holding her wrist in a viselike grip. "I may not be as stinkin' rich as the old man you've managed to latch on to, but I'm not penniless either."

Reaching past her, he picked up her drink. Iris jerked her hand free, after leaving the money in his pocket, but he seemed to have already forgotten about it. She wondered briefly if he might actually be on something other than alcohol, he was acting so strange. Matt was suddenly preoccupied with stirring her drink and for a moment, she was afraid he was going to drink it himself.

But instead, he just smiled sort of sheepishly and handed the glass to her saying, "I'm sorry, Iris. I shouldn't have said that. After all, what business is it of mine?" She was a little surprised as drunk or stoned or whatever he obviously was, given his behavior, that he even remembered her name.

She had only danced a part of a dance with him the first night onboard the ship, and it had been the next day, Sunday, that he had sent her the flowers. Other than the argument between her and William about the bouquet, she had not thought of him since.

"You're right again." She looked at him this time when she said it. "It is none of your business, and even if it was, what makes you think he's rich? And by the way, he's not old and I didn't latch on to him, as you so rudely referred to our relationship."

Her eyes flashed into his and her chin tilted upwards in her anger. She took a big gulp of the margarita and waited for him to say something. After all, he wasn't much more than a boy as far as she was concerned, and she wasn't going to take any shit off of him, no matter how much the flowers had cost.

Turning his beer bottle up, Matt took a long pull from it, before answering. Giving her a contemplative look, he tilted his head to one side. He was deciding on how much to tell her, knowing that very soon now, she probably wouldn't remember what she heard anyway. Iris took another gulp of her drink, wondering why Matt was looking at her funny. The margarita was strong and she was already feeling a buzz.

"Because I know who he is," Matt said slowly. Iris wondered why his words sounded long and drawn out like that. Maybe he was more wasted than she had at first thought.

"His name is William Pendleton and he owns Pendleton Manufacturing in Franklin, Tennessee. Like you didn't know," he accused. He took another long drag off of his beer and even though Iris didn't normally like her drinks this strong, she took a sip anyway. She was extremely surprised to hear that Matt knew William, because she felt pretty certain that William did not know him.

"He's a sixty year old widower, with an extremely profitable business, a mansion, and no heirs. You probably knew all that though, didn't you

Iris?" he practically spat at her. "You wasted no time sinking your claws into him, the very first day of the cruise. It wouldn't surprise me if you came on this trip for that very purpose. Why else would a looker like you go on a trip alone?"

Iris tried to stand up, forgetting about the slot machine and the money she still had in it. She was going to find William and have him squash this guy like a bug. "I'm no treasure seeking whore, Max...Mac, whatever the flying fuck your name is," she stammered. What was wrong with her? Why couldn't she think of his name and where had she been going when she stood up to leave? Matt shot her an evil grin and took her by the arm to steady her.

"Let go of me," she said, but it didn't sound convincing, even to her own ears. "I'm going home." But, when she took a step, she unwillingly found herself leaning against him for support. Matt gently but quickly, guided her out of the casino. They had been sitting close to one of the doorways and he shuffled her, using a firm grip on her arm, to a nearby elevator.

Just as they stepped inside, Iris thought she saw William enter the casino from the opposite hallway. She saw him stop and look around briefly, and then acting as if he recognized someone, he walked quickly across the room. But who had he seen?

Opening her mouth to call out to him for help, she was horrified that no words would come. Her mind screamed for him as the elevator door closed and she felt helpless and alone. But, she knew unfortunately, that she wasn't really alone. Someone was holding her up against a corner of the elevator. But who? And where in the hell was David? The bastard must have deserted her again, just when she needed him most. That was the last she remembered, just before her legs gave way beneath her.

William spotted Wilma and though Iris didn't appear to be with her, he hurried in her direction. He wanted to assure her that Fred was fine and find out if she knew where Iris was. She was probably at a machine nearby since he didn't think she would stray out of Wilma's sight.

Just as he got within speaking distance of her though, there was suddenly a loud noise and a big light on top of Wilma's slot machine started flashing. She let out a yelp and then noticing William had come up beside her, jumped up and starting shouting, "I won, I won, William, I won!"

Several other people gathered around her then, grinning happily at the little old lady's exuberance, and offering her their congratulations. William hugged her affectionately and teased her about not telling Fred about her winnings if she split it with him.

A casino attendant came over and asked her name and congratulated her, as well. He mercifully turned the sound off and then verified the amount she had won, but only after the spectators had gone back to playing their machines with renewed hope, and Wilma and William were the only ones to hear him. He asked them both to come with him to the cashier after telling Wilma she had a little more than eleven hundred dollars coming to her.

The attendant was glad to see a younger man with her. Otherwise, he would have been concerned with the elderly woman having that much cash on her, especially this late at night. The various hallways, where all the cabins were located, could sometimes be all but deserted by now, and he voiced his concern while giving her the money. Wilma assured him that the big, strong, handsome young man with her, would escort her safely to her suite. "Won't you, dear?" she asked, looking up into William's pleasant face.

"Of course I will, but first I'd like to find Iris. We might as well all go together. Do you know where she went?" he asked Wilma, looking concerned for the first time. He thought she would have come running when Wilma's machine hit and started going off like that. The sound had been loud enough to wake the dead. Maybe she was playing a good paying slot machine herself, and just hadn't wanted to walk away from it just then.

"Well, I did see her when she first sat down and began to play." Wilma looked at William apologetically and continued. "But, I'll admit, I was so into my machine, I lost track of everything else around me for a while. But, I can show you where she was the last time I saw her," she offered eagerly.

William placed her arm securely through his and patted her hand. "Don't worry, Wilma. We'll find her. She may have gone to the restroom or the bar and has come back by now." He didn't want to cause her any worry or make her feel guilty because she had lost track of Iris. After all, he thought, Iris should have been the one keeping an eye on Wilma, not the other way around. This was just so uncharacteristic of her that he was puzzled.

When he said "bar", that triggered a memory, and Wilma stopped and shook her head at William. "No, I don't think she would have gone to the bar; perhaps the restroom, though." She felt a little uneasy telling William about the man she had seen talking to Iris. She wasn't one to tattle, but then he could be someone they both knew and he wouldn't mind after all, so thinking it might help locate her, she decided to tell him and take that chance.

"Why don't you think she would have gone to the bar, Wilma?" William had seen a light come on in her eyes, and she suddenly seemed nervous about something. "Did you remember something you haven't told me?" They had started walking again, but when they came to the machine that Wilma had last seen Iris at, and she wasn't anywhere around, Wilma stopped and pointed.

"Here. She was playing this machine, and a few minutes later I glanced over and a young man had sat at this one right next to her. As a matter of fact, I couldn't really see Iris very well, because he blocked my view, but I could tell she was still here." She tried to act as though it was unimportant, what she saw next, so she shrugged her shoulders and told him the rest.

"I don't think she went to the bar, because the gentleman sitting at this machine," she emphasized her words by laying her hand on the stool next to where Iris had been sitting, "appeared to be buying drinks for both himself and Iris, when I next looked over."

Instinct filled William with dread, but he didn't want to frighten Wilma. "What did the guy look like?" he asked her calmly. "Maybe it's someone I know, too. Iris probably wouldn't allow a stranger to buy her a drink."

William refused to dwell on the fact that five days ago, he and Iris had been strangers and look what had happened since. But, he also knew, without a doubt, that Iris wouldn't cheat on him. He wasn't worried about that, but now, he was very worried about her.

"Well, let's see," Wilma held one finger up to her cheek, as if that would improve her memory, and cast her eyes upward. "He was very young, and blonde and kinda tall. Oh yea," she added, "nicely dressed, too. You know, not all sloppy looking, like young men often dress these days. He looked very much the gentleman," she assured him. "Do you know the man I've described, dear?" she asked hopefully.

Before William could answer her, Wilma suddenly pointed to the slot machine Iris had sat at. "Look William! Iris forgot to cash out her winnings. She's got over a hundred credits. That's about twenty five dollars. I wonder why in the world she didn't take her money when she left? Do you think she became suddenly ill?" she asked, looking more than a little concerned herself.

"Yes, I think that's possible, Wilma. And I'm pretty sure I know the guy she was with, as well. Do you mind if I see you to your suite now?" he asked politely. "I'd like to first check her cabin, even though I feel certain she would have told you if she was leaving the casino." Just then, he spotted something that was barely visible, sticking out from between the two slot machines.

William bent down so he could better see what it was. Feeling sick, he pulled on the strap and Iris' little coconut purse came into view. Wilma's hand went to her mouth and she let out a small gasp, clutching William's arm tightly with her other hand.

Opening it and looking inside, he found a lipstick, her room key and a little money. Maybe ten or fifteen dollars he guessed, not taking time to count it. It was a very small bag, but held all her basic essentials. She would have never left it behind and could not have gone to her suite without the key, so that answered that question.

"Son-of-a-bitch!" William said emphatically, giving each word equal time. Wilma had put the money the cashier had paid her in her handbag, but still had some quarters left in a bucket she had placed on the stool where she had last seen Iris sitting. William snatched it up and held it under the slot, and pushed the payout button on Iris' machine, letting them fall noisily, making a few heads turn in their direction. It only took a few seconds and William could tell Wilma didn't want to just leave the credits on the machine for someone else to get. It just wasn't natural.

As soon as the last quarter hit, he grabbed the bucket and hurried Wilma from the casino, taking the same nearby elevator that Iris had been in just a few minutes earlier. Of course, William had no idea how long Iris had been missing, but he knew it had to be longer than the ten minutes or so he had spent with Wilma, because he had surveyed the room pretty thoroughly when he had first entered the room, and there had been no sign of her.

The elevator door had almost finished closing, when William noticed the ladies restroom sign just outside the casino. He stuck his substantial foot out, to keep the door from shutting and pushed it open again. Taking Wilma with him, he crossed the hall as quickly as he could, with her in tow.

"Let's just make sure she didn't get sick and go in there," he said, pointing to the bathroom door. "Do you mind taking a quick look around?" William reminded her what the shoes looked like that Iris had worn this evening, so Wilma could glance at feet beneath the stall doors, without disturbing anyone.

But, when Wilma willingly and hopefully entered the restroom, it was empty. There were only two stalls and both doors stood open, leaving Wilma both disappointed and more anxious than ever. If only she had noticed Iris leaving the casino, she could then at least have given William something to go on.

But, her machine had been paying out small amounts pretty consistently and she had gotten caught up in the excitement of it. Tonight was the first chance she had really had to gamble since Fred didn't care anything about it, and he usually wanted to retire to their suite right after dinner each evening, after perhaps a stroll on deck.

Tonight, they had stayed up later than usual, and since Iris had wanted to play the slots too, she had taken advantage of the opportunity. If only she had gone to their cabin with Fred, then Iris would not have become separated from William and this would not have happened.

She hurried back out to tell William the bathroom was empty. He saw the worry in her expression, and knowing at eighty six, she didn't need to become too upset, he tried to appear much calmer than he felt. He knew something was terribly wrong and only wanted to see Wilma safely to her suite as quickly as possible so he could search for Iris.

They returned to the elevator and thankfully nobody stopped it along the way to their level. Passing Iris' cabin, William couldn't resist knocking loudly on her door, just in case she had gotten the room steward to let her in. There was no answer or sound whatsoever. They reached Fred and Wilma's room a short time later and he waited as she took her key from her purse. Just as Fred had done, she handed it to him, knowing he would be quicker at getting the door unlocked than she would be. Normally, her hands didn't tremble, but she was visibly shaken at Iris' disappearance.

Figuring Fred was probably already asleep, they were as quiet as they could be. "Don't lie awake worrying about Iris, Wilma. I promise I'll find her and we'll both see you tomorrow." Kissing her soft, wrinkled cheek, he then gave her a big smile and a wink. "It's probably a good thing I got you away from the casino, anyway. Another half hour in there and you might have bankrupted the joint."

Wilma relaxed a little, knowing William didn't blame her in the least for what had happened. Even still, she blamed herself enough for both of them. At least he felt sure he knew the man Iris had been talking to, so that was something. She didn't want to hold William up any longer, but she couldn't resist paying him a well deserved compliment.

"I wasn't lucky enough to have a son, William, although my daughters are wonderful. But, if I had, I would want him to be as kind and thoughtful and decent as you." Her eyes welled up with tears and she hurried inside before he could see them.

As soon as she was safely inside, William sped down the hall to his own cabin, quickly going inside and straight to the inhouse telephone. He called the four digit code that would page his cabin steward. He and Iris were right next door to one another and therefore this young man serviced both suites, along with a few others across from and to either side of theirs.

William was hoping that perhaps he had seen Iris or could at least help him find information on this Matt guy. He was going to need help from someone to find Iris. He was certain of that. And the cabin steward seemed liked the most likely person to start with. He paced the floor nervously, awaiting his return call, looking at his watch every five seconds or so.

It was ten minutes before one in the morning and he felt sure that Iris had been taken somewhere at least twenty minutes ago, and against her will. He had arrived at the casino at twelve thirty, but after finding her purse about ten minutes later, it had seemed like forever from then, until now. He quickly searched the purse he had thrown onto his bed upon entering the room, one more time. But seeing Iris' room key again, did nothing to reassure him.

The telephone beside his bed rang and he jumped and grabbed at the receiver. Looking once again at his watch as he answered, he saw that it had only been two minutes since he had sent the page. It was indeed the cabin steward and he sleepily agreed to meet William in his suite right away.

He could tell something was amiss, but could only assume it was in relation to the cabin itself. He was on call twenty four hours a day, but most of the time, he was undisturbed between midnight and about seven in the morning. Even the guests had to sleep sometime, but he knew there were those who partied into the wee hours and slept until noon or after. He had actually been asleep about two hours before getting this particular page. He hoped it would be a quick fix, whatever it was, and he would be able to quickly return to his bed.

William was standing in his open doorway watching the cabin steward come down the hall towards him. He had spoken to him a few times, in both his suite and Iris'. His name was Phillippe and he was originally from Guatemala. Iris, being the exuberant, outgoing and kind person she was, had politely asked him one morning about himself and his family.

He had been a fisherman on his father's boat, ever since he was a small boy. He was the only son out of seven children and he and his father, along with his cousin, went out every day the weather allowed. They fished from the first light of day until early afternoon, when villagers and restaurant cooks, would meet the various boats at the dock, to buy the day's catch.

They would always keep something nice tucked away for their own family and for his cousin to take home to his mother for supper. Working long, hard hours, they made a decent living. Phillippe's mother and six sisters cleaned and cooked, tended a small garden and kept a few laying hens for eggs.

So, after the day's catch was sold, and the boat and gear cleaned in preparation for the next day, he and his father could relax on their little front porch, while the girls prepared their supper. Life was pretty good until one day a storm came up very suddenly and they couldn't get back in. The boat capsized and Phillippe and his cousin, being young and strong swimmers, survived, but his father drowned and the fishing boat sank.

Phillippe became responsible for his mother and younger sisters and without a boat and with no money to buy one, he got a job on a cruise ship and left home for the first time. Now, more than ten years later, he had worked himself up to his current position on a new ship, and continued to care for his mother and youngest sister, who had not yet married.

He was usually gone for nine months to a year at a time, then would have a couple of months off to spend with his family back in Guatemala. Because he was gone so much, he had never married, but had managed to save quite a bit of money and planned to go home for good within a year or two and settle down.

He wanted to build a nice house, get married and have children and move his mother in with him. Still a young man, in his late twenties, he seemed to have a good head on his shoulders. That was one reason William had paged him.

Knowing Phillippe liked Iris and also knowing he knew the ship's ins and outs like the back of his hand, he would know who to contact and how to go about finding out where Matt's cabin was. Hopefully, he could help get William access to it, with perhaps assistance from the cabin steward responsible for that room.

As he approached, Phillippe could tell by the look on the big man's face, that this was no casual summons. He was at least twice the size he was, and with the very grave, stern expression he wore, was rather intimidating. Immediately he wondered where the pretty, blonde lady was, whose suite was next door. He had very seldom seen one without the other, and other than the first night of this week's cruise, he knew the big man had not stayed in his own suite overnight. And yet, it was almost one in the morning and here he was, taking up the entire doorway of his own cabin. He quickened his pace.

Stepping aside, William motioned for him to come in. He very quickly explained the situation to Phillippe, showing him Iris' purse with her room key inside. "I think she was possibly drugged Phillippe. There's no way she would have willingly left the casino without telling her friend or taking her purse, if she was in her right mind and in complete control of her actions." If possible, William's expression became even darker. "What's even scarier than anything else, is the fact that she's probably been with this guy for at least half an hour now."

"You say this guy's name is Matt? What is the last name?" he questioned William, heading toward the telephone. He knew the ship's operator would give him the cabin number of this passenger under the circumstances, and he had a pass key that would allow him access to any cabin.

"That's the problem. I don't know it," he admitted with obvious frustration. "But I do know the name of the young woman he's been hanging out with this week. She's actually an employee of mine and this whole situation has got to be more than mere coincidence. I think they're up to something together."

After racking his brain while waiting for Phillippe, he had finally remembered Allison's last name, knowing it was critical information that would be necessary to find Iris as soon as possible. "Her name is Allison Daniels. Can you get me her cabin number? I'll make her tell me who her boyfriend is, to save her own skin."

Surely, he thought, Allison wasn't a party to what Matt had done tonight. Why would she be, William asked himself? If they were sharing a cabin, why would she allow him to bring another woman to their room? No, that didn't make sense. They must be in separate rooms, but he figured she would know which one was Matt's. For Iris' sake, she had better know.

Phillippe spoke briefly into the phone and gave William the cabin number of Allison Daniels. Sure enough, she was listed in a room all by herself. There was no record of a second guest staying in her cabin. William wasted no time in calling her room. It would be much faster than going there. Her cabin was two levels beneath his and on the opposite end of the ship, according to what Phillippe told him. He said he knew the layout of the *Whimsical* so well, he could find her cabin blindfolded if necessary.

The phone rang three times, much to William's annoyance, before Allison picked up. Thank God, he thought, at least she was in her room. If he had not been able to reach her by phone, he would have had to go physically search for her in the bars and clubs, and that would have wasted valuable time, even if he was able to eventually locate her.

"Hullo," her grouchy and sleepy voice answered. Her greeting did at least give William a surge of hope and great relief. "Who is this? Matt, if it's you, I'm going to kill you," she threatened. Allison suddenly came fully awake as she heard William's voice when he answered her.

"No, Allison, it's not your friend Matt. It's William Pendleton and I need you to wake up and listen to me." He had said the name "Matt" like he would have said bastard, and it had not gone unnoticed on Allison's end. He must have seen her with Matt somewhere on the ship, even though she thought she had been careful.

Since Matt had been interested in pursuing William's lady friend, Allison had not wanted him to connect the two of them. She didn't understand Matt's attraction to the older woman, but since she wanted William for herself, she had encouraged him to chase after her. She smiled now, thinking this might be her chance to seduce William. Perhaps Matt had finally gotten lucky with Iris tonight.

"Don't be silly, darling," she purred in her sexiest voice. "I have no romantic interest in Matt, or anyone except you, for that matter. Why don't you come on over, since you obviously took the time to find me, and I'll prove it to you." She sat up on the side of the bed and looked at her reflection in the mirror. Maybe, she was thinking, I'll have enough time to brush my teeth and fix my hair before he gets here.

"Shut up, Allison, and listen very carefully. I have reason to believe your boyfriend drugged Iris, and then took her from the casino, against her will, about half an hour ago. Now, tell me what his cabin number is and don't try to pretend you don't know it. This is serious, and unless you want to be considered an accomplice, you better give him up now." Allison couldn't believe what she was hearing, but could tell by the fury in his voice, that William wasn't joking.

"You've got it all wrong, Mr. Pendleton," Allison said, rushing to defend herself, and also to save her job. She could almost see her ten year career go down the toilet. "Matt's not my boyfriend, he's my brother, and I promise you, he wouldn't do anything as stupid as you just described."

"His room is directly across the hall from mine, E162. I'll get dressed and go over there right now, but I'm sure you must be mistaken. Women are drawn to Matt like bees to honey. He would never have to drug a woman just to sleep with her." She didn't want to piss William off further, but felt compelled to defend Matt. Besides, she didn't want to think of her brother as a rapist.

"Get dressed, but stay where you are," William instructed her. "I don't want you warning him or spooking him into doing something even worse than he already has. I'll be there in two minutes." Having said that, he slammed the receiver down and both he and Phillippe flew as fast as their legs could carry them to the opposite end of the hall.

Phillippe said the stairs down to the Empress level would be quicker than taking the elevator and they would arrive just a short distance away from cabin E162. Even though William's legs were much longer, Phillippe was younger and more agile, and he had no difficulty keeping up with William's frantic pace.

Both men were silently praying as they rushed down the steps, taking two at a time, that they would find Iris unharmed. They both also knew, even without the words being said, that William would either kill him or make him wish he was dead, if Matt had forced himself on Iris, or worse.

Chapter 11

When Iris collapsed in the elevator, it made Matt concerned that someone would see her like that and alert a crew member, but riding the elevator down to his level, they encountered no other guests. It was after all, half past midnight and Matt couldn't have been more pleased at the timing of his unexpected opportunity.

Not letting her hit the floor when her legs gave way, he held her up with both arms wrapped around her in an embrace-like position, with her head resting on his shoulder. Matt wasn't quite as tall or as solidly built as William, but at forty, was still in good shape. If someone did see them exiting the elevator, he would just laugh and tell them his girlfriend had had one too many to drink and he was putting her to bed.

He smiled at his own joke as the elevator stopped at the Empress level, where both he and Allison had rooms. He planned on getting Iris in bed alright, eventually anyway, but he would rather she wake up just a little so that she could enjoy it too. In the past few nights on the ship, he had been with two different young women, barely more than girls actually, but they had eagerly pursued him, not the other way around.

The doors opened and Matt looked around unconcerned. Not a soul in sight and Iris wasn't making a sound, but for her light breathing. Walking backwards, he was literally dragging her to his room, which was only one cabin over from the elevator. He had turned her around so that his arms were around her torso, just beneath her breasts and the heels of her feet dragged quietly across the carpeted hallway. Her slides had come off and he held them by their leather straps, between his fingers.

He fished his key out of his pants pocket, where he conveniently kept it and quickly unlocked the door to his room, dragging Iris in with him as he entered. He locked the door behind them, dropped her shoes on the floor, and carefully picked her up in his arms and placed her sideways across the bed.

The rooms on this level were not suites and were quite small. His was just large enough for the bed, a small dresser with three drawers, one metal straight chair and tiny table and a closet, if you could call it that, directly across from the bathroom. The bathroom was about the size the closet should have been and the closet was not much more than a cupboard.

Although, Matt had paid a hundred bucks extra to get an outside cabin, that at least had a decent sized window to see out of. Whereas his sister's room across the hall, was an inside cabin with only a fake window with curtains over it for effect. He was way too claustrophobic for that, though. He had to be able to see out or the close quarters would have been unbearable for an entire week. The curtains in his room were open and an almost full moon reflected off the water and made the room bright enough to see, even with the lights off.

Matt went in the bathroom and brushed his teeth and washed his face and hands. He had been drinking beer pretty much all day and his mouth tasted funky, even to him. He didn't want to make a bad impression on his date.

Even though his bundle hadn't been very heavy at all, he was still hot and sweaty from his exertion. It was just a warm, tropical evening and besides, he always got hot in the elevators. Probably just another claustrophobic thing, although he really didn't think they piped nearly enough air conditioning into them.

Laying his slacks across the single chair, after slipping off his loafers, he looked down at Iris lying peacefully across his bed. Slowly, he unbuttoned his shirt and threw both it and his socks into a pile on the floor. Wearing only his boxers now, he returned to the bathroom, which was literally two steps away, and ran a clean wash cloth under cold water. He took what his grandmother used to call, a whore's bath, at the sink and afterwards, felt like a new man.

Stepping once again into the bedroom, he stood looking at the way Iris' blonde hair was spread out on the snow white comforter. His sister seemed to think Iris was older than him, and a whole lot older than the barely legal girls he usually dated. But the very first night of the cruise, when he had danced with her, he guessed her to be about his own age. Seeing her asleep on his bed, he still thought Allison was wrong. To him, she could easily pass for forty, but even if she was a little older, so what? It's not like he wanted to marry her.

As a matter of fact, he had never been involved with one woman long enough to even consider marriage. He was a confirmed playboy, and as soon as a woman started talking about the future, she was history. A little slap and tickle, a dinner and a movie, or dinner and dancing, was as close to commitment as he was interested in getting.

Iris stirred slightly and turned her face a little more in his direction. She really is very pretty, he thought, no matter how long in the tooth she might be. After all, he reminded himself, his sister was just about to turn thirty and she was panting after a freakin' sixty year old man. How sick was that?

Matt had jokingly told Allison that he doubted if William could still even get it up. But, if this spicy little mama was spending all her time with him, then evidently he could still cut the mustard, or could at least still lick the jar. He grinned, enjoying his own brand of humor.

Stepping out of his boxers, Matt freed his erection and got down on his knees beside the bed. He leaned across Iris and not being able to resist, ran a hand through her golden hair. He moved closer still, so that he could bury his nose in the long strands that felt like silk in his hand.

Breathing her scent in deeply, he thought she smelled sweet and clean, with just a touch of something else. He breathed her scent in again, and thought he recognized a type of perfume he had smelled before. Matt hated the smell of cheap perfume, but loved to smell the really good stuff, and this was definitely the good stuff. Chanel perhaps.

When he drew his hand away, a few hairs got caught in his watch band, and when he tugged them free, Iris' eyebrows shot up and she frowned slightly. Matt looked at the time before taking his watch off and laying it on the tiny, round table that barely fit between the bed and the dresser. It was fifteen minutes before one.

No hurry, he thought. Nobody knows where she is. How could they? Earlier, in the casino, he had carefully looked around the room, and hadn't recognized a single face and he knew for sure that William hadn't been there. Perhaps Iris had grown tired of him already.

That would certainly make Allison happy. She was determined to get William in the sack, and was confident that if he had her once, he would throw rocks at every other woman after that. She was thirty years younger than him, half his age, and could give him the children that his goody-two-shoes wife had never been able to. Once she produced an heir, she would live on easy street for the rest of her life.

When Allison had first told Matt about the cruise, and her plan to use this perfect opportunity to seduce William Pendleton, he had complimented her on using her head for once. Well, giving head would probably describe what she would be doing more accurately, he crudely told her.

But she didn't care how she had to do it, nor did he. There was just the two of them and had been for a long time. Their dad had been a drunk and ran off with some bimbo when Matt was fifteen and Allison only five. Their mother worked two jobs and Matt practically raised Allison on his own. He was very proud of her.

She was beautiful, smart, and determined to marry money. She had never allowed herself to get caught up in the sappy romances that other young girls did, or get herself used and abandoned with a kid to raise on her own. Matt had taught her well. Somebody had to. Both of their parents had set lousy examples.

Their mother had never remarried and died in her early fifties. Allison suspected, she had confided in him, that she had waited as long as she could for her husband to come back, and when he didn't, she had simply given up and died of a broken heart. Allison was bound and determined that would never happen to her. Surely, no man was worth that.

Iris mumbled something and turned onto her side. Matt ran a hand over the curve of her slim hip and down her thigh. He wanted her to at least be able to feel him, even if she didn't wake up enough to know it was him. He didn't want it to be like screwing a corpse. Even though he had never done that, it didn't hold a lot of appeal, even to someone like himself, who enjoyed kinky sex.

Part of him wanted Iris to realize who he was and what he was doing to her. If she would just give in to him, he knew he could please her and then maybe she wouldn't try to cause him trouble by claiming rape. He had only used the date rape drug on one other woman, and he had known her intimately already. She had finally agreed to let him use it on her, because he thought it would be thrilling to have that kind of power over a woman. She was one of the stupid ones who had actually thought that if she only let him have his way about everything, he might actually marry her.

Just like now, after he got the girl in a hotel room, he had played with her until she became conscious enough to participate somewhat. However, the following morning she had told Matt that it was like a dream or a memory of something that happened a long time ago. But, she had seemed no worse for wear, so Matt brought some with him on the cruise, just for kicks. Just knowing he could use it if he wanted to, made him feel powerful.

Of course the twenty year old and then the twenty two year old he had fucked on the second and third nights of the cruise, had practically raped him, so he'd had no use for it. He was single, very good looking and women chased him even more often than he chased them.

That's what had made Iris a challenge and a turn on. He had never really been blown off before or even rejected sexually. He just wanted to give her a sample of what she could have more of if she wanted it and let her know what she had been missing out on all week.

He knew she would enjoy it and probably ask him to do her again, if she could only realize it was him. He was pretty sure when they danced closely that first evening onboard the ship, that Iris had been attracted to him. But William had come between them that time. But not now.

Matt had almost finished unbuttoning her tunic, thinking how cute the outfit was with the wooden animal buttons and all. As he undid the last one, Iris rolled over on her back again, making things even easier for him.

He peeled the long top wide open, revealing a white lace bra and more bosom than he had expected to find on such a small woman.

To make things even better, the bra had a front hook, which he unfastened with one, quick movement. He was in his element now and had undressed more women than most men had ever even dreamed of. Not bothering to remove the delicate bra, he opened it and gently freed each plump breast from it's lacy cup. The air conditioning made Iris' nipples tighten up and stiffen, but Matt assumed it was in response to his touch.

"See there, Iris," he whispered softly. "Your body wants me, even if your mind doesn't know it yet." He tugged slowly on her pajama style bottoms and having an elastic waistband that was a little loose on her, Matt got them down and off without disturbing her in the least. For the moment, he had left her matching white lace panties on. He liked the way they looked against her tanned skin.

Kneeling on the bed beside her, he held his erection in one hand, while he ran a finger of the other hand across the silky lace of her panties, allowing it to slide between her parted thighs. Briefly, he touched the warm, soft folds of flesh that were barely covered by the strip of cloth between her legs.

He didn't dare to slip his finger beneath the fabric, into her wetness just yet, because he didn't trust himself to not lose control and ejaculate before he got what he was truly after.

So instead, he cupped a breast in his hand and enjoying the contrast between the round softness in his one hand and the long hardness in his other, he closed his eyes so he could indulge himself in this pleasurable sense of touch. From experience, he knew that sometimes how someone felt could be more pleasing than how they looked, although with Iris, he was extremely pleased with both.

Just as he closed his eyes, Iris opened hers. She thought she heard someone whisper to her earlier, but had been unable to respond. And then, she felt someone touch her, down there, but who was it and why were they doing that while she was sleeping? The voice and the touch was all wrong, she felt certain, but again she couldn't bring herself to respond. Was she dreaming?

Then a hand held her breast and she knew it was real. Her memory flooded her mind with flashes that frightened her; the casino, an elevator, then a man, and then darkness. She struggled to make sense of it. Her instincts told her she was in great danger and she had to wake up. But, who would want to hurt her and why?

William's face came to mind and she wondered where he was and why he wasn't with her. Somehow she knew she desperately needed him. Then she remembered going to the casino with Wilma. Was Wilma in danger too? That thought made her sick with worry.

The more Iris forced herself to remember, the wider awake she became, but as of yet, her body had not received the message. At first she wanted to scream, but a sixth sense told her not to. Besides, when she tried to move her lips, nothing happened. It was like a horror movie she had watched once with her kids, where this guy was on an autopsy table and was about to get cut into, except he wasn't really dead.

The terror of that memory is what made her eyes fly open at last. But now, she was really confused. Still, she had not made a sound and now she was glad, because she recognized Matt and remembered he was the one who had practically dragged her into the elevator. But where were they now and why was he sitting beside her with his eyes closed?

At first, she thought he looked like he was meditating or something, but as her eyes became fully focused, Iris realized with horror that he was naked and holding his penis in his hand. With equal dismay, Iris slowly became aware of his other hand on her breast. Her eyes darted around the room, looking for anything familiar, but saw nothing she recognized.

It was dark, except for what appeared to be moonlight shining on the bed. So there must be a window, but she couldn't yet turn her head enough to see everything. They were definitely on a bed in a small, dark room. Matt's room evidently, because it most definitely wasn't hers. And thankfully, nobody else seemed to be there with them. At least he didn't have an accomplice and it wouldn't be two against one.

Iris saw Matt's eyelids twitch and she quickly closed her own eyes again, before he could realize she was awake. She had only had them open for several seconds, while he was having his moment of reflection, or whatever the hell he had been having, she thought with disgust.

She could feel her body begin to tingle, like a foot that had gone to sleep and now was beginning to wake up. It felt as if her blood was flowing again, after having her circulation cut off. She was beginning to figure out that Matt must have put something in her drink. She remembered him reaching for it and stirring it thoroughly, before handing it to her. Why would he go to this much trouble to be with her, she wondered? He was young and handsome and half the women on the ship would probably be flattered at his attention.

But, maybe that was too easy, she thought worriedly. Maybe rape was the only way he felt like a man. But as she felt her strength returning, she was determined not to become his victim. He placed his hand on her other breast and kneaded and squeezed like he was trying to make biscuits. She could feel it now, where before, she had only been aware of him touching her, but not really knowing to what extent.

Even though it made her sick to know what he was doing, she was glad the feeling in her body had returned. She knew she could move now if she tried, but was waiting for a better opportunity to catch him off guard. At the moment, he was positioned over her and she was flat on her back. It would be too easy for him to pin her down.

Matt's hand trailed down her belly and it was all she could do, not to slap it away. He was breathing heavier now and Iris felt the bed move as he stood up. At least he's not touching me at the moment, she thought with relief. But what was he doing? Not daring to open her eyes, she was relying on her ears to keep her informed. A drawer was being opened and she realized he was probably getting a condom out of it. Well, if this was his version of safe sex, she wasn't interested.

Iris had noticed the tiny metal table right next to the bed and the small dresser just on the other side of the table. Her heart was pounding as she realized this might be her only chance to fight him off, and God willing, escape from this crazy son of a bitch. She didn't care if she had to run screaming down the hall, naked. Anything would be preferable to what he was planning to do to her next.

With speed and strength born of fear and determination, Iris bolted upright and grabbed the table firmly in both her hands. Matt turned towards her, eyes wide with shock. He was definitely in an awkward position. He had been concentrating on opening the condom and had placed the package between his teeth to rip it open, holding the wrapper in the fingers of one hand and holding his own throbbing package with his other.

Adrenaline coursed through her body as Iris' head began to spin with her sudden movement. Don't faint now, she warned herself, or it's all over. With every ounce of strength she could gather, Iris brought the table down hard across Matt's face. It was metal, but not heavy and she had been worried upon lifting it, that hitting him on top of his head wouldn't do enough damage.

Matt dropped both the condom and his cock and grabbed his nose with both hands, as blood spurted from it like a fountain of wine. "Bingo!" Iris shouted and brought her knee up sharp and fast into Matt's quickly softening crotch. She wanted to puke at the way his equipment felt on her knee and also from the sound he made.

Dropping to one knee and letting go of his nose in order to cover his balls, Matt made a noise like Iris had never heard before and hoped she would never have to hear again. She moved away from him as he tried to grab her ankle and pull her down. Quickly positioning herself behind him and grunting loudly with her effort she brought the table down again, this time on the back of his neck.

He fell forward, bracing his head against the side of the bed. Now he held his squashed balls with one hand and placed the other on the back of his neck. Iris giggled hysterically and shouted at him to say his prayers while he was down there.

"You stupid whore!" Matt screamed at her. "I think you just broke my fuckin' neck!" He was struggling, trying to use the bed as leverage to get to his feet. Iris saw her bra and the clothes she'd had on, lying beside him on the floor and snatched them up in her left hand, but still holding firmly to the table with her right. She still held it as high as she could, in case she needed to whap him with it again.

"Who are you calling stupid?" she screamed back at him. "I'm holding a table over your head and you're holding your nuts! And, if you don't stay down, I'm going to really hurt you," she warned him, backing quickly toward the door. She didn't want to stay in that room long enough to get dressed, but now she could hear sounds coming from the hallway, and didn't want to open the door naked, either.

She could hear muffled shouting and running footsteps and seeing the familiar white bathrobe the cruise line provided, hanging on a hook, she slipped into it quickly and tied the sash around her waist tightly, never taking her eyes off Matt.

Evidently, all the racket had awakened the neighbors. Iris had no idea what time it was, but the curtains were open on the window above Matt's bed and except for the moonlight, it was still very dark outside.

Matt was still holding his neck and trying to pull his boxers on, one handed, while still kneeling beside the bed. He was busy too, working out a story in his head, to place the blame on Iris. After all, he was the injured one here. He would say she willingly came to his room for a good time, but once he became vulnerable, she attacked him and was going to rob him, before witnesses showed up. He would get Allison to vouch for him and tell her to say she had seen him and Iris laughing and drinking and entering his room kissing.

But, when Iris yanked the door open, Matt looked up, and seeing William standing in the hall along with Allison and a crew member, his heart sank. Evidently William had used Allison to find him and when Iris told them her side of the story, he knew they would believe her. He mostly knew he was fucked. Well, no actually, he hadn't been, and that only added insult to injury. Oh well, at least she couldn't claim he raped her. Good thing too, because he had glimpsed murder in William's expression.

Iris threw the table in Matt's direction, barely missing him and ran from the place that had become her hell. But, she ran straight into a wall, almost knocking the breath from her body. No, not a wall, a man. Massive, strong arms wrapped around her and for a split second, Iris thought she was being captured and taken back to the nightmare of Matt's room. Maybe he did have an accomplice after all.

She began to struggle, but then felt a huge hand stroking her hair and then heard the voice of the man she loved, as William attempted to calm and soothe her. "It's o.k., Iris. It's me, sweetheart. You're safe now. Everything's going to be fine. I love you, precious."

Iris pressed her face into his chest and clung to him, her delayed emotions overtaking her now that she was free. Her body began to shake uncontrollably and then the tears came.

A few people stuck their heads out of their cabins to see what all the ruckus was about, and Phillippe efficiently shooed them back inside, insisting that this was a private matter and being taken care of. "No worries, no worries," he assured them. "Go back to bed. All is well."

Allison stood frozen for just a minute and then crossed the threshold into Matt's room. Her brother was sitting on the side of the bed in only his underwear and he looked like hell. His nose was bleeding profusely and he was holding the back of his neck and his crotch. She also took in the overturned table, the condom lying unopened on the floor, and what she supposed were Iris' shoes. Simply glaring at him, she picked up the shoes and closed his door. At least with it locked, William couldn't easily get to him.

Allison's own door was open across the hall, where she had been standing in the doorway, waiting for William. He and the crew member had come from the direction of the stairs. She had been watching for the elevator to open and had been looking in that direction when she heard shouts and crashes coming from Matt's room. At that same moment, she had heard footsteps running and then William had appeared suddenly. Before they even said a word to each other, Iris had bolted out of Matt's room and straight into William's arms.

Phillippe asked Allison then, if they could go inside her room for a moment and clear the hallway. "Of course, of course. I'm sorry. I guess I just don't understand what's happening." She motioned for William to bring Iris into her room. He looked at her briefly, standing barefooted in her pajamas and robe, holding Iris' shoes. She looked a little like she was in shock herself, he thought.

He would rather have taken Iris directly to her suite, instead of to this crowded, little cabin with barely enough room for the four of them. But, she was in no condition yet to go anywhere, so he accepted Allison's offer and picking Iris up effortlessly, he carried her in his arms to Allison's bed.

Allison smoothed the sheets and propped the two pillows up behind Iris' back and shoulders. She had refused to lie down completely, and had only agreed to get in the bed at all, if she could sit up.

William, sensing the reason for her reluctance, sat her up as straight as possible and covered her up to her neck with the comforter. Phillippe brought Iris a drink of water. There had been an unused plastic cup in the bathroom and finding some ice that had not yet melted in the bucket, he poured water from an unopened bottle of Evian the cruise ship provided daily to each cabin.

Iris drank the entire cupful, without stopping. Evidently the drug had dehydrated her. She had stopped crying and wanted to go to her own suite, but William asked her to tell what had happened, to the best of her memory. He wanted both Phillippe and Allison to witness her story. Besides, Matt was still only a few feet away and accessible to William if he decided to rip him apart. How he punished Matt would depend on the extent to which he had abused Iris. However, other than being an emotional wreck, and wearing the ship's bathrobe instead of her own clothes, he thought she seemed unharmed.

"Please, sweetheart, while we have witnesses, please tell us everything you remember. Did Matt force you to leave the casino? Wilma and I found your purse." Iris blinked at him in surprise. She had completely forgotten about her little coconut handbag and was glad they had found it.

"Wilma found a machine she liked and I moved away to give her some space. I saw the kind of quarter slot machine that I prefer to play and stuck a twenty in it." Here, she stopped and looked up at William, who sat beside her on the edge of the bed. "I had money in the machine I was playing. I must have left without cashing it out. Oh well, it wasn't much."

William smiled at her. He was relieved to hear that she remembered such a small detail as that. That was a good sign, in his opinion. She was obviously thinking quite clearly. "Our friend Wilma noticed the credits still on the machine you were playing. She had hit her machine for a nice sum of money, and after collecting it, she took me right to where she had last seen you. I cashed out your quarters into her bucket and found your purse stuck between two slot machines. That's when we knew for certain you had left in a hurry, and I immediately suspected, against your will."

Iris smiled back at him when he said Wilma won big. She was happy for her and wished she had been there to see it. "Good for her," she said to William and Phillippe smiled too. Iris was looking better and appeared to be recovering quickly from her ordeal. Allison remained sitting in the only chair in the room, with no expression. She desperately dreaded hearing what Matt had done and was mostly concerned about how all of this would ultimately affect her.

"As soon as I began to play," Iris continued at William's urging, "Matt sat down at the machine beside me and started talking. I all but ignored him, thinking he would go away, but he smelled like a brewery and was being belligerent and seemed to be enjoying himself." Holding the plastic cup up to Phillippe, he filled it again.

"Thank you, Phillippe," she said kindly. "Thank you for coming with William to rescue me." There were tears in her eyes again, but she wiped them off her cheeks as soon as they fell. Phillippe felt tears sting his own eyes, but didn't shed them. He didn't want to upset her further, so he just smiled back and nodded his head in acknowledgement of her thanks.

Iris went on, even though the rest of the story was going to be more difficult for her to tell. "A server came by and we both ordered a drink. Matt tried to pay for mine but I wouldn't let him. I stuck the money in his shirt pocket and I remember that made him angry." She looked at William apologetically for what she was about to say next. "He said even though he wasn't rich like you, he wasn't poor either, and accused me of chasing after you for your money." Nobody looked her way, but when Iris told William what Matt had said, Allison blushed beet red, because that was exactly what her plan had been.

Iris saw William's jaw twitch and his grey eyes grew a darker shade. "I assured him we had a real relationship, and it has nothing to do with money. I realize now, he was just baiting me, and there was no reason for me to defend myself against his ridiculous claim, but it just made me so mad."

She sipped her water and drew her brows together in a frown, remembering what had happened next, and wishing she had been more suspicious of Matt's actions, realized now what he had done and when he had done it. "He reached behind me to where the waitress had set my drink down, picked it up and stirred it for a while before handing it to me. I took a drink and looked over to check on Wilma, then played my machine for a minute, then took another drink. It seemed to only make me thirstier each time I drank from it, and suddenly it was as if I was hearing Matt speak from a long way off, and his words sounded slow and garbled."

William and Phillippe glanced knowingly at each other and then William once again gave Iris his full attention, but Phillippe was watching Allison. She had turned pale beneath her tan and yet her cheeks were flushed with either anger or embarrassment or both, he guessed. Remembering that William had told him earlier that Allison was an employee of his, he couldn't help but wonder for how long.

"The next thing I remember is trying to stand up. I was going to look for you," she explained, and it broke William's heart that he hadn't been there for her. "But suddenly, Matt was grinning like a possum eatin' briars, because I had to lean against him for support." William laughed softly at her description and felt Iris relax a little. At least she hadn't lost her sense of humor.

"Everything happened very quickly and unexpectedly then. Matt whisked me out of the casino into a nearby elevator and I remember him having to keep me propped up in the corner, to keep me from falling." Here she hesitated, trying to remember how she got to Matt's room, but she couldn't.

"What's wrong, Iris?" William asked gently. "I know this isn't easy for you, reliving what happened, but it's very important that the three of us know everything you can tell us, so that Matt can't talk Allison into trying to cover for him." Iris looked at Allison for the first time, and both women blushed deeply, and quickly averted their eyes away from each other.

Allison knew that William suspected her being party to this crazy stunt, but she was just as disgusted by it as they all were. "I hope you don't think I would participate in any way in any of this," she directed at William. "Matt's my brother, and I love him, but I refuse to be held accountable for something I had absolutely nothing to do with." Seeing the look on Iris' face, Allison realized that Iris had had no idea whatsoever that she and Matt were connected in any way. She greatly wished William hadn't figured it out as well, but then if he hadn't, she shuddered to think what might have happened to Iris. If they hadn't been standing just outside the door when Iris ran from his room, would Matt have caught her and punished her for what she had been able to do to him?

"Her brother?" Iris asked William, her golden eyes flashing. "And you knew and didn't tell me?" she accused him. "Is that why you got so mad when you found out the flowers were from Matt? Did you already suspect the two of them were up to something?" Iris wasn't really mad at William, but still, if she had known, she would have avoided Matt like the plague. Especially after witnessing how Allison had played up to William in Saint John. Surely though, Allison had not known about Matt's abduction of her. Even a sister wouldn't allow another woman to be treated as abusively as Matt had treated her.

"No, Iris, I didn't know then. I swear I only found out they are related, tonight. I figured out it was Matt, based on Wilma's description of the guy she saw talking to you. But, not knowing his last name or how to find him, I called Allison. I had seen the two of them arguing up on deck one morning when I went for a run, and thought she might be involved romantically with him. That's why I was confused when she came on to me and Matt pursued you. I didn't care how they knew each other, but only wanted to locate his cabin because I felt certain that's where I would find you."

William wished even more so than Iris did, that he had told her about seeing the two of them together that morning. He had only found it a little strange, but had definitely had no idea that it would be worth mentioning. And maybe it wouldn't have changed what had happened anyway. There was no way to know for sure. It just pained William to think that he might have lost Iris' trust in him.

Allison, seeing how much in love with Iris, William really was, knew now that she had never had a chance of coming between them. But still, she hated seeing the doubt in Iris' eyes as she questioned William, and didn't want him to lose her, because of Matt. Maybe, she thought, if she spoke on William's behalf, she could still hang on to her job at least, even if she had lost her dream.

She hung her head, not looking at anyone when she spoke. "It's true, Iris. Mr. Pendleton had no idea who Matt was. I didn't even know, until he called tonight looking for Matt, that he had ever even seen us together. I didn't want either of you to know that I knew him. I knew Matt was interested in you after the very first night onboard the ship, but I even tried to dissuade him from approaching you. I didn't want anyone to think I had put him up to it, because I figured it would hurt my chances for a relationship with Mr. Pendleton." Allison raised her head then and looked Iris squarely in the eyes, smiling a small, nervous smile.

"But, seeing the two of you together, I know now, I never had a chance with him anyway. It's quite obvious to me, the two of you are in love and meant for each other. I'm so sorry for my own behavior, but I promise both of you, I had nothing to do with what happened tonight." Tears spilled from her eyes. "I'm afraid to hear what else you have to say about what took place in Matt's room, and ashamed that it's my brother who's responsible. I hope he didn't hurt you, Iris, really I do."

Allison's chin was quivering and tears flowed unchecked, down her face. She was surprised at her own genuine regret over what Matt had done. She knew it must have been a terrible experience for Iris. She still couldn't understand why Matt had taken her against her will. He never had a problem seducing any woman he wanted. What was so special about Iris, that neither William nor Matt had been able to resist her?

All three, listening to Allison's apology, believed what she was saying and looked at her a little more kindly, even though none of them said anything to her. The two men were much more anxious to hear the rest of Iris' account of what happened, so they would know for certain that she hadn't been hurt and how best to deal with Matt. As of yet, neither of them knew about Matt's extensive injuries at the hands of Iris. Phillippe knew it would be his responsibility to handle it from a professional standpoint and William was anxious to handle things his own way. Little did he know, there wasn't much about Matt that hadn't already been handled. But, right now, Iris was their only priority.

Iris was relieved to know William had not purposefully kept secrets from her and was ready to get through the rest of her story, so she could return to her suite and get in her own bed. Suddenly, she was exhausted beyond imagination. The clock in Allison's room told her it was already one thirty five in the morning. She and Wilma had gone to the casino about midnight. She couldn't wait to put the last hour and a half behind her forever. William held both her hands in his and coaxed her to finish so they could go. He sensed the exhaustion that had overtaken her. "What do you remember after getting in the elevator sweetheart?"

"That's just it," Iris said frowning, trying to force herself to recall more than she was able to. "I don't remember anything else until I became aware of someone touching me." With closed eyes, she tightened her grip on William's hands. He dreaded what he would hear next. "I didn't know who it was and was completely unable to move or speak, but I could hear a man's voice and somehow I knew it was all very wrong and I was afraid." She still kept her eyes closed, but William could feel the tension build in her body and heard it in her voice. Once again, he and Phillippe exchanged a worried look. They had all three forgotten Allison's presence in the room.

"I tried to scream but couldn't make a sound. As it turns out I think that's what saved me, because Matt had no idea that I had regained consciousness even a little bit." She chewed her lower lip and tried to explain how she had felt, but it was humiliating. "Then, I felt him touch my naked chest, but at the time, I still didn't know who he was or where I was or why I was naked." This time she felt William's grip tighten and she didn't dare look into his eyes.

"Finally, I was able to open my eyes somewhat, and couldn't believe it was Matt who was kneeling beside me on the bed. I could feel the bed under me now, when just a moment before it had been as if I was suspended in mid air. I could tell I was on my back because I was looking directly up into his face and could see the ceiling over his head. But he had his eyes closed and didn't see mine open, thank goodness. I could feel his hand cupping my breast and then it hit me that he was nude and holding himself in his other hand." Allison made a small sound of disgust from the corner where she sat, but nobody paid her any attention.

William was growing more furious by the moment, and sickened, it was all he could do to listen to the rest. Phillippe, who had a strong sense of respect and admiration for women, could never have imagined a man doing the things Iris described. But he knew from his life in Guatemala, that these things often happened to women and sometimes much worse.

Some of the female crew members he knew had left their various countries to escape lives of abuse and degradation.

"I felt that Matt was about to open his eyes and I instinctively knew that the best thing I could do in my current position was to feign sleep, so I quickly shut my eyes again. The feeling was starting to return to my body rather quickly now, and I could tell when he began to fondle my other breast, because he was rough and it started to hurt. I heard him breathing harder and then mercifully he released me and got up off the bed." Iris had begun to talk faster and she became more agitated as the fear she had felt flooded her memory.

Opening her eyes, Iris pulled one hand free of William's grasp and took a drink from the glass of water. She clasped the comforter tightly in her fist and held it firmly against her chest, remembering her former nakedness and how helpless she had felt. Sinking back into the pillows, she closed her eyes again. It was just too embarrassing to look at anyone at this point of the story, especially William.

"I heard a drawer open and the crinkling sound of foil or cellophane or something and I was pretty sure Matt was getting a condom. I knew I had to act quickly, because in another minute, it would be too late. My only chance was to take him completely by surprise and I did." Iris made a choking sound, somewhere between a laugh and a sob, as she recalled what she had done. She still didn't know where her strength and her courage had come from.

She opened her eyes then and smiled at William, which surprised him, but pleased him too. Evidently she had gotten away before Matt had raped her because he could tell she found something amusing in what she was about to say. Relief washed over him, replacing the dread that he had been feeling. Relief felt a lot better.

Iris both laughed and cried as she described how she had smashed Matt's nose with the metal table. "Blood flew everywhere and there he stood with the condom wrapper in his mouth and his pecker in his hand." Both men and even Allison laughed along with her at her descriptive account. Iris wiped her tears from her cheeks and eyes, but they were tears of relief and humor, at least. She almost couldn't believe that she had actually escaped without a single injury, to herself anyway. Nothing hurt but her pride, and she knew she could live with that.

"He let go of everything and grabbed his nose, leaving his manhood unprotected." She glanced over at Allison and said, "I hope you're not planning on having any nieces or nephews any time soon, because I racked him pretty hard with my knee, and he hit the floor so hard, I'm surprised he didn't bust his knee caps." By then, all four of them were laughing hysterically, and reminding each other to keep the noise down. It was the middle of the night and most people were trying to sleep, after all.

"The rest, you pretty much either heard or figured out on your own," Iris said, shrugging her shoulders to emphasize she was almost done. When he went to the floor, I ran away from him. Oh yea, he tried to grab my ankle, but I hit him again with the table. That's when Matt started yelling and saying I probably broke his neck. And then I yelled back and grabbed my clothes off the floor and ran like hell for the door."

"On my way out, I saw this robe hanging on a hook next to the bathroom and not wanting to run into the hallway butt naked, I took a second to put it on." Iris looked seriously at William, and even though she had survived this entire thing remarkably well, he saw everything she had been through in her eyes. "When I ran into you, the reason I fought you, is because I had this crazy notion that you might be Matt's accomplice and I was terrified to go back in there. After what I had just done to Matt, I thought he might kill me given the opportunity."

William touched Iris' cheek with his hand. "Are you really all right, Iris?" he asked her, looking deep in her eyes for something she may have hidden there. The ordeal she had been through had been terrible, but at least the bastard had not been successful in raping her. William didn't think Iris would have recovered from that.

Even though he knew her to have a healthy sexual appetite and was fun in bed with him, he knew that before him, there had only been her husband of more than thirty years. Regardless of the fact that he and Iris had met less than a week ago and had been sexual partners since the second day, neither of them was promiscuous. They had simply fallen in love and had both, somehow, known it was real. There was no doubt in William's mind that Iris was a good, decent, kind, moral person, and he considered her every inch a lady.

Looking at her now, he was so very proud of her for keeping her head and rescuing herself. Mentally adding intelligent and brave to her list of attributes, he also thanked God for helping her when he had not been there to protect her. He didn't know if he and Phillippe would have reached her before Matt had really hurt her and it made him sick to his stomach, to think they may not have. They had been about to enter the room when they heard all the commotion and Iris barged through the door.

After he asked if she was really alright, Iris thought very seriously for a moment before answering. "Yes, William, I do believe I am. After what I did to Matt, he's the one who's going to require medical attention. I'm sure right now, knowing you're right across the hall, he's afraid to come out of his cabin, though. Let's go to our suite," she suggested. "I'm ready now. It helped me to vent, but I'm absolutely worn out."

William looked at his watch and was surprised to see it was two o'clock. He stood and gathered up Iris' clothes and shoes and asked her if she wanted to get dressed before going up to what they both thought of as their room.

"Yes, if Allison doesn't mind, I'll get dressed in her bathroom. I have no desire to keep this robe as a memento of my eventful evening." Allison blushed and ushered Iris into the tiny bathroom, again apologizing profusely for Matt and herself.

William and Phillippe walked out into the hallway, where they spoke in low tones so neither Allison nor Matt could hear them. "What do you want me to do, Mr. Pendleton?" Phillippe asked seriously. "I can call security and they can restrict this man to his cabin for the next two days until we reach Miami. There, he can be taken into custody by the local authorities and arrested if Ms. Corrigan wishes to press charges. But if I involve security and tell them what happened, the cruise line may press charges even if Ms. Corrigan does not. It's your call."

William placed a huge hand on Phillippe's slight shoulder and thanked him for coming to his assistance so quickly. "I apologize for keeping you up until two in the morning," he added, "but I appreciate your help and am glad you stayed to hear what happened from Iris herself. I'll speak to her in private, and see how she wants to proceed. It's not like Matt can get away." He didn't want to divulge any personal information about Iris to Phillippe, but so he would understand if she decided not to press charges he added, "She's been through a lot recently, before the cruise I mean, and I can't be certain how she'll feel about getting involved with his arrest and a possible trial."

Phillippe nodded his head in understanding. He knew sometimes women were so anxious to put this type of experience behind them that they did not do anything about it legally. But, he hated to see that scum get away with attacking a nice lady like Ms. Corrigan. Or any woman for that matter. "Whatever she decides to do, I'll honor," Phillippe assured William. "But one thing's for certain. I'll see to it somehow that this man's name and photo will be on the cruise line's alert list. He'll never be allowed on one of their ships again."

Iris came out, fully dressed, and amazingly enough she was smiling. She looked tired, but otherwise, no worse than anyone else did. She glanced, only once, at Matt's closed door, but made no comment. William and Iris both thanked Phillippe one more time, and Iris kissed him on the cheek. Phillippe told Iris how sorry he was and apologized on behalf of the cruise line, even though, they all knew that it was nobody's fault, except Matt's. The decision had not yet been made whether or not to report the incident to an officer of the ship.

Allison stood just inside her room, restlessly waiting for them to leave. Iris knew she was concerned about Matt, and even after what he had done, he was still her brother. She turned to her after Phillippe was gone, and with William's arm protectively around her, Iris considered how she would feel in Allison's predicament. She had to not only feel anger and concern towards her brother, but it only made sense to assume, she was afraid she would lose her job and livelihood, as well.

"Allison," she spoke softly and looked at her with compassion, which astonished both Allison and William. "For what it's worth, I have mixed emotions as to what to do about Matt's punishment. He shouldn't be allowed to get away with what he did to me without some penalty. However, after the injuries he incurred, I'm pretty sure he might think twice before drugging and abusing some other woman, and perhaps has already learned his lesson."

Tears streamed down Allison's face. She was afraid for Matt and herself, in shock over his treatment of Iris, and completely embarrassed in front of William. He was her employer for the moment anyway, and someone she had secretly been in love with for almost ten years. At least he seemed to be unaware of her true feelings for him, but she was convinced by the way Iris looked at her, that she understood everything. Women were perceptive that way.

"I know you're anxious to see about him and I understand all about loving a family member, even when they hurt and betray you." William thought Iris must be thinking of David when she said that. She had spent almost her entire lifetime with him and had given him three children, after all. Surely, she still felt some love for him, even now, he assumed. Iris, William believed, was truly as generous and compassionate a woman, as Rebecca had been. Perhaps even more so he reasoned, because to his knowledge, Rebecca had never been hurt or abused by anyone.

Iris wiped a tear from her own chin before it could drip off. "I just want you to know, I have no hard feelings toward you, and neither do I hold you responsible in any way for your brother's behavior. Thank you for allowing me to rest and recover in your room. It's very late and I know you're tired and worried and embarrassed. I see it all in your face, and then some," she knowingly added.

The two very different women exchanged a long look and Allison was relieved and grateful to hear what Iris had said. She knew it would carry a lot of weight with William. Iris knew it as well, and hoped he would allow Allison to keep her job. She was single and self supporting and ten years of employment and experience, was a lot to throw away in her opinion, for either William or Allison.

Allison thanked Iris and said she was sorry to both her and William. William simply nodded. Her fate, as far as he was concerned, would depend to some degree, upon what Iris decided to do about charging Matt. Besides, his thoughts and concerns were about Iris, not Allison. He and Iris walked the short distance to the elevator and the doors opened as soon as he pushed the button. At that time of the evening, or morning now, there were few people about and no wait.

They both heard Allison knock on the door to Matt's room, but neither of them turned around. As they stepped inside the empty elevator and the doors were closing, Matt's door opened and Allison disappeared inside.

Chapter 12

Iris had never been so glad to see her suite. Even though it was small, it was at least twice as big as the two rooms she had just come from. Opening the door to the balcony, she stepped outside, breathing deeply of the warm, sea air. William brought her a single shot of tequila, which she gratefully accepted. He poured himself a shot of Jack Daniels, and afterwards they both felt a little calmer. They stood side by side on the balcony, each lost in their own thoughts, but neither of them spoke.

After a moment, Iris went into the bathroom and William could hear the shower running. He turned down the bed and undressed and was lying there awake when she came out. He knew she had needed a few minutes alone and also understood her desire to shower.

She hadn't taken the time to shampoo her hair because it took so long to blow it dry, but Iris felt cleaner, as if she had been able to wash away Matt's touch. Getting into the bed naked, William pulled her into the comfort and safety of his arms. She lay her head on his broad shoulder and he stroked her hair.

"Thank you," Iris whispered. "I don't know how you found me exactly, but I'm so glad you did. I've just been wondering what I would have done if you hadn't been there when I ran from that room. I was half crazed with fear and disgust. I also had no idea where I was or how to get back here. I was obviously still under the influence of whatever he put in my drink, to a certain extent. Not to mention I had no key, even if I had been able to eventually find my cabin. You really are my white knight you know." She tilted her head up and kissed him on the chin. It was the only part of his face she could reach, and she was too content to move.

William didn't feel like he had done nearly enough. It had taken him too long, in his opinion, to get Wilma to her cabin, obtain Phillippe's help and reach Iris. And that's what he told her. "I'm sorry I didn't get there sooner, sweetheart. I had to see Wilma to her suite because she had all that cash on her, wait for Phillippe to answer my page and then it took a moment longer to locate Allison's room number. I'm just glad she was in her room and could tell us who and where Matt was. I was as surprised as you were to learn he's her brother. Boy, what a pair of siblings. Thank God you weren't seriously hurt Iris. I think I would have gone ballistic and killed him." He laughed softly and squeezed her even closer to him. "You know there's still time for me to do it, yet. Just say the word."

But Iris didn't hear that part. She had fallen asleep listening to the sound of his voice. Exhaustion, the drug, her ordeal, and the fact that it was two thirty on Thursday morning, had at last taken its toll.

William was glad she was able to sleep and so thankful to have her safely beside him. He lay awake for several more minutes. It seemed impossible their day had begun in Sint Maarten. So much had happened since Wednesday morning, when they had awoke in each other's arms. Now he wished they had never gotten out of bed.

But he had been truly happy to see Greg and the rest of the gang at Splash Jewelers. And at least, he did now have the perfect engagement ring tucked away in his safe in his own suite. As in all of life, he knew, you had to take the bad with the good. He fell asleep then, remembering the desire that had brought them back to the ship earlier than scheduled and the passionate afternoon he would always remember.

They would spend all of Thursday and Friday at sea, for which both Iris and William were grateful. It was noon when they awoke and without so much as a 'good morning' being said, they reached for one another, and made love slowly and more gently than they ever had. The events of the previous evening had brought them even closer together.

Only hunger made them stir from their love nest that afternoon. They ordered a late breakfast to be sent to their room, and quickly showered together before it arrived. William removed the DO NOT DISTURB sign from the outside handle of the door, so Phillippe would know they were up and about. They didn't want to worry him that something might be wrong.

It had been about sixteen hours since they had eaten dinner the night before and they ate everything that wasn't nailed to the breakfast tray. A short time later there was a soft knock at the door and William opened it to find a very worried looking Fred and Wilma.

Wilma had filled Fred in on what little she knew from the night before and Fred, just as William did, wished they hadn't left the women alone for quite so long. But he had already told Wilma about stopping at William's suite to see the ring and she was thrilled to learn that the proposal would take place on their wedding anniversary. Wilma promised to keep it a secret from Iris until then.

William invited them out to the verandah to sit with him and Iris. He left the empty food tray outside the suite, on the floor so they wouldn't be disturbed. There was barely enough room on the balcony for the four of them, but they huddled around the little table and enjoyed the breeze.

After hearing as much of the story as Iris was willing to tell, Fred and Wilma were sickened by what had happened to her. Even though she had left out some of the more graphic details, they were wise enough to fill in the blanks. They were just so thankful that she had escaped before something even more dreadful had happened. And then, they were even happier to hear that Iris had beat the living hell out of him with a table. They both praised Iris for keeping her wits about her, and William, for reaching her as quickly as he had.

About an hour after Fred and Wilma had arrived, there was another knock at the door, and William was glad to see it was Phillippe. He was there, not only to service Iris' room, but to give them some information he had learned, as well. He had a good friend who was in charge of cleaning the infirmary and his friend had told him about the man who had come in early that morning for treatment.

Phillippe hadn't let on that he knew anything about the man, and his friend was not the least bit informed, he assured them, of what had really happened to the patient. He told Phillippe the guy had confessed to the doctor that he had become drunk and had fallen down a flight of stairs.

His injuries consisted of a broken nose, two black eyes, a busted lip, a laceration on one cheek, a huge lump on the back of his head, right at the neck, and most interesting of all, his friend had confided to him, hugely swollen testicles.

"The doctor seemed to think all of the other injuries were typical of a serious fall," Phillippe told them, "but he evidently admitted to his patient that he had never seen an injury to the groin like the one he had, from a fall down some stairs. My friend described the patient as a blonde, white guy, maybe around forty, when I asked what the guy looked like."

He laughed as he continued, and his audience laughed, as well, including Iris. They were very pleased with the amount of damage she had been able to inflict on her abductor. "My friend said when the doctor checked him down there, the guy almost screamed with pain. My friend had to leave the room and finish cleaning later because he was getting a little squeamish."

William had assured Phillippe when he came in that he could speak freely in front of their guests. William told him that it was Wilma who had seen Matt with Iris in the casino. "Without her help," William praised her, "I wouldn't have known where to begin looking for her." It was very important to Iris and to William that neither Fred nor Wilma feel the least bit responsible for what had occurred last night.

Phillippe set about cleaning the suite while the two ladies talked about the dresses they would wear to the captain's cocktail party and dinner that evening. Everyone could sense and fully understood that Iris was anxious to put the unpleasant parts of the previous evening behind her. Up until Matt had ruined it, the time they had all spent together last night, had been very enjoyable.

Iris asked William, Fred and Wilma to not mention any of it to the young newlyweds. "Why spoil their honeymoon for them in any way?" she asked sensibly. "I don't want anything unpleasant to interfere with our formal night either. I've looked forward to this evening all week."

"Besides, I feel wonderful, like the entire thing is a distant memory now. It must be a side effect of the drug or something, but it almost seems like a very bad dream I had, than anything that actually happened." Iris couldn't help but notice the relieved expressions the other's now wore, and smiled lovingly at all of them.

"You know," Iris said, looking into the now familiar and dear faces, "I haven't even known y'all a week yet, and already William feels like my soul mate and Wilma, you and Fred treat me like a daughter." Her eyes grew misty with tears but she was smiling as she marveled at the fate that had brought them all together. "I love you all very much, and I won't be able to thank my children enough, for giving me this cruise as a gift. It's turned out to be one of the biggest blessings of my life."

Fred and Wilma hugged and kissed Iris and then William, and promised not to mention to anyone the unfortunate treatment Iris had suffered at the hands of Matt. They agreed to meet them in the hallway at seven sharp, so they could all go together to the cocktail party.

The two women were as excited as if they were attending their first school dance and the men grunted and rolled their eyes and complained profusely about the "monkey suits" they were expected to wear. But in truth, they were all looking forward to the evening's festivities.

"It's nice every now and then to play dress up," Iris directed at William. "Besides, it'll give me the perfect excuse to show off my necklace you got me in Sint Maarten and the earrings from our stop in San Juan. And," she jumped up and down like a little girl which made the other three laugh, "I have this gorgeous new dress that I've been dying to wear all week!"

Wilma and Fred left, saying they were going to go nap for a while before getting ready, but promised they would be back at seven on the dot, bright eyed and bushy tailed. Once again, they told Iris how glad they were that she was alright and she thanked them for their concern.

Iris told William that she would require more time to get ready tonight than usual, because she wanted to wear her hair up. It was late afternoon by then and they were going to have to be dressed a full hour earlier than normal, so they didn't have but an hour or so more to relax before she wanted to start getting ready.

William poured himself a generous amount of the Tennessee whiskey over ice and made Iris a margarita that she swore was the best one so far. "I'm convinced you could have a successful career as a bartender if you ever get the desire to retire from the corporate rat race," she complimented him. They had taken their drinks back out to the balcony where they sat, feet up, holding hands and enjoying the beautiful afternoon in peace and tranquility.

"I've been thinking about doing that very thing lately," William said, in a serious tone, which surprised Iris. He wouldn't mention his plans for Jake to her, until after he proposed, though. He didn't want anything except her feelings for him to influence her decision. Besides, he knew there was the possibility that Jake wouldn't be interested, anyway. It would probably depend on how well he accepted William's presence in his mother's life. Thanksgiving was exactly one week from today and William was excited about meeting the entire family. Hopefully, he thought, soon to be his family as well.

Iris grinned at William with raised brows. "What? You've been thinking of becoming a bartender? Fantastic! Now I know I'm in love!" she teased him. He turned toward her and gave her his best idiotic moron expression which sent her into a fit of laughter. "Stop it!" she screamed at him. "Didn't your mama ever tell you your face could freeze that way? If that happens, then no respectable bar will ever hire you."

They stayed outside until five, when Iris told him she was throwing him out. "It'll take me two full hours to shower, shave, shampoo, condition, blow dry, moisturize, dress, fix my hair, and make up my face. Not to mention get my jewelry from the safe and touch up my nails." She was counting it all out with her fingers, emphasizing everything she had to do by seven o'clock.

"Shit!" William exclaimed. "I'm exhausted just listening to you. I never would leave the house if I had all that crap to do just to get ready. I'm pretty sure building the pyramids took less effort." Iris giggled as she pushed him out the door.

He told her to wait there for a second, and he went to his cabin and returned a moment later with the little coconut purse. "Your room key and lipstick is in there," he said, handing it to her. "I thought you might need them." She had given him her extra room key a few days ago, which he had used to let them in early that morning.

She thanked him again for finding both her and the purse, and for a moment, they stood holding one another in an embrace that was loving and comforting and made no further words necessary. They were just so thankful that all had ended well, at least for them, and could peacefully put the ugliness of last night behind them.

William kissed her tenderly and told her he would miss her for the next couple of hours. "It seems I'm only happy," he whispered into her hair, "when you're within my reach." Reluctantly, he let her go, but stood outside her door until he heard her bolt it. He was paranoid about leaving her alone, even though he was right next door.

Iris on the other hand, was thinking of nothing other than how she would wear her hair and which shoes and bag to use with the beautiful new dress she was so anxious for William to see on her.

She showered, shampooed, shaved and moisturized and laughed out loud as she recalled William's comment about the pyramids. She had not yet done her hair, makeup, dressed or gotten her jewelry and accessories together and already almost an hour had disappeared.

After applying only a little more makeup than usual, Iris finished blow drying her hair and swept it up and away from her face and neck into a french twist, securing it with lots of pins, so it would stay up when she danced. Using a curling iron, she created a few tendrils of curls to hang loosely around her face. Giving her hair an extra shot of spray, she prayed it wouldn't fall until at least after dinner.

Finally, she was ready to get dressed. She took the evening gown out of the closet and unzipped it from the protective plastic cover that she had kept it in all week. She had wanted to be sure William didn't see it before tonight. As she slipped it on, she remembered the other gorgeous dress she had worn on the semi formal night. She smiled as she was also reminded that nobody, except William, had even seen it that evening. That was the first night they had made love and that dress had been cast aside like yesterday's news, as they had been more interested in the gift of one another, rather than the wrappings.

Tonight however, Iris knew they would dine and dance and enjoy the company of their friends, because they had already committed to doing so. Taking her jewelry from the safe, Iris chose the opal and diamond necklace and earrings William had bought her and the diamond dinner ring that she had brought with her. She carefully returned the rest of her jewelry to the safe and double checked to make sure it was locked.

Looking at herself in the mirror, she was delighted to see how the opals had picked up the coral color of the dress. They really did have a lot of fire and flash to them, she noted with pleasure. The fire came from the opals themselves, and the sparkling diamonds surrounding them, provided the flash. She knew William would be pleased she was wearing them.

The dress was long, almost to her ankles, except for the very front of the hem that came up about mid calf and was gathered there with a large rosette of the same fabric. It was sleeveless with a low cut neckline and back and had a dropped waist to it, in a vintage design. It was a beautiful light coral color with beads of a darker coral in a rose pattern, placed at the breast on one side and also at the lower back, on the opposite side. Iris had always been told this was a very good color for her, whenever she had worn anything that was close to this same color in the past. With her deep tan and sun lightened blonde hair, she thought it was even more so now.

Her high heeled, strappy sandals and beaded evening bag were the same dark coral as the beaded trim of the dress. She remembered Sarah telling her to be sure to get her picture taken on formal night. Well, she would, but not alone. William would be in the photograph with her. She could hardly wait to see him in a tuxedo.

And, she didn't have to wait long. Just as she finished putting herself together, she heard his knock. He was such a gentleman and so respectful of her privacy and space. Iris found herself holding her breath with anticipation as she hurried to meet him.

Iris let her breath out slowly as she opened the door, but sucked it in quickly again when she saw William. While it is true, clothes do not make the man, she thought this man definitely did wonders for these clothes. He wore a black tux with a silver grey vest and tie, over a basic white tuxedo shirt. No ruffles or cummerbund, she noticed, just refined elegance. He could have graced the cover of GQ and done it justice in her opinion, and her heart agreed. It was pounding so loudly, she was certain he must hear it.

But the only thing William could hear was the rush of his own blood in his ears as he took in the vision before him. In her heels, Iris still barely came up to his chin, but with her hair swept up and the long dress she wore, she looked like a beautiful actress from the forties or fifties era. She was the most feminine woman William had ever known, except perhaps his mother, he thought reverently. She had been a beauty as well.

"I wasn't sure I would like your hair up," was the first thing William could think of to say. Iris just smiled radiantly up at him as if he had just paid her the highest compliment of her life. They were both feeling a little giddy in each other's presence. "But, I love it," he added. "It makes me anticipate the moment I can take it down for you. As a matter of fact, standing here looking at you, I'm anticipating all sorts of moments." His eyes took in every detail, from the delicate beadwork on the old fashioned style dress, to the way light reflected off the opals he had given her. The total effect was mesmerizing.

Iris saw him lean down to kiss her and closed her eyes. But, instead of crushing his lips to hers as he normally did, and as she longed for him to do, he barely brushed the surface of her mouth with his. Her skin tingled at the hint of more to come. When she opened her eyes, he had already straightened up and stepped back. He didn't trust himself enough to place his arms around her and kiss her like he wanted to.

Iris saw the look in his eyes and understood that if she wanted to leave this room tonight, she had better do so now. His step back had placed him more in the hallway than in her room, so she joined him there, closing the door behind her. They had already promised the others they would spend the evening with them, and if they were going to keep that promise, they needed to distance themselves from her suite. Otherwise, their passion for each other was going to leave yet another gorgeous dress unseen by anyone other than the two of them.

Slipping her hand through his arm, they turned to walk the few doors down to Fred and Wilma's suite, but just then, their door opened and they emerged in all their finery. Fred was wearing a more traditional tuxedo with ruffles on his white shirt and sporting a red tie and cummerbund. Wilma was wearing a red chiffon evening gown that made her appear much younger than her eighty six years. Both William and Iris noticed right away, the ruby jewelry she wore at her ears and throat, wrist and hand. How could they not? It was stunning.

After exchanging hugs, handshakes and compliments, they cheerfully headed for the elevator. Fred and Wilma led the way with William and Iris patiently taking baby steps behind them. Exchanging a tender look, they both secretly hoped that thirty years from now, that would be them. Still together, still relatively healthy, and so obviously, still in love.

All four of them were delighted to find the newlyweds waiting for them at the entrance to the theatre where the captain's cocktail party was taking place. A photographer was set up there and Julie and Julian had wanted the six of them to be photographed together. They all agreed that was a wonderful idea and thanked them for waiting. The photographer posed them in various ways, placing first one couple in the center and then the others. Each of them said they wanted a picture for themselves, so he was very friendly and accommodating.

After the photo shoot, the three couples found a table that all of them could share in the theatre. A server carne around with complimentary drinks soon after, and directly behind him, another server followed with saucers, napkins and treats. They used toothpicks to spear cheese cubes, spicy meatballs and egg rolls. There were also grapes and strawberries and chunks of pineapple.

Wilma and Iris told Julie they were jealous of her youth and beauty and Fred and William praised her as well, but assured the other women that they were still quite beautiful themselves. Julian quickly agreed with his elders and told both Iris and Wilma that he would be very pleased if Julie maintained herself as well as each of them had. Julian was wearing a charcoal grey tuxedo with pinstripes and Julie, a long, shimmering, silver dress that molded her exquisite figure.

The band had been playing while everyone filed into the room, found seats, ate, drank and talked among themselves, but stopped as the cruise director took the stage. She welcomed everyone, thanked them for spending the week on board the *Whimsical*, and then introduced the captain and his officers.

It was amazing to listen as she told their names and where they were from. There were so many different countries represented, that it was impossible to remember them all. After the captain said a few words in English, with his heavy Italian accent, which the ladies found sexy, the crowd applauded respectfully while the crew left the stage. The cruise director then introduced the band and said they would play another few songs, and invited those who wished to dance to take the stage.

It was surprising to their little group that so few people got up to dance, but not being shy, the three generations of new friends led the way. The first song was a waltz and only a few other couples joined them. Then came a perfect song to dance the rumba to, and a few more couples came up onto the stage. After each dance, the audience clapped in appreciation for both the band and the dancers. The last song they played, invited a traditional slow dance and finally the stage was crowded with "belly rubbers", as Iris referred to those who would only dance an occasional slow dance. This usually occurred after the men had a few drinks and their wives had threatened divorce.

The band quit playing and most of the crowd was already charging the doorways, hurrying towards their respective dining rooms. William and Iris, along with their friends, went back to their table, where they sat and finished their drinks, allowing the masses to clear out. They weren't in any hurry to be jostled and have their feet stepped on, as often happened when hundreds of people crammed into stairways and onto elevators at once. "It's not like we don't have an assigned table in an assigned dining room," William pointed out, and the others readily agreed.

"Besides," Julian spoke up, laughing. "Most of the time we get in one of those situations, some guy uses the opportunity to grab Julie's ass." Julie flushed with embarrassment and the others laughed when she playfully slapped him. The crowd had thinned out significantly and crew members were beginning to clear the glasses, plates and trash from the tables, so they joined the last of the stragglers leaving the theatre.

The waiter and his assistant greeted them at their table, seating the ladies and lavishing them with compliments on their appearance. This was what they were trained to do, however they were sincere in this case, and enjoyed this table of guests very much. Dinner was as enjoyable as always, as was the company, and once again they were among the last ones to leave the dining room.

Their little entourage stopped at a quiet piano bar, where the background music was nice, and yet they could still carry on a conversation. At dinner, they had each only had one drink, so they ordered their coffees spiked with amaretto. The conversation was primarily about how much each of them had enjoyed the week, and how quickly it had passed.

"So much has happened since I boarded this ship last Saturday that it doesn't seem possible that it hasn't yet been a full week," Iris said, smiling at William. The others exchanged a look among themselves that Iris didn't see. Everyone knew about the ring and the proposal that would come tomorrow night, and could hardly wait.

William saw the look being shared among their friends and felt a surge of anticipation. Nobody was more excited than him about the possibilities tomorrow would bring. He understood how Iris felt about how quickly things had changed in six days. "My life has definitely taken a turn for the better," William added.

"I really enjoyed the first week of marriage," Julian teased, trying to peek down the front of Julie's dress. She slapped at his fingers, but only halfheartedly. "I'm pretty sure we made a little son or daughter too, so I'll need your e-mail addresses to send pictures of my very fat wife and then the baby." Julie turned every shade of red imaginable and slapped his hand harder.

"I'm just glad the ship stopped at three islands," Julie threw back at him. "Otherwise, we would have no pictures of our honeymoon that we could actually show anyone." Everyone laughed in appreciation of the two youngster's playfulness. They were so perfect for each other and both older couples would genuinely miss them.

"I'd love to receive pictures from you," Wilma directed at Julian. "But, you'd have to mail them the old fashioned way. Fred and I don't have e-mail. Neither of us are very mechanically inclined. Fred does well just to use his electric shaver." She looked very sweet and serious when she spoke, but her eyes twinkled mischievously.

"You better let me write down our address for you, Julian," Fred threw in. "Wilma's handwriting reminds me of muddy prints made by chicken's feet." He shot the men a sideways look and shrugged. "But then, she does write better than she cooks." Fred took Wilma's ruby clad hand in his and kissed her palm, then gave her a hint of the once radiant smile that had won her heart seventy years before.

"However, I didn't marry you for your handwriting or your cooking did I?" He almost whispered the question, and they smiled upon each other with the tenderness that came from a lifetime of love and happiness, compromise and understanding.

"You two certainly set a shining example for our young newlyweds," Iris said with a sigh. She felt like a failure in the department of lifetime commitment when she thought of her divorce from David. She had desperately tried to be a good example for her children. But maybe she and their father just hadn't had that special something that Fred and Wilma had been blessed with. She sincerely wished Julie and Julian a lifetime of happiness, and looked longingly at William, wondering if they would really have a future together.

William heard the sigh that escaped Iris and knew she must be thinking about her failed marriage. If you could call thirty-something years together, a failure. Even if it was, it hadn't been her fault, and he had no reservations about asking her to be his wife. He understood the look she was giving him now, and although he wanted to reassure her that their relationship was solid, he wasn't willing to give away his surprise just yet.

Fred stood up and announced that it was half past his bedtime and pulling Wilma to her feet, thanked them all for yet another wonderful evening. William and Iris said they were also ready to call it a night and offered to accompany them to their suite. Julie and Julian bid them goodnight and said they were going to one of the clubs to dance for a while, but looked forward to seeing them tomorrow.

As the elevator opened on their level, Iris remembered the horror of that other elevator she had been on with Matt, just last night. She gripped William's hand tighter and he placed a protective arm around her shoulders, once again sensing the direction her thoughts had taken her. They walked on past their suites and waited as Fred unlocked theirs.

"Oh, I almost forgot, Iris." Wilma went in and motioned for them to follow her. Iris and William entered and watched as Wilma unlocked the safe and took a small plastic shopping bag out. Handing it to Iris, she smiled somewhat apologetically. "Your quarters. I meant to bring them to you earlier today, but I was in such a hurry to see how you were doing, I forgot them."

Iris laughed, and after feeling how heavy they were, handed them over to William. "Believe me, Wilma, these quarters have been the last thing on my mind. But thank you for keeping them for me. Maybe I should apply them to Matt's medical bills." The other three groaned in unison.

"He's lucky he doesn't have a funeral fund you could donate to," William grumbled. "And I'm lucky you were able to get out of his room before I could get in, because I would have done something stupid, I'm sure. You probably kept me out of jail and it would have taken a lot more quarters to get me out."

Fred saw them to the door and gave William a wink and a handshake when Iris turned to walk away. "I know you don't need it but good luck just the same. Me and Wilma and the French kids are all very excited about tomorrow night." Iris stopped and turned around, waiting for William to catch up.

Of course she didn't have long to wait, because three of his long strides brought him to her side, where he wrapped her in his arms and finally gave her the kiss she had been wanting since first seeing him that evening. William had been courteous of her hairdo and makeup long enough, and was now very anxious to claim what he already considered his.

The urgency of his kiss matched her own rising passion and reaching Iris' suite, William didn't wait for her to produce her key, but quickly used his own, not wasting a moment. Barely waiting for the door to close behind them, he backed her against the wall and kissing her again, began to pull pins from her hair, laying them on the table in the tiny foyer, where he had already placed the bag of quarters. As he loosened her hair, Iris was unbuttoning William's vest.

Finally, Iris' hair was free and flowing around her shoulders. William had located the hidden zipper on one side of the dress and after pulling it down, he was able to slide the straps down off her shoulders, allowing the exquisite dress to fall to the floor.

Quickly appraising what she had worn beneath her dress, he was delighted to discover it wasn't much. A pair of lavender thong panties and a matching bra that was just a piece of stretchy lace, barely covering her ample chest. While he looked, he shrugged out of his jacket and vest, removed his tie, slipped his shoes and socks off and finished unbuttoning the shirt that Iris had already got started for him.

She pulled the shirt away from his broad, brown shoulders and only had to lower her head slightly to flick his nipples with her tongue. William removed his shirt while Iris first unbuckled his belt and then unfastened his trousers. She unzipped him carefully, because his erection was straining so hard against his pants, she was afraid of pinching him with the zipper. His briefs barely restrained him, and Iris thought with just a little more effort, his penis could puncture the fabric.

William unhooked the bra and as his slacks hit the floor, he pulled the lacy material away from her. Grabbing the cheeks of her round bottom in both of his hands, he raised her off her feet, bringing her breasts up far enough for him to suckle first one and then the other. Iris wrapped her legs around William's waist for support, and leaned her head back against the wall with her eyes closed.

She sucked her breath in sharply when he dipped a finger inside of her soft wetness. The small strip of panty at her crotch was easily pushed aside, giving him access. Iris' legs were spread wide around William's middle and he used the wall to support her, as well as his other hand beneath her bottom. With her arms and legs clinching him tightly, she wasn't going anywhere. William pushed the panties aside further and using two thick fingers, stroked her until she moaned loudly and soaked him with her orgasm.

Iris was kissing William deeply and passionately when she came and he could not only hear, but feel the moans that erupted from her very core. Her vagina spasmed around his fingers, clinching and releasing. He gently removed his fingers and still holding her against the wall with one arm supporting her, he pulled his briefs off, and his long thickness sprang to full attention as if his penis had a mind of it's own and knew it's target was very close at hand.

Iris had her head resting on William's shoulder, breathing deeply to replenish the air in her lungs, but suddenly her breath was forced out of her once again. William ripped the thong strap of her panties to get it out of his way. Sliding both hands beneath her, he used his fingers to spread her open and lowered her suddenly onto the full length of his erection.

A shock wave ran through her, as he thrust himself so deep inside of her, she thought she would lose her mind. Iris made a noise that was half scream and the other half a painful grunt.

Trying to speak, the only word that she could manage was William. Over and over she said his name, sometimes in almost a whisper and at other times, loud enough to surely wake the neighbors if they'd had any. Thank goodness William's suite was on the other side of this wall.

But William wouldn't have cared at this point, if they woke the entire ship. He was like a wild animal of some kind that had finally tracked down the female, whose scent he had been following for days. He raised and lowered her with his arms and using the tremendous strength of his legs and buttocks, thrust up and plunged into her again and again.

He could hear her saying his name, but he couldn't tell if she wanted him to stop or was begging him for more. But, since stopping wasn't an option for him at this time, even if she did want him to, he convinced himself that she wanted more. So, he gave her all he had, which was significant.

This morning he had made love to her slowly and with great tenderness, like it was her first time, but now he took her almost fiercely. Since last night when another man had infringed on William's territory, he had felt the need to restake his claim and mark her for his own. He didn't quite understand it himself, and yet he was aware of something in his very soul that needed to be fed. After tomorrow night, she would wear his ring upon her hand to show the world that she was his, but for now, he would possess her in the only way he knew how.

Something very powerful and a need as old as time, had overtaken him. All the love and desire he felt for Iris and his anger and loathing for Matt had merged together in his gut and when he finally came, it was with such force that his knees almost gave way beneath him. Iris felt him burst inside of her and heard him make the sound that was more animal like than human.

She didn't come with him this time, however, as she normally did. She felt raw and sore and swollen and when he finally pulled himself out of her, she gasped with pain. Her strength was completely gone and she could barely bring her legs down to the floor.

Resting her head against William's chest, she could feel the drumming of his heart and felt herself tremble with weakness. William felt it too, and using what he could muster of his own remaining strength, he gently scooped her up and carried her the few steps into the bedroom. Luckily, for him, it wasn't any farther away than that, because Iris was dead weight in his arms.

He knew she must be exhausted and now that he could think more rationally, he understood that he had hurt her. That had never been his intention but knew that was no consolation to Iris at that moment. Stretching her out on the bed, with her head resting on a pillow, he slipped her sandals off and what remained of her panties. They were the only things she was still wearing except for her jewelry.

Walking quietly across the carpeted floor, William went to the bathroom and washed himself off. He then took a clean wash cloth and ran warm water over it and then wrung it out. Returning to the bed, he placed the damp cloth between Iris' legs, which she opened slightly to accommodate the comforting feel of the cloth. She couldn't have walked to the bathroom just now if her life depended on it. The damp cloth was very soothing and seemed to absorb most of the heat that radiated in waves from between her legs.

Sitting beside her on the bed, he took his watch off and put it on the bedside table. William then began to stroke Iris' hair with his hand, in the gesture he knew comforted her. "Sweetheart, I know I hurt you and I'm sorry. And while there's no good excuse I still want to explain." Iris opened her eyes and seeing the seriousness of his expression, smiled at him so he would know she wasn't angry.

"There's nothing to be sorry about, my love," she assured him in a voice as soft as the touch of a feather. "I was as hungry for you as you quite obviously were for me." Iris laughed a little at the understatement. "It just happened that way. I'll be good as new by morning, I assure you. After all," she added, reaching up to caress his face, "it's not like I'm complaining. That was some pretty amazing stuff." She grinned at him and saw William visibly relax.

"You're the one who's amazing," he said tenderly, bending down to kiss her forehead. "I really did live up to my barbarian status this time though, didn't I?" he asked, chuckling a little. Joking about it was a lot easier than trying to explain what he had really been feeling. "Guess I just woke up on my redneck side this morning."

Iris scooted over in the bed, giving him room to lay down beside her. She dropped the wash cloth onto the floor on her side of the bed. She would pick it up later. Right now, she just wanted the luxury of snuggling next to William's body, while he held her in his arms. A touch of fear gripped her heart as she realized the cruise was almost over, and she had only tonight and tomorrow night to be with William this way. Then what? She couldn't bear to think about it just yet.

After the week they had just spent together, the possibility of living without him in her life, and in her bed, was unthinkable. Iris remembered Scarlett O'Hara in Gone with The Wind, saying she would worry about everything tomorrow, or something like that. Anyway, if she was going to get any sleep at all tonight, she certainly couldn't start worrying about anything right now. "I love you, my prince," she said sleepily to William. But all she got in response was a soft snore. She smiled to herself, thinking even barbarian princes had to have their sleep.

Iris snuck out of bed without waking William and picked up the wash cloth she had thrown in the floor. She was about to bust she had to pee so bad. Quietly closing the door, she used the restroom and put the lid down to flush, so it wouldn't be so loud. The noise the cruise ship's toilets made, with their special plumbing, was so loud it was embarrassing. There was no way a person could sneak and use the toilet. Hopefully though, William was so out of it, the flush didn't wake him.

Iris removed her makeup, washed her face and brushed her teeth. Using a soapy, warm cloth, she washed herself off gently, but thoroughly, cleaning especially well between her legs. She thought she understood a little why William had been so rough and forceful in his lovemaking tonight. She had felt all day the anger and frustration of last night, and knew that William had kept his true emotions bottled up for her sake, as she had to a certain extent, for his.

But at least she had been able to carry the satisfaction with her of the pain and injuries she had been able to inflict upon Matt. She knew William had wanted to tear him limb from limb, but since she had escaped virtually unharmed and considering Matt's sister was his employee, he had felt it necessary to restrain himself. Tonight, some of his negative energy had mixed in with his passionate nature, and even though Iris knew he had not been angry with her, she had been the recipient of William's combined emotions and strength.

It had been easier for her to laugh it off and tease him about it, than it would have been for her to listen to him try to explain it. She thought correctly, that he had been a little embarrassed, and again correctly, that he wasn't quite sure how to put his feelings into words. Iris knew they both had already learned how to read each other, in a very short period of time. As corny as it sounded Iris knew that she and William were made for each other, in every way that mattered. Physically, mentally, emotionally and even spiritually, they always seemed to be singing from the same song book, as her grandmother used to say.

Opening the door carefully, she crept on silent feet to her side of the bed, and barely disturbing the sheet, slipped in next to William. He lay on his side facing her and she stared at his handsome, rugged features. Whether it had been fate or karma or the proper alignment of the stars, she was thankful to everyone and everything involved, that had conspired to bring this wonderful man into her world.

They had only one more day together before Saturday morning would intrude upon them, making it necessary to leave the ship. A whole new group of cruisers would replace them and some other couple would perhaps sleep and make love in this bed she had so willingly shared with William. Feeling a new surge of panic, Iris wondered what William would say if she suggested they purchase a cabin together and sail for another week.

The *Whimsical* alternated weeks between the eastern Caribbean and the western, she knew. The itinerary she had picked up a copy of this week, showed it would go to Cozumel, Mexico, then Grand Cayman, and Ocho Rios, Jamaica, before returning to Miami a week from Saturday.

Then she remembered that next Thursday was Thanksgiving. Not that some of her family had never been out of town before on a holiday, but this year all of her children had assured her they would spend Thanksgiving with her. At the time, they had assumed the holidays would be difficult for her with David gone, but then nobody, including herself, could have foreseen a new love in her life by then. Not to mention she wanted William to meet her family as soon as possible, and he seemed to want to, as well.

That settles it then, she thought with a sigh. Maybe when the damp, cold Tennessee winter settled in after the holidays, she would see if William could steal himself away from work for another week. She grew excited thinking of that possibility. They both loved Sint Maarten and Aruba. She would start checking flights and accommodations for both places as soon as she got home.

Since this trip hadn't cost either of them too much, except for all the clothes she had bought before she left home, and of course the earrings and necklace William had bought her, she reminded herself sensibly, then maybe she could even give him the trip as a Christmas present. She wouldn't have to buy more clothes and she could possibly use her air miles she had saved up, for at least one ticket. The kids would gladly give her a little spending money, instead of having to shop and wonder what to get her for Christmas. She fell asleep finally, with a smile on her lips, satisfied with her plan.

Chapter 13

For once, Iris was the first one to wake up. She had gone to sleep smiling and woke up smiling, but she couldn't yet remember why. Something about Aruba she was thinking, and then her plan came to mind. That brought her fully awake and her grin grew bigger. Even in the morning light, it still seemed like a good idea. She watched William sleep for just a moment, noticing how his lips almost puckered when he exhaled. He breathed in through his nose and out through his mouth.

Knowing she should be depressed because this was Friday, and the last day of the cruise, she was filled with optimism instead. Her secret plan enabled her to push all negative thinking from her mind. Today, she promised herself, she would enjoy to the fullest. Besides, tomorrow night her family was meeting her at the airport and she was looking forward to seeing them. They had said they would wait and have dinner with her at nine when her flight got into Nashville.

Getting out of bed slowly so as not to wake William, she felt only a slight soreness from the night before. Heat coursed through her, as the memories of him pounding into her made her flush. She went into the bathroom and washed her face and hands and then set about making their coffee.

Since it had already been early morning when they had gone to bed, Iris was proud of herself for being up by nine. This was the first time she had made coffee for William, instead of the other way around. When it was ready she fixed hers first, since it took longer, and then poured a steaming cup for William. He must have heard her stirring about, because he opened one eye and looked at her.

Still with only one eye open, he looked at the clock and noting the time, his second eye flew open. He applauded as she handed his coffee to him, and she stuck her tongue out and said, "Smartass." He pretended to be scared to taste it. After all, he had never tasted coffee she had made. "See if I get up earlier than you again," Iris playfully threatened him. Then she remembered that tomorrow morning could be the last time that she would have that opportunity, and her smile quickly faded.

Even though he had only had one sip of coffee, William was awake enough to notice the sudden change in Iris' expression, and to react to it. "You can make my coffee anytime, beautiful," he said, patting the bed beside him. "As a matter of fact, it's even better than mine. What did you do, stick your finger in it and make it sweet?"

"Flattery will get you anywhere you want to go, big boy," Iris teased, in a terrible Mae West impersonation. He laughed so hard it was difficult to keep from sloshing his coffee. Iris held her nose, in admission that her performance had stunk, and then keeled over on the bed, when William laughed so hard, he farted. Then she held her nose again, even though he was still under the sheet and she couldn't really smell anything. They were both wiping tears from their eyes and trying to compose themselves when the phone rang.

They each looked at the telephone, wondering who would be calling, but since it was Iris' suite, she answered it. "Hello?" she answered, still giggling. "Oh Julie, I'm glad it's you. I've got my tickle box turned over this morning." She listened for a moment, then William heard her say that something would be great and that they would appreciate it. Then she hung up.

"How do you know that "we" appreciate it, when I don't even know what it is I'm supposed to appreciate?" he asked, pulling her down to give her a kiss. "I think I like a woman who makes all my decisions for me. How would you like to come to work for me? You could save me hours and hours of deliberation." He was joking, but she wondered if he minded that she had spoken for both of them.

"I'm sorry, William. You're right. I should have asked you first. Julie just said they were going to the pool at eleven to hang out today and wanted to know if we would like for them to save chairs for us." She blushed and shrugged her shoulders. "I guess I just thought since it's our last day, we would probably want to get some sun. Especially since we stayed in here all day yesterday. If you don't want to, I'll call her back," she offered.

He took her face in both his hands and drew her down to him again. He kissed her forehead and her nose, then her lips and her chin. "I'd love to hang out with you and the kids at the pool today, Iris." He really had been only toying with her, and didn't mind at all that she had accepted on his behalf. But he could tell she was feeling insecure today, and knew he would have to be careful what he said to her. He could have easily put all her doubts to rest, and he was feeling a little guilty that she was unsure of their future relationship, and yet he still wanted tonight to be special and a big surprise for her.

Iris was relieved that he didn't mind that she had answered for both of them and also glad he wanted to go to the pool today. It would be too cool when she got back home to lay in the sun, and she wanted to go home with a nice tan. She got up and handed William the room service menu. "I'll make you a deal," she told him, handing him the phone. "Since I have already made one joint decision today, I'll let you decide what's for breakfast for the two of us."

William would have settled for him and Iris having each other for breakfast, but knew it was too soon after the stunt he pulled last night, to even suggest it. Besides, he was hoping that tonight they would have cause for a celebration, and he could wait until then.

After ordering their breakfast, William gathered up his clothing that was strewn around the floor, and giving Iris a kiss, went to his own suite to shower and change. Promising her he would be back by the time breakfast arrived, he told her he could get ready faster without her as a distraction.

"You better get yourself back here in time, because I'm so hungry I could eat the entire thing by myself," she warned him. And it was true, she thought after he had gone. Their sexual high wire act last night had zapped every ounce of go juice she had possessed. She couldn't even imagine how weak and famished William must feel. After all, he had done all the work.

There was really no point in washing her hair just to go to the pool. Besides, it would never be dry before breakfast arrived, so she pulled it back and worked it into a braid. Since her hair was only shoulder length, it didn't hang down very far, but she thought it was still cute and at least it would be out of her way when applying suntan oil. Hopefully, she thought, as she was deciding which bathing suit to wear, her man would offer to oil her up.

Iris knew William had spoiled her rotten this week, and she now expected it. She felt like she could no more live without him in her life than she could live without air to breathe. What if, when they returned to the real world, and he went home to the house and business he had shared with Rebecca, he didn't feel the same way about her anymore? She had barely been able to get over losing David, and he had been an asshole. Iris was sure she could never recover if she lost William. He was the man of her dreams. The kind of guy she had only read about in romance novels. Now here he was, in the flesh, and he had said many times that he loved her.

She chose a chocolate brown tankini with beige fringe around the hem of the top and little wooden beads that trimmed the low neckline and the waistband of the bottoms. The material was a faux suede that actually was very light weight and dried quickly. She put on beige moccasins that were delightfully soft and comfortable. The wrap that she tied around her waist was the same fabric as the swim suit, with fringe around the bottom. Looking in the mirror, she was glad she had decided to braid her hair. It was the perfect style for what she was wearing.

She hurried to brush her teeth and then squirted just a little touch of perfume in her hair. Room service knocked at the door, and Iris let her in, almost fainting at the delicious aromas emanating from the tray. William showed up just in time to tip the lady as she was leaving. He really is Johnny-on-the-spot, Iris thought, as William joined her on the balcony. He always managed to be at the right place and do just the right thing at precisely the right time. She had never known anyone like him.

William had a fit over Iris' outfit and hair and swore she could pass for a woman in her thirties. Which reminded Iris that she still didn't know William's age, and then she remembered the article she had read about him and it suggested he was older than she had initially thought. She had figured him to be about her age, and even though Matt had mentioned the other night that William was a sixty year old widower, Iris remembered nothing of that part of the conversation. After experiencing his energy both in and out of bed, Iris was still leaning towards the notion that he was not much older than her, if any.

Well hell, why not just ask him, she reasoned. We know each other well enough now and there should be no secrets between us. They were quietly eating their breakfast when Iris blurted out, "William, I've been wondering all week how old you are. I told you that I'm fifty on the very first night. Not that it matters," she added quickly. "But, I admit to being curious."

The moment of truth had come, William knew, and decided to tell her. The woman he was about to propose to had a right to ask him anything she desired, and expect an honest answer. "I didn't want to make a big deal about it, sweetheart, but today's my birthday." He smiled sheepishly at her, feeling guilty that he had not already told her.

"What?! No way! You're shittin' me," Iris accused him, convinced he was pulling her leg. But, he was shaking his head like he really wasn't feeding her a load of crap. "Oh my goodness! We'll have to celebrate your birthday along with Fred and Wilma's anniversary tonight," she rattled on, her breakfast totally forgotten. But then she remembered that he still hadn't told her his age. She grinned at him, leaning on her elbows across the table, only inches away from his face. "And which birthday will we be celebrating, handsome?"

William stopped eating and looked her squarely in the eyes. "I turned sixty about an hour ago." He watched her reaction carefully when he told her. First her eyes grew bigger, but then Iris squinted at him and shook a finger in his face.

"Oh you. You had me going there for a second," she reprimanded him. "You're no more sixty years old than I am. A big stud muffin like you? Yeah, right." She rolled her eyes in exasperation. "O.k., so don't tell me. Like I said, it doesn't matter anyway." She went back to eating her breakfast.

Calmly, William reached in the pocket of his swim trunks, and produced his wallet. Taking his driver's license out of it he scooted it across the table so Iris could read it. She picked it up, her eyes big once more. "Holy crap," she said quietly, looking at him with a straight face. "You weren't jokin', were you?"

William shook his head. "Are you disappointed?" he asked her. "I should have told you right from the start, but I was hoping if you fell in love with me, that it wouldn't matter. Was I wrong?" He looked so genuinely concerned and serious, that Iris was taken by surprise. She had been worried that she was too old for him, and as it turned out, he had been afraid that she would think he was too old for her. How ironic, Iris thought, and how stupid we both have been.

Getting up from her chair, she went to sit in William's lap. Wrapping her arms around his neck, Iris gazed into his eyes and gained his full attention before she spoke. "I love you, William Pendleton. At sixty, at eighty, and if we're lucky, at one hundred. Age is only a number. When I boarded this ship, I felt like a used up fifty year old. But your love has completely restored and revived me. If possible, I'm even more impressed by how terrific you are. I had you figured at about my age, and I admit, I was afraid you would consider me too old for you."

Iris was smiling happily, more relieved than she would let on. She was actually delighted to learn that William was ten years her elder. Maybe that's why he wasn't interested in Allison when she practically threw herself at his feet. And, if they did have some kind of future together when the cruise was over, maybe he wouldn't leave her, as David had, for some child.

William had been holding his breath and now let it out in a huge sigh of relief. He was terribly glad to have that over with, and he believed Iris really didn't care about his age. That would make his proposal come a lot easier for him. "I love you too, Iris Corrigan, and I'm flattered that you didn't try to push me overboard when I confessed my age. That's a definite step in the right direction and very encouraging. But let's not make a big deal out of my birthday at dinner tonight, o.k.? I don't want to take anything away from Fred and Wilma's seventieth wedding anniversary," he suggested generously.

"That sounds like something you would say," Iris told him, standing up and placing her hands on her hips. "But I have to at least be allowed to acknowledge it, so we can toast you. And I won't take no for an answer." Sitting back down in her chair, she spread some jelly on a piece of toast.

William looked at his empty plate and noticed that Iris still had another piece she hadn't touched. "O.k., sweetheart, I'll agree to a toast. And speaking of toast, can I have your other piece?" he asked, pointing to her plate. "It is my birthday, after all." Iris burst out laughing and handed him the piece she had already put jelly on.

"I can see you're not above using your birthday to the fullest advantage," she accused him, putting jelly on the other piece for herself. "First, you'll hardly admit to it and now you want to be a ham about it." Iris was mentally racking her brain to recall if there was anything in the gift shop that might make a suitable spur-of-the-moment present. She would have to sneak away from him for a little while today and check out the possibilities.

Finishing breakfast, they hurried up to the Lido deck, where it was already crowded around the pool. Julian spotted them and whistled, waving a hand in the air. Iris waved back in acknowledgement and she and William picked their way between the chairs and around the people, until at last they reached them. They had managed to snag four chairs on the first row, right by the pool.

"You make a pretty good cabana boy," Iris praised Julian. "What did you do, sleep out here all night to reserve this spot?" Julie giggled and Julian thumped his chest like Tarzan.

"No actually, I didn't sleep at all last night," he proudly confessed. "We went dancing until about two thirty and when we went to bed about an hour later, I got my second wind." He did his eyebrows up and down in a you-know-what-that-means expression and Julie giggled again. Iris was thinking that she and William weren't the only ones whose tickle boxes had got turned over today. They both grinned broadly at the young lovers. They really were adorable.

"So right after breakfast," Julian added, "we came up here and spread four towels out on four chairs, and fell fast asleep. That was about an hour and a half ago and now I feel brand new," he said, holding up his hand. "As a matter of fact," he gestured to a waiter as he spoke, "it's time for my first beer of the day. Can I get you something, little one?" he asked Julie, nuzzling her neck.

She ordered a bottle of Evian as did William and Iris. Julian raised a questioning eyebrow at William and he laughed. "Don't worry, Julian, I'll catch up to you before the day is over. We just now finished breakfast. But when I was your age, I would have already been working on a case by now." Both men laughed, but Iris only rolled her eyes at Julie.

"A word of warning, honey," Iris directed at Julie. "They never do grow up. That's why there is a saying that goes, "boys will be boys". If they actually changed, it would go "boys will become men". I'm not saying it's necessarily a bad thing, I just thought you should know." The guys just looked at one another and shrugged and Julie only giggled again.

The sun was hot and the breeze was perfect. They oiled one another up and used sunscreen on their faces, necks and ears and stretched out like they were daring anyone to disturb them. Today they claimed this little strip of the ship as theirs, and everyone agreed that the day, so far, was surely like heaven itself.

About an hour later William asked Iris if she wanted to get in the pool with him. Julie and Julian had fallen asleep, but they had just turned over, so Iris wasn't worried about them burning. She nodded and got up, leaving her pool bag in her seat and placing her moccasins in William's, hoping nobody would steal their chairs. She didn't trust Julian to wake up, unless someone attempted to make off with Julie.

The pool was crowded but the water was so refreshing that neither of them cared. There wasn't really room enough to swim, but it felt great just to sink down into the water up to their necks and cool off. Seeing a little dark haired boy in the pool, Iris was reminded of her five young grandsons and her little granddaughter, and felt a pang of homesickness. William noticed her looking longingly at the child and smiled at her.

"You miss them, don't you?" he asked gently. She smiled and nodded, never taking her eyes off of the bright blue trunks that the little boy wore with a white, short sleeved shirt. At least his parents were taking precaution against sunburn, she was glad to see. Although he was dark-skinned with jet black hair and eyes. Iris wondered if he was perhaps Hispanic. Whatever he was, William and Iris agreed, he was beautiful.

They sat on the side of the pool dangling their legs in the water, talking about the Thanksgiving holiday they planned to spend with her family. "I'm very excited about you meeting them, and so happy that you want to," Iris admitted. "I'm having a late supper with them tomorrow night and I'm going to tell them all about you." William laughed and she blushed. "Well maybe not all about you, but everything they need to know," she quickly amended.

When they returned to their chairs the kids were still asleep, so Iris woke them up. "I'm sorry to disturb you, but I'd hate to think y'all would get sunburned and not be able to celebrate the last night of your honeymoon," Iris apologized, feeling like a mother hen.

Julie thanked her profusely and began to apply sunscreen all over, which she would wear the remainder of the day. She was the most fair skinned of the group, even though she tanned easily and well. They all then agreed it was officially five o'clock somewhere, and while the two guys ordered beers, the ladies got the drink special of the day.

When the waiter brought their drinks, which William paid for, the girls were delighted with the pineapple chunks and orange slices that lined the rim of the bright yellow glasses. Even though they were only plastic, they boasted the ship's name on them and William had paid a dollar extra so they could each keep their glass as a souvenir. They made such a big deal over them that William said he could have saved a lot of money and bought Iris a thousand or so plastic glasses, instead of opals and diamonds.

They all laughed, including Iris, but then she threatened him within an inch of his life if he tried to take back her jewelry. "I love my necklace and earrings!" she exclaimed. "And since I've already worn them, I believe they are legally mine now." Julie and Julian agreed with her and so William, being outnumbered, said that she could keep them.

The drink of the day was called a "yellow bird", and was an immediate success. Both Iris and Julie started begging for another as soon as they had slurped the last drop through their straws. William and Julian looked at each other and winked, gladly ordering refills for their lady loves. Since William had already paid for the glasses, the refills cost a little less, so they all agreed he had made a wise investment.

By the time the second "yellow birds" were empty, Iris and Julie were giggling like school girls, and the guys were getting a kick out of their innocent fun. William, being the oldest and taking responsibility, went to the nearest lunch counter and brought back a tray of hot dogs and little bags of chips. He knew between the drinks and the sun, they all needed something in their bellies besides alcohol.

"The hot dogs and chips were really good, William," Iris admitted with a frown, "but lunch killed my buzz." Julie agreed on both counts and with exaggerated lip pouting and a lot of eyelash fluttering, they convinced William and Julian to order them just one more "yellow bird" apiece. They swore there was barely any alcohol in them and that they were perfectly sober having had lunch.

After the next round of drinks, the four of them got in the pool to cool off. The guys held the ladies in their arms and floated them around the pool. They laughed and splashed and told funny stories about themselves and nobody watching them would have ever guessed there was a thirty or forty year age difference in their little group.

Late in the afternoon the crowd started to thin out, much to the four friends' delight. They now had room to swim, and they raced and played horse, with Iris and Julie on William's and Julian's shoulders. The object of the game was supposed to be for the girls to try and knock each other off their "horse's" shoulders, however, they had secretly agreed not to do that. Their private goal was to splash and dunk and attempt to soak their mounts as much as possible, while remaining high and dry themselves.

Eventually the men got wise, and after consulting with one another, devised their own scheme. At a signal from Julian, they each grabbed the girls feet and flipped them backwards, off their shoulders, carefully checking to make sure they would land safely in the water. Iris and Julie came up spluttering and squealing, just in time to witness a high five being exchanged by their riderless horses.

Many of the other guests had already gone to their cabins to get ready for the early seating dinner time of six thirty. Parents with young children had long since taken them out of the hot, late afternoon sun. The remaining guests were thoroughly enjoying the peace and relative quiet of the breezy, virtually cloudless afternoon. The four amigos were included in that number.

Having a little more wiggle room now, they moved their lounge chairs so that William and Iris were facing Julie and Julian. They had played in the pool for over an hour and had worked up a substantial thirst. The "yellow birds" were flying once more, but even though it was the fourth time, the drinks had been consumed over a period of about five hours. So the guys, after giving them the very technical how-many-fingers-am-I-holding-up test, agreed to buy their sweeties just one more.

William and Julian had worked off their beers as well, so they also indulged themselves one more round. "It would be quite rude to allow the ladies to drink alone, William," Julian said seriously. "I'm not sure if we could ever forgive ourselves if we didn't follow proper protocol."

Julian toasted William with his beer, and giving him a private wink, started talking about their dinner plans. "Julie and I have been wondering whether or not to get Fred and Wilma an anniversary gift. We don't want to embarrass them with anything extravagant, since we've only just met them, but we want to get them something," he explained. "After a week of marriage I'm beginning to see what a challenge seventy years with one person could be."

Taking one of her flip flops from beneath her chair, Julie threw it at him, almost knocking his beer out of his hand. After following up with a long string of expletives to Julian in French, she seemed satisfied at last and went back to sipping her "yellow bird" like nothing had happened.

"I rest my case," Julian said calmly to William and Iris, making them laugh. Julie only grinned around her straw. "Anyway as I was saying just before I was assaulted, Julie and I would like to give them some type of gift tonight at dinner. Do you have any suggestions for us?"

William and Iris exchanged a guilty look. William couldn't say so, but he had been so focused on his own proposal to Iris he hadn't given their friends' anniversary a lot of thought. And Iris, after finding out today was William's birthday, had been planning to steal away and buy him a gift when he went to his own suite to shower before dinner. Not wanting to give away their individual plans, they sat there not saying anything, like two bumps on a log. But now, Iris came up with a new plan. She wanted to kiss Julian for making things so much easier for her.

"I have a great idea!" Iris suddenly shouted, making both men jump. Julie only smiled at her from around her straw. "Julie and I will go right now," she said, gathering her stuff together and cramming it in her pool bag, "and get them something nice from the four of us. It's almost time to go in anyway, and it may take us a while to decide on something, so why don't we just meet y'all back in the rooms afterwhile."

Julie began to put her cover-up on over her bikini, and was slipping her flip flops on at the same time. Everyone heard her suck the last of the "yellow bird" through the straw and then she handed the empty glass to Julian. Holding her hand out, palm up, she never said a word, but evidently Julian could read sign language, because he reached in his wallet and pulled out a credit card. He refused to hand it over though, until she gave him a kiss.

That being accomplished, the girls hurried off, arm in arm, in the direction of the retail shops. William and Julian smiled at each other after they had gone and clicked their beers together in a salute to their good fortune. "How in the hell," Julian inquired of William, "did we get lucky enough to avoid shopping with them? I could kiss Iris! Would you mind terribly?" he asked William earnestly.

William patted his buddy on the shoulder and looked him in the eyes, just as seriously. "Not if you'll promise to kiss terribly." Julian got the joke and laughed with more appreciation than it called for. But they were each feeling a fine buzz and it had struck Julian as funny as hell. But then, he was operating on very little sleep too.

William suggested they go to their respective cabins and nap while the ladies were taking care of business, and Julian thought that an exemplary idea. They walked as far as the elevator together after cleaning up their mess poolside, and Julian wished William good luck in his proposal to Iris that evening. "Man, I can't wait," Julian admitted with a huge grin, "to see her expression when you pop the question. Julie will probably cry though, I warn you. She's just mushy like that."

William thanked him for his support and then shook his head and laughed. "You know Julian, the girls were pretty ripped when they left to go shopping. It kind of scares me to wonder what they'll choose as a gift from the four of us." Julian laughed too, remembering Julie's slightly glazed look when he had given her his credit card. "I'll order a nice champagne at dinner," William decided, "just in case Fred and Wilma open a beautifully wrapped package that only holds a stuffed whale or something."

This time, Julian didn't laugh, just rolled his eyes and looked at William as if nothing Julie did would surprise him at this point. After arriving in their suites, both men fell asleep within five minutes. William dreamed of stuffed whales in various colors and sizes. Julian was too tired to dream.

As soon as Iris and Julie got out of sight and Iris felt confident William couldn't hear her, she stopped Julie and said, "You're never going to believe what I am about to tell you." Julie leaned up against one of the big, decorative columns that marked the entrance to the retail area and looked eagerly at her friend, in anticipation of some juicy tidbit.

"I thought something was up, the way you were in such a rush to get away from the guys," Julie said, looking a little less foggy. Her eyes were big and bright and blue as she gave Iris her undivided attention.

Iris thought as she looked at Julie, that she couldn't remember ever being that young and carefree. She had gone from childhood straight into motherhood, while still a teenager. Perhaps that's why she had abandoned all caution and fell so hard and fast for William. She was finally ready to pursue a life for herself.

"I just found out this very morning, that today is William's sixtieth birthday. And I was frantic to find an excuse to slip away to buy him a present. Julian offered me the perfect cover when he asked what to get for Fred and Wilma's anniversary. Please thank him for me. It was perfect timing on his part, as if we had planned it." Iris was obviously pleased and excited, but Julie was looking a little glazed again.

"What? I must have not understood you correctly. I sometimes get numbers wrong in English." But Iris was smiling and shaking her head, letting Julie know she was not mistaken. "But you said sixtieth birthday. That can't be right. Not a hotty like William. I knew he was old enough to be my father, but my grandfather? No fucking way," she argued bluntly. She was convinced that either Iris had made a mistake or that William was playing a joke on her. Either way, she wasn't buying it. William was the most handsome, sexiest, old guy, she had ever seen, even in France.

Iris was still shaking her head and laughing at Julie's denial. "I know just how you feel," she responded sincerely. "I thought he was as full of shit as a Christmas turkey when he first told me, but then he showed me his driver's license. I thought he was about fifty, the same as me, and yet something I had read about him in the newspaper back home, made me think he might be a little older. But when he said sixty, I was truly shocked. And, to tell you the truth, I am a little relieved, as well. I was afraid I was too old for him," she confessed.

"Well, in the first place, I'm almost as surprised to hear that you are fifty years old. You are amazing, Iris," Julie complimented her in her carefully pronounced English. "But how can you be relieved that William is sixty? I mean, you know," she blushed slightly, but continued, "can he still lay the pipe down?" Julie looked a little concerned and confused and Iris didn't know why. Whatever did she mean about laying pipe? Did Julie think somehow that's what William did for a living? Now Iris looked both concerned and confused too.

But Julie's flushed cheeks and obvious embarrassment at asking Iris that question finally made a light come on in her head, and laughter erupted from her so abruptly that it startled Julie and made her jump. "Do...do you...do you mean?" Iris tried to talk to Julie but was so tickled at her obvious concern that William was too old to get it up, that all she could do was laugh hysterically. Finally, she controlled herself long enough to compose a sentence.

"Honey, don't worry about a thing," she said, patting Julie's arm in a consoling gesture. "Not only can he still lay the pipe down as you so eloquently put it, but he can lay it down often and for hours." A smile spread across Julie's face and she looked so genuinely happy for her that it made Iris crack up all over again.

Then Julie's tickle box got turned over at Iris' obvious amusement at her expense, and before long they were both howling and crossing their legs and leaning against the column for support. People passing by, either gave them a look of amusement or shot them a you-need-to-hold-it-down look of disapproval.

The two women finally got a grip and wiped the tears from their eyes. Thank goodness there was a ladies room close by, because between the "yellow birds" and the laughing, they were both about to bust. After using the restroom, they stood at two sinks, washing their hands and feeling like two school girls with a secret. No one would have guessed there was almost thirty years difference between them.

Determined now to find the perfect birthday and anniversary presents, they hurried, not to the gift shop, but to the ship's jewelry store. Iris and Julie fell in love with an exquisite Lladro figurine that they agreed would be perfect for Fred and Wilma. It was two swans with their necks intertwined in a gesture of love and an inseparable existence. At least that was how it made them feel when Iris and Julie discussed the piece. But then, they were two women, both desperately in love themselves and it was easy for them to find romance in everything they saw.

Iris knew that the only jewelry that William wore was a Rolex watch and a black onyx ring. The ring had a single small diamond in its center and had belonged to his father, he had told her. Although Iris didn't like a lot of jewelry on a man, she noticed a masculine gold bracelet that she thought would look great on William. With his thick wrists and big hands, there was no way it could look feminine on him, she thought, and when she consulted Julie, she agreed.

It was heavy and rugged looking. The man behind the counter opened the case and handed it to Iris, so she could better see the quality and workmanship. While Julie thought it would be too big and bulky on her younger, slimmer husband, she too believed it would look great on William. Iris consulted with the salesman about price and asked if they did engraving. He assured her that he would have it engraved and gift wrapped in time for her to pick it up just before dinner.

Leaving the figurine to be gift wrapped also, they paid for it, splitting the amount on their separate credit cards. Of course Iris put the full price of William's gift on her card. Feeling a great sense of accomplishment, they hurried from the store to the elevators.

"I need to start packing our things," Julie told Iris. "I can not believe we have to leave in the morning. Tonight will be both a little sad and very exciting at the same time." More exciting than Iris even knew, she thought to herself.

"I don't want to waste time later on packing. I will have to force Julian to help me so we can get most of it done before dinner. We brought so much shit and then bought even more on the islands! I hope we have room in our suitcases," she added, looking as if that thought had just occurred to her.

Iris knew how young people often acted on something and thought of the consequences later. After all, she had three grown, but still young children herself. She could just picture one of them in Julie's situation. "Well, don't try to over pack your suitcases," Iris gently warned her. "The zippers could bust open and then you would have a mess. If you find that you've bought more than you have room for, send Julian to the gift shop. They sell small suitcases and duffel bags there and you might even save money in the long run by buying an additional bag, because the airlines will slap a hefty fine on you if your suitcases are overweight."

Julie lit up like a sparkler on the fourth of July. "I didn't even think of that. What a great idea! Iris, you may have just saved my marriage. I could just hear us arguing over whose stuff went where and who bought too much. With an extra bag, there should be room for everything, even Julian's junk," she giggled. Julie told Iris that she and Julian would stop by and pick up both gifts on the way to dinner, so that William would not see the present from Iris to him, until she was ready to give it to him.

Iris gave Julie a hug and thanked her for her help in choosing the gifts, then exited the elevator at her level. She had a lot to do in the couple of hours left before dinner. Pausing briefly at William's door, she didn't hear any sound, so she let herself into her own room without disturbing him.

She removed her swim suit and hung it outside even though it was barely damp. She didn't want to pack anything even remotely wet, in with her good clothes. Pulling the suitcases from the closet, she opened them up on the bed. As Julie had said, she couldn't believe they would wake up in Miami tomorrow morning and have to leave the ship. Iris was almost as nostalgic as she was when she had said goodbye to her family last week.

It was hard to believe that she had not wanted to come on this cruise and now she hated to leave. What a week it had been! There was so much to tell her kids and she was anxious to see her babies, but if it had been a ten day or two week cruise, instead of only one, it wouldn't have hurt her feelings any. Remembering the plan she had devised early that morning, about giving William a trip with her for Christmas, she felt somewhat better.

The clothes she had worn this week, went in one bag and all the clean clothes and souvenirs and things she didn't want to get messed up, went in another. The packing went fairly quickly but then she had to decide what to keep out to wear tonight at dinner and keep something to wear home tomorrow, too. Iris thought about the long drive that William would have ahead of him from Miami back to Franklin, Tennessee, and almost wished she was riding back with him.

If he had flown, they would have probably been on the same flight. She couldn't help but wish he had. That would at least have given them a couple more hours together. Snap out of it, Iris, she told herself. The poor guy's probably ready for some alone time. They had spent almost every waking and sleeping hour together, since the second day. She wondered if she would see him before Thursday, when he would be coming to her house for Thanksgiving.

Then it occurred to her that William hadn't even asked for her telephone number or address yet. Iris felt another stab of panic but forced it down. She would worry about that tomorrow. She refused to waste her last evening on board the *Whimsical*, worrying about anything. Tonight she would devote herself to loving William and squeeze every moment of happiness she could, out of their last hours together. Tomorrow, and all her doubts and fears, would have to wait.

William felt great when he awoke from his nap and felt even better when he realized that the night of his proposal was here at last. He had only bought the ring two days ago in Sint Maarten but it seemed as if he had been waiting far longer than that to offer it to Iris. He could hardly wait a moment longer, in fact, getting it out of the safe and opening the box to stare at it, for what must be the hundredth time.

Picking something to wear to dinner from his remaining clean shirts and slacks, he then began to throw everything else in his suitcases. He had worn nearly everything he had brought with him, so he didn't have to be particular about packing. He left out his cowboy boots, a pair of jeans and a white shirt, to wear home tomorrow. Now he sort of wished he had flown instead of driven. He would have probably been on Iris' flight, and maybe they would have been able to switch seats with somebody and sat together. Oh well, he shrugged as he packed, her family was meeting her at the airport anyway, and she would have a lot to discuss with them.

Smiling to himself, he was thinking that she would have even more to talk to them about after tonight. His smile turned upside down for a brief moment, as he allowed himself an unusual twinge of doubt. William shook his head, as if trying to wake up from a bad dream. No, enough of that, he admonished his subconscious. There was no way he would take no for an answer anyway, so why waste a moment worrying about it.

Iris was all packed up and ready for the evening when William came by for her. They were both dressed in black and white and laughed when they saw each other. They had a way of coordinating what they wore without consulting each other that had amused them all week. Iris wore a knee length, black pencil skirt with a slit in the back at the hem, and a white blouse with feminine lace at the collar and cuffs. Her black, open toed slides and black evening bag completed the outfit. Her hair was parted slightly to one side and hung just past her shoulders in soft curls at the ends. William said she looked very pretty and sort of like a teacher he'd had a crush on when he was in junior high.

They hadn't seen each other in approximately three hours, so they took the time for a lengthy, deep kiss, before leaving Iris' suite. "If you had kissed your teacher like that the two of you would probably have been the first teacher/student relationship to make the news," Iris teased him, when they finally came up for air.

"Considering I was in junior high in the fifties," William said, laughing, "that would have been considered almost pornographic and would never have been publicized anyway. Besides, once my father found out and kicked my ass from Franklin to Nashville, they would have had to interview me from a hospital bed." Iris thought of her daughter, Rachel, and was suddenly glad she taught second grade.

Entering the dining room, they found the other two couples being seated and hurried to join them, so as not to inconvenience their waiter. By the time he was through seating Wilma and Julie and giving menus to the four of them, William and Iris arrived at the table. William ordered a special bottle of champagne when the bar waiter came to their table and also informed their waiter that it was Fred and Wilma's seventieth wedding anniversary. He knew a group of servers would come to their table and sing to them and thought they deserved acknowledgement in front of the entire dining room.

Little did either of them know that Julie had informed the others of William's sixtieth birthday, and the waiter had already been asked to get a group together to sing happy birthday to him. Fred already knew but had been sworn to secrecy by William, but Wilma and Julian had been as shocked as Julie to learn William's age. They only believed it because Julie said Iris had actually seen it on his driver's license.

None of them mentioned the proposal to the waiter however, because it would have been awful if they sang to Iris before William had even proposed. Everyone could feel the electricity in the air at their table. There was so much to celebrate, after all; an anniversary, a honeymoon, a birthday and an engagement.

Dinner was once again delicious and they toasted Fred and Wilma with the champagne when the dining room staff came over to sing to them. Everyone seated around them applauded as Fred gave Wilma a loving kiss. Then Julie brought the gift from the four of them out from under the table and presented it to them making sure they knew it was from not only Julian and herself, but Iris and William too.

Fred fussed, saying they had spent way too much, when they saw it was a Lladro, but Wilma only cried and said she loved it. They knew Fred was just as thrilled with the gift though, as Wilma was, by the way he kept looking at it. He was just trying not to get too emotional. There was going to be plenty of time for that before this night was over.

William was very surprised and a little embarrassed when the group of singers came back to their table five minutes later to sing happy birthday to him. He rolled his eyes at Iris and everyone laughed at his discomfort. But, when Iris planted a kiss on him that Ajax couldn't take off, he quickly forgave her. Then Julie handed his present to Iris underneath the table and when she gave it to him, William was surprised once again.

"Now I know you didn't have that with you when you came in here," he accused her, as he reluctantly unwrapped the box. "This was the kind of thing I was afraid of when I told you it was my birthday. So who was your conspirator?" he questioned Iris, raising an eyebrow at Julie. As usual, she only giggled.

But when William took the bracelet out of the box and read the inscription, he had to admit, it was a great gift. On the inside of the bracelet, all the way around, was engraved, "So you will never forget the cruise, or me. Love, Iris." After passing it around the table for everyone to admire, he allowed Iris to fasten it on his wrist.

Between the size of his wrist, his deep tan, and the masculine design of the gold bracelet, it looked better on him than he had originally thought it would when he first saw it. He had never worn a necklace or bracelet of any kind, other than dog tags in the service, and had always been of the opinion they should only be worn by women, but he would wear this one, if for no other reason than that Iris had given it to him. Everyone assured him that he couldn't look like a sissy even in a dress, and even he had to laugh at that picture.

The moment of truth had come. They had just ordered dessert and coffee and now everyone, except Iris, was looking with barely concealed anticipation at William. While Iris was happy thinking the evening had been a huge success, the other two couples were about to bust with excitement.

William stood up and Iris assumed he was about to excuse himself to go to the restroom. However, the other four suspected otherwise, and found themselves looking at one another and holding their breath collectively, without even being aware of it.

In one precise, fluid moment, William removed the ring, minus the box, from his pocket and knelt beside Iris' chair. Wilma and Julie instantly got tears in their eyes at his gallantry, but Iris just thought he had dropped his napkin on the floor. When he took her left hand that had been laying in her lap and didn't stand up again, she looked at him with a quizzical expression, afraid for a moment, that something was wrong with him.

William held the ring concealed in one hand, and was amused that Iris was clueless as to what in the hell he was doing down there. Iris heard a sniff and turned to see Julie wiping a tear from her cheek and the other three grinning like politicians on Election Day. She was about to ask Julie why she was crying, when William's voice broke the silence. Turning to face him, Iris searched his eyes for some kind of explanation. She couldn't help but notice that even on bended knee, he was taller than her.

"Iris," William said seriously. And, in that moment, hearing him only speak her name, she knew. Everyone heard her intake of breath as William continued. "I know we've only known each other for one week, but with God and our friends as witnesses, I promise to love you and take care of you for all the remaining days of my life." By now, Iris was trembling from head to toe and tears streamed freely from all six pairs of eyes. "I'm not just asking, sweetheart, I'm begging you to marry me. Please say you will and make me happier than I've ever been in my life."

Iris was crying openly and people from all the surrounding tables had grown quiet as they witnessed William's proposal, and were waiting, as he was, for Iris' answer. At first they could barely hear her reply, but with each yes she gave him, her voice rose in volume. "Yes, yes, yes!!!" she cried, flinging herself into his arms. Everyone burst into a mixture of laughter and tears and well wishes and congratulations. The maitre d' sent over another bottle of champagne with the ship's congratulations, and the servers hurried over to sing "happy engagement" to the now official couple.

William had pulled Iris from her chair and now held her in his lap, as he sat back down in his own seat. Without saying a word, he kissed her and while she was thus occupied, he slipped the sparkling diamond ring on her finger. When she felt the ring on her hand, she pulled away from him and holding her hand out, she looked to see what he had chosen for her engagement ring. Not that she cared. It could have been a cigar band and she would have thought it the most beautiful piece of jewelry she had ever laid eyes on.

"Oh William, you didn't!" she screamed in his ear, as she recognized the two carats plus, diamond ring from Splash in Sint Maarten. The two ladies squealed with delight when Iris showed it to Julie and Wilma. Fred was the only one, besides William, who had actually seen it. Of course Iris herself had chosen it, without realizing it at the time. Julian was as impressed as was everyone else and pouring the six of them champagne from the complimentary bottle, declared a toast to the newly engaged couple. Several people seated nearby joined in the salute and several of the women came over to admire the stunning ring, and the men to offer their congratulations to William on his stunning fiancé.

Finally, they settled down to enjoy their postponed desserts and freshly poured coffees amid pleasant conversation with just the six of them. Cell phone numbers, e-mail addresses and home addresses had all been passed around, with promises made to stay in touch. Julie and Julian begged William and Iris to honeymoon in Paris, so they could spend time with them, and they said they would consider it when they got that far along in their plans.

They all knew the day of departure was hectic and they might not run into each other before debarkation, so they hugged and kissed and laughed and cried after they left the dining room, before going their separate ways.

The love that was made between William and Iris that night, was a perfect blend of both the passionate sex they had shared the afternoon in Sint Maarten and the romantic, slower, lovemaking they also enjoyed. Iris hoped it would always remain so between them, since it was both the sexual and emotional release and fulfillment that satisfied her completely.

She and William stayed awake most of the night talking about everything from Thanksgiving and him meeting her family, to when and where to have the wedding and where to go on their honeymoon. Since they wanted to go to Europe, but just as much, wanted to go on another cruise, they decided to plan a two week Mediterranean cruise. That way, perhaps Julie and Julian could meet up with them in the south of France on one of theirs stops.

"What do you think about Valentine's Day, Iris?" William asked, bracing himself for her wrath, and smiling to himself. He remembered back to the first night they had met and what she had bluntly said to him, concerning that particular day.

"What about it? I hate fuckin' Valentine's Day, or have you already forgotten?" Iris couldn't imagine why William would bring up such negative memories for her at a time like this. If this was his idea of humor, she wasn't laughing. It had always been one of her most favorite days of the year, but now, even with William's engagement ring on her finger, she didn't know if she could ever feel totally happy on that day ever again.

"I was thinking that since last Valentine's Day was so horrendous for both of us, that maybe we should get married on February the fourteenth, so that it will once again, and for always, be a happy, loving day of celebration for the two of us. So what do you say, sweetheart?" He pulled her even closer to him and whispered in her ear. "Iris Corrigan, will you marry me on Valentine's Day?"

Iris felt terrible about the comment she had just made to William, and in a pretty nasty tone too. But then, he had set her up and she knew it. She had wondered how long he would want to wait before getting married, but hadn't wanted to pressure him for an exact date. Now she suspected that he had had this day in mind from the very beginning.

Raising up on one elbow and looking into his laughing eyes, she kissed him sweetly and tenderly at first, and then with increasing passion. She circled his nipples with her tongue, and gently and slowly moved her hand down his belly toward the erection she knew would be waiting there. Just before closing her hand around him, she gave him her answer. "Of course I'll marry you on Valentine's Day, William Pendleton," she crooned sweetly. "Didn't I tell you? I just love Valentine's Day. It's my favorite day of the year."

Epilogue

Iris sat at the head of her dining room table and looked lovingly at her family. Jake sat directly opposite her at the other end, with the turkey platter in front of him. She had asked him to do the honor of carving the Thanksgiving bird this year. He accepted, knowing that it was just for this one time. His daddy had done it for as long as he could remember, and by next year, William would take over in that capacity.

The six grandchildren were standing by the adults' chairs until after the blessing was said, and then they would have their dinner served to them at the kitchen table. William sat at her right and Sarah to her left. Her children and grandchildren had not only accepted William into her life, but had welcomed him into theirs, as well. The adults were very happy for them both and her babies just thought it was very cool that their nanny had brought them a new grandfather back from her trip.

Jake and William already seemed more at ease with one another than Jake and David ever had. William had hinted to Jake, just before sitting down to the table, that he had a business proposition to make him, but it could wait until tomorrow. His plant was shut down for the long holiday weekend, and he suggested he and Jake take a tour of it on Friday and talk shop.

William had not yet spoke of his hopes and plans where Jake was concerned, to even Iris yet. He had however, promoted Roger on his first day back to work. He and Allison very seldom saw each other, and when they did, neither of them acted any different toward the other, as if nothing had happened. News had quickly spread of his engagement and upcoming marriage.

Everyone joined hands and bowed their heads in preparation of the thanks that Iris always gave on this day. She had never in her wildest imagination thought she would be this thankful or this happy today. She had to fight back tears just to get through her prayer. Both Sarah and William squeezed her hands when they heard the tremor in her voice.

"Dear Lord," she began, "please forgive me if my words are inadequate in expressing all that I'm feeling thankful for today. I'm undeserving of all the blessings you've given me, although I humbly and gratefully accept them. Most of all, I thank you for my family and our love for one another. I thank you for William, and the door you've opened for us into our future life together, and whom we all consider family already. Thank you for this meal that you've provided as nourishment for our bodies and the love you show us, as nourishment for our souls." Here, Iris paused for only a second, but smiled thinking what could it hurt. "And, I'm not sure if it's totally appropriate, but thank you also for the cruise."